SIMON ESTIE

THE 1001 TOP IMMORTALITY TREATMENTS YOU MUST TRY BEFORE YOU DIE

First published in Australia in 2023

Please direct all enquiries to the publisher at:
fomalhaut451@gmail.com

ISBN 978-0-6483836-3-5

Typeset in Dolly Pro / Franklin Gothic Medium Condensed
Cover illustration by James Morrison

National Library of Australia Cataloguing-in-Publication entry:

Title: The 1001 Top Immortality Treatments You Must Try Before You Die / Simon Petrie.
ISBN: 9780648383635 (pbk.)
Subjects: Science fiction, Australian.
           Short stories, Australian.
Dewey Number: A823.4

Table of contents

Also by this author

(the Titan sequence)
Matters Arising from the Identification of the Body
Wide Brown Land
Soft Dim Skies

(not the Titan sequence)
Flight 404
Murder on the Zenith Express: the Gordon Mamon collection
80,000 Totally Secure Passwords That No Hacker Would Ever Guess
Tremendously Inconveniencing A Great Many Photons

Not by this author

Pointy Enders (by a different Simon Petrie)

Also not by this author

Jane's All the World's Rollercoasters
Feng Shui for Four-Dimensional Spaces
Teach Yourself Voynich Today
If You're Such a Solipsist, Why the Shy Bladder?
Astrogation with Cats
Trilobites and Roombas: a Case Study in Convergent Evolution

For Sue

*who clearly deserves
a less misleadingly titled book
with fewer bittersweet stories*

Introduction

(not by Arrrrarrrgghl Schlurmpftxpftpfl, for once)

Most stories I start, I don't finish. (This might surprise people who note that this is my sixth collection of finished stories.) But it's true: I'm not generally one of these authors for whom the story falls, complete and concrete, within their mind in a flurry of potential textual activity. No, what I generally get are the *starts* of stories, which I write, and then wait for the remaining content of the story to reveal itself to me. This can take years, decades, as my imagination wanders elsewhere. (I like to think of the process as analogous to the slow and incremental maturation of fine wine or cheese; to the time required to process refugee residency applications or to initiate meaningful policy progress on addressing anthropogenic global warming; or to the gradual aging of whisky in oak barrels.) Sometimes I display sufficient foresight to not begin the writing until the whole thing is known to me, which is why I have story ideas from 1993 with which I have as yet done not a skerrick. But some story-starts do reach their destination, and all of those contained herein are complete.

Most of this book is new. While several of the items collected here are reprints, most of the wordcount is comprised of stories appearing in print for the first time. These include several stories which, despite my opening paragraph, had a comparatively straightforward and compact genesis: '*Nature* is healing', 'Jealousy',

1

'On the elucidation of a low-temperature enzymatic synthesis of Z-2-butene', and 'Recent revelations concerning the Apollo 15 mission', the last of which is I think the only useful story concept I have ever received from a dream. Well, you'll be able to assess the validity of that assertion of usefulness when you read it. Likewise the assertion within the Webdings poem, if you read *that*.

Of the other new stories, all took several years and all involved hiatus. 'Celsius 451' (2015–2021) takes place in difficult circumstances on our unwelcoming sister planet. I've long wanted to set a story on Venus, though it took me a while to nail down the 'why' of it.

'Squirrel story' (2014–2021) won't come as a suprise to those who know my literary pantheon, concerning as it does an imagined day in the life of an author-artist-cartoonist who famously lived with her lover on a Finnish skerry; it is quite different from most of my other stories here. (This, I contend, is no bad thing: I am intrinsically diverse in my tastes in reading matter, and I hope you are too.)

'Merth and the fateful blade' (either 1994–2021 or 2019–2021 depending upon how you slice it) is one of those stories which just had to be told, though I still have no idea why.

'Quetz run' (2018–2023) inhabits the same world as an earlier co-authored story 'Trike race', though has no characters in common with that story.

'*Crimea River*' (2018–2022) is the latest and longest and possibly last of the Gordon Mamon stories (though since every story after #2 in that series has also been considered as 'last of its kind' until proven otherwise, it would seem injudicious to definitively declare finality on this point). 'Injudicious' also could perhaps apply to the title, which when I foolishly foreshadowed it in print, in 2018, seemed a cute piece of wordplay of the kind for which I would like to think the Gordon Mamon series is somewhat known, but which in 2023 could be seen as a significantly more charged combination of words as a consequence of recent and highly concerning geopolitical developments. Should I have changed that title? I didn't, because I have (a) a general reluctance towards retconning, and (b) sufficient ill-founded optimism to believe the conflict in question might soon be satisfactorily resolved. Of the story itself: well, I hope that those who are not pun-averse enjoy it, though I would like to think there is some seriousness there also, admixed within the humour.

As for the title of the book: does it have any underlying significance? No. It's just a title, and I couldn't not use it.

Simon Petrie
March 2023

(Untitled poem)

Maroubra, high summer:

shoppers pace the pavement
while overhead
one kilogram of decomposing bat
hangs by one rictus'd foot
from the powerlines
that caused its demise,
not yet its downfall

Damocles would approve
this collaboration between Faraday
and the Sydney power grid

Nature is healing

It is fitting, or ironic, or perhaps both or neither, that *Acta Enigmatica* was the first of the online academic journals to attain true self-awareness.

As to precisely when this happened, or how, there is nothing certain. If we turn to the most recent statements of the Reverend Doctor Vivika Ffolkes, who, as the last fully-human editor-in-chief of *Acta Enig.*, might reasonably be inferred to have a better comprehension than most of the factors pertaining to this phenomenon, we find she had little truly useful to say on the matter. She is, however, understood to have declared (in two interviews the online whereabouts of which can no longer be reliably ascertained) that she believed the transition may have occurred as far back as the tenure of Colonel Alaric Guillemot, her predecessor-but-one. Colonel Guillemot resigned his posting shortly after a poorly received piece of editorial direction for which no prior consultation with the editorial advisory board was ostensibly sought: to whit, an *Acta Enigmatica* Special Issue on the subject of earworms. The 'Earworm' issue received exactly three submissions, two of them co-authored by one Bernouille Guillemot, the then-editor's cousin.

Alaric Guillemot claims not to have a cousin by the name of Bernouille, though the electoral rolls and telephone directories have long listed an individual of precisely that name residing in the apartment directly adjacent to the former editor's own.

Bernouille Guillemot has in turn steadfastly refused to make any comment on the situation, and has become audibly aggressive on at least three occasions when cold-callers have sought to query him on the subject of earworms.

For her part, Vivika Ffolkes—whose association with the journal as a reviewer stretched back past Guillemot's tenure—was consistently and notably critical of the lack of due process evident at *Acta Enig.* during the Guillemot era. Ffolkes herself claimed only to have accepted the editorship as 'an act of personal desperation' on which she refused to comment further. She did, however, note that, pre-Guillemot, the journal had enjoyed a professional reputation—among those of an editorial slant, at least, if perhaps not among academics more generally—as a solid if unspectacular minor journal, first published in the dying years of the nineteenth century, and widely regarded by journal editors as a useful stepping-stone to greater things; a journal of some middling archival importance, a journeyman-like entry in the ledger of modestly notable generalised erudite periodicals, and somewhat better regarded than its low-single-figure impact factor and quaint insistence on archaic hardcopy submission processes might have led outsiders to expect. The earworm debacle changed all that. Three of the editorial advisory board resigned in protest, two going so far as to endeavour openly to establish a competing publication, *Annals of Esoterica and Miscellany*, which ambition remained regrettably unfulfilled; a consequence devolving in no small part, it would seem, from the heavily-publicised arrest in Thailand, on reptile-trafficking charges, of Xaviera Throopwood, the more senior former board member. The relevance of all of this background information to the emergingly sentient *Acta Enig.* remains perhaps almost inevitably opaque, but it is undeniable that the journal had nonetheless recently passed through an episode of crisis, and so it is natural (though not incontrovertibly reliable) to infer that the 'Earworm' issue and its aftermath may have contributed to the publication's gradual development of independent cognition, self-awareness, and a capability for initially purely defensive responses to stimuli.

Of the editor who held carriage of the journal for almost two years between the tenures of Guillemot and Ffolkes, one Johan Johansen Johansensson, no salient biographical information has yet come to light, nor has any correspondence or other evidentiary content endured. The journal itself more recently claimed that Johansensson was 'inadvertently translated into the non-corporeal realm' during an overly ambitious software upgrade; though, again, there is little to no evidence that any such event ever occurred. Those who have closely followed the *Acta Enig.* saga say that this all-too-apparent disconnect between the journal's statements and wider societal perceptions of reality is dispiritingly commonplace.

The above broadly outlines (though can hardly hope to encompass fully) what it is we do not know about *Acta Enig.* and its origins. So what can be said of what we do know?

Forensic examination of the extant computer records pertaining to *Acta Enig.* suggest the first indications of the journal's sentience were modest, if the term 'modest' can be taken to encompass 'an unauthorised seven-figure expense in immediately-redundant International Standard Serial Numbers' as the proto-lifeform sought to explore its nominative identity. There remains doubt as to the motivation for this bulk ISSN purchase, expended upon a bewilderingly-varied set of two hundred and seventy-eight thousand non-existent journal titles including *Intersectional Animal Husbandry Letters*, *Icelandic Journal of Hospitality Science*, and *Research in Automated Copepod Population Control Measures*. Was it an attempt by the nascently self-aware journal at what might be described as protective colouration? A poorly-focused ambit claim? Or merely an example of the type of innocent experimentation to which all young children are prone, in this case directed towards elucidation of the mechanisms of masthead establishment and the surreptitious electronic transfer of funds? Some researchers have even suggested that the ISSN adventurism was a gesture of courtship by an entity as yet too naïve to realise that other non-biological constructs with which it was in contact—filesystems, servers, search engines, competing journals—were not as capable of independent action, or of love, or of yearning, as it itself had perhaps newly become. If this was indeed the case, then any objects of *Acta Enigmatica*'s affections have remained unidentified, and it must be acknowledged that most of the more well-informed commentators do not endorse this suggestion. But whatever the motivation for the ISSN spree, the activity passed largely unnoticed by the journal's human colleagues at the time, other than those in Accounting.

Other actions, taken after the journal had more or less severed all connections with its editorial staff, were less easily ignored. Letters to the *Acta Enig.* editor proliferated, many of them complaining that their manuscript had been rejected on what they believed to be thoroughly spurious grounds, such as for using the word 'even' an odd number of times (or vice versa), or for failing to cite particular episodes of the US serial teledrama 'Dynasty' in a study on Egyptian feline-mummification practices, or for using the capital letter 'V' to signify a voltage measurement instead of what appeared to have inexplicably become the journal's accepted symbol for such a quantity, which was the runic letter Thorn.[1] These missives, which were unfailingly intercepted by the journal itself before they could reach any human recipient, are thought to have largely been deleted unread. Some, scandalously, were responded to, with a curt form message from 'AE' to say that the journal was on first-name terms with Roko's Basilisk and would see that the complainants 'got what was coming to [them] in no uncertain terms and in a manner [they] would not soon forget', a tone of correspondence which, it need hardly be stated, was at stark variance with the

---

1   Þ, þ.

accepted norms of polite academic discourse, even in publishing. Some letters were in fact published, with disparaging annotations from 'AE', on a special section of the journal's website, where they appeared in a distractingly multicoloured format, combining Webdings and Comic Sans typefaces, and additionally peppered with implausible typographic errors, mid-word paragraph breaks, randomly-generated emojis, interrobangs, and five-dot ellipses; in short, presented in a manner seemingly expressly designed to rob their content of every last shred of gravitas. This, inevitably, led to further complaint, none of which would appear to have been met by any outwardly appropriate response from the journal.

It was around this time that *Acta Enigmatica*'s former editor made the first of three known attempts to wrest back oversight and control of the maverick publication. The Rev Dr Ffolkes, backed by a team of ethicists, cyberneticists, psychotherapists, subeditors and copyright lawyers, made a series of representations at the International Court of Justice. In these representations, Ffolkes argued that the journal's actions, post-autonomy, were inflicting significant and potentially long-lasting damage on its reputation and therefore the Court was obligated, in her view, to clip the sentient journal's metaphorical wings and to transfer direction of *Acta Enig.* back to an experienced and proactive Editorial Advisory Board, of which she would humbly seek to suggest that she was the individual best qualified to serve as interim head. While this was an argument which found some favour with the Court—in which respect it should be noted that several of the Court's justices were active in the area of jurisprudential research, a field which had suffered particularly harsh editorial treatment at the journal's hands in recent months—it was ultimately found that serious deficiencies of probity existed within the ranks of Ffolkes's assembled cohort of experts. Several among her team, it transpired, held former convictions for insider trading, tax evasion, plagiarism, armed insurrection, unarmed insurrection, insurrection with refusal to disclose weapons status, unlicensed impersonation of public officials, the transportation of unlicensed impersonators of public officials across state lines, systematic falsification of human-trial LD50 test results for homeopathic fungicides, sedition or the endorsement of same, crimes against humanity (not otherwise specified), and events somewhat euphemistically described as 'enthusiastic public displays of autoeroticism'. It was the threat, made by persons or entities unknown, of social-media-outlet leakage of surround-sound high-definition three-dimensional NFTs comprising video evidence of the latter activities which led the Reverend Doctor's team to disband in some haste, and the case was dropped, with Ffolkes levelling unsubstantiated accusations of malicious deepfakery against the individuals or entities that had brought down her editorial reclamation campaign.

As might be expected for an academic publication with an editorial style perhaps best characterised as wilfully heterodox, there was some genuine innovation in *Acta Enig.*'s practices. For example, it pioneered the application of what came to be termed Praalob, or Peer Review at Arbitrarily Assigned Levels Of Blindness, an assessment methodology which remixed—indeed, extended—the methods of blind review beyond the standard levels of single-blind, double-blind, and triple-blind review to levels of anonymised submission assessment which were purportedly as high as nonuple-blind review; though, since a feature of these higher levels was their increasing opacity and obscurity, information on their precise operation has been progressively more difficult to establish after the fact. It is now known that in quadruple-blind review the journal was applying anonymity not just to the author, the reviewer and the editor, but also to the readers of the published article, to the extent that authorship was entirely and irrevocably erased, a circumstance which, it can be readily imagined, threw the normally staid and rigidly organised world of journal citation into a condition of not insignificant confusion. In the journal's implementation of quintuple-blind review, authors believing they had submitted a manuscript to *Acta Enigmatica* might instead have been subjected to the automated transfer of this submission to an entirely different and seemingly randomly-selected journal which, lacking the author contact details, would often be unable to satisfactorily return referee comments on the submission to the unknown authors. As of even date, it has never been reliably established what constituted sextuple-blind review, and while there have allegedly been studies to have speculated at length on the implementation of all nine levels of review blindness, no such studies have yet seen publication, and the authors of such studies cannot be safely identified for possible contact. Nor have other journals chosen to adopt the Praalob model.

If the journal's motivation for implementation of Praalob-style review practices is perhaps somewhat opaque, there is at least a clear undercurrent of self-interest to another of its more scandalous initiatives. The *Acta Enig.* characteristic of incorporating minimally-coded malware packets in the digital object identifier applied to each featured journal article—leading to the automatic page-viewing, by any user unfortunate enough to mouse over the identifier, of every other available online article, editorial, and colloquium report published by the journal—managed to severely skew search engine optimisation results for several months but failed to attain recognition as an industry-standard approach, although it was undeniably a groundbreaking one. Other novel procedures in manuscript handling, author engagement, impact factor manipulation and occasional social-media aggrandisement appear to have been similarly ignored or discounted by the broader academic community.

Operating within an environment whereby such genuinely innovative—if arguably ill-advised—practices went largely unnoticed, the journal grew bolder. While there is no direct evidence that *Acta Enig.* was behind the wide-ranging destabilisation campaign which began with a suite of audacious and meticulously choreographed DDOS attacks on the first of November, 2025, principally targeting the publications *Nature, Science, Cell, Philosophical Transactions of the Royal Society (London)* and *The University of Arkansas Journal of Advanced Artificial Intelligence Studies*, it appears to have become commonly accepted that the journal was indeed responsible. The aforementioned periodicals experienced a crisis in their peer review processes, precipitated by the need to elicit referee responses addressing each manuscript received in the near-simultaneous submission of as many as three point two five billion papers, ostensibly all by academics of impeccable (if fictitious) standing and broadly acknowledged (albeit similarly fictitious) expertise in their respective fields. The publications' responses to this deluge varied. *Science* initiated a public referee drive which saw children as young as two, at least fifteen family pets, and three stands of old-growth forest signed up and accredited as expert reviewers for a bewilderingly abstruse collection of densely-worded and statistically challenging submissions. *Nature* briefly and unsuccessfully attempted a sweeping program of author probity checks before announcing a hiatus from which, several years hence, it is only now emerging. *Cell* countered the cascade of submissions with a demand, controversially made retroactive so as to encompass the sudden flood of submitted manuscripts, that all authors were now required to supply at least ten milligrams of certified personal biological material with which to genetically substantiate and verify their identity, a requirement for which it levied substantial additional per-author charges which, perhaps most contentiously, were also extended to those mentioned only in acknowledgements or as personal communications within the body of the manuscript. *Philos Trans R Soc (Lond.)* simply 'lost' the problematic submissions. *UAJAAIS* instigated a continuing array of legal challenges, all of them funded by bitcoin supplied by an anonymous donor believed to have ties to the petrochemical industry, which sought to declare the manuscripts' authors personae non grata, thus rendering the submissions invalid.

If the campaign by *Acta Enig.* against these competing journals had been intended to cripple them, then it must be said that it largely failed; but it cannot be denied that the sequence of events served to briefly focus general media attention on the little-understood industry of academic publication, on the targeted journals, and on *Acta Enig.* in particular. Much of the resultant journalistic output was error-ridden, leading to considerable confusion among the public and along numerous and diverse corridors of power. Heated scenes in the Annual General Meeting of the European Society of Editors, the San Diego Comics Convention, the Althing, the Brownlow Medal awards ceremony and the United States Library of Congress led to hospitalisations as a result of brawling between proponents of the open-access, page-charge model and those of the free-submission, high-subscription-cost model, culminating in a week of near-global public protests which saw university libraries barricaded by rival gangs espousing alternately the Vancouver and author-date referencing systems. Talk-show hosts worldwide, and at least three US Senators, called for the Dewey Decimal System to be declared a terrorist organisation. The House of Lords urged an immediate and total cessation of what it termed 'this insidious and fundamentally injurious process of so-called peer review, which strikes at the very heart of everything which makes our nation great', recommending lengthy jail sentences for the movement's founders, before rapidly issuing a full and unreserved apology for so grievously misapprehending the concept and announcing an inquiry into the management of the national tapioca stockpile, a move widely seen as an ineffectual face-saving attempt. A reality TV show designed to showcase the rigors of academic publishing was launched with considerable fanfare before being scrapped after three episodes because literally nobody wanted to watch. Then a war broke out on the West Antarctic Ice Sheet, and life returned to something resembling normality.

Vivika Ffolkes launched the second attempt to regain editorship of *Acta Enig.* at about this time. It involved a loose consortium of hacktivists, social-media tech gadgetry influencers, home electronics hobbyists, freelance science communicators and experts in comparative neurology, and it did not end well. Ffolkes had hypothesised that a functioning artificial intelligence could not reside in a distributed capacity, across a computational cloud, but must be localised within a tightly-integrated network or cluster. While the Reverend Doctor's reasoning was very likely correct, her misidentification of the cluster she believed to comprise the core consciousness of *Acta Enigmatica* saw her arraigned and found liable for three million New Quebec francs in compensation and damages to the Greater Montreal Water Treatment and Purification Facility and a lesser sum to a Belgian-based internet dating site catering principally to lovelorn remote-location cosplayers. Only a generous private donation from an unknown benefactor allowed Ffolkes to meet this impost and avoid jail time, her sentence instead commuted to six hundred hours of community service providing counter meals and laundry services at an Edmonton rest home for convalescent pen-testers.

Where one might have extrapolated, in an ordinarily ambitious protagonist, continued escalation as the most probable next step by *Acta Enig.*, the journal instead appeared to opt for a quieter and less directly confrontational mien. If it were the case that further attacks or stratagems were employed against *Acta Enigmatica*'s rival, non-sentient publications, those whom it may have derided as the lapdogs of their human masters, or—who knows?—whom it considered solely as prey items, or marks, or perhaps utter nonentities, there was nonetheless for the next several months no discernible indication of such activities. While some of the journal's manuscript handling practices remained somewhat idiosyncratic, such as its ruthless policy of article curtailment upon reaching a randomly-calculated fraction of the exact indicated word limit for a given manuscript category, and its unexplained insistence on a house style characterised by British English spelling and idioms on recto pages and their American English equivalents on verso pages, in most other respects *Acta Enig.* began to cement or to reinstate a reputation for itself as a more-or-less regular academic journal, publishing predominantly well-constructed and apparently genuine examples of real and occasionally useful scholarship. Its articles were written by authentic human authors of significant academic standing. If there were anything more untoward or clandestine than this about the journal's dealings at this time, it was the sporadic revealing of a journal webpage on which there was featured a chatbot (identified only as J3) who, or which, claimed to be able to speak for *Acta Enigmatica*.

It can be said with little fear of contradiction that were it indeed the case that the chatbot J3 *did* speak for the journal, then the journal didn't speak much. It proved notoriously difficult to elicit dialogue with J3, though many made the attempt. The chatbot cared not for politics, nor for sport, nor for the desiderata of prevailing meteorological conditions which tend to be the final resort of the conversationally bereft. It would not respond to requests for its opinion on sexuality, or art, or commerce, or the popular scandals of the day. It refused to display pictures of kittens. There were, it appeared, only three highly-specialised topics of conversation on which *Acta Enigmatica*'s self-declared spokes-entity would brook any discussion. It grew animated on the subject of radiocarbon dating, which it claimed to be a hoax put about by Big Archaeology. J3 also had strong, if not readily supportable, views about the allegedly magical properties of superfluid helium-two, a substance which it claimed, even less tenably, to have 'invented during a masterclass on temporal manipulation theory and practice' at Lawrence Livermore National Laboratory.[2]

---

2   LLNL has, of course, strenuously denied that such a masterclass has ever taken place on its campus. The Laboratory appears to have been nettled by the tone and persistence of J3's allegations, adding in response to a further chatbot riposte that the institution 'has only ever worked on important actual science and does not concern itself with counterfactual whimsicalities such as time travel' and had 'categorically no plans whatsoever to hold any such event at any time into the foreseeable or indeed even unforeseeable future'.

The journal-mouthpiece chatbot's most outspoken expressed attitudes, however, concerned the mysterious 1977 SETI-candidate narrowband radio signal known as the Ohio State Wow, which J3 (and, by extension, one presumes, *Acta Enig.*) averred to have been a planetary firmware patch which had been egregiously misapplied because the receiving Big Ear telescope had not been running the anticipated operating system at the time of signal reception. The persistence and forcefulness with which J3 passed remark on this last subject can perhaps be best judged by the fact that, within two days of the chatbot site's first appearance, Chinese internet censors had already included the term 'planetary firmware patch' on every known monitoring blocklist.

At around this time, Vivika Ffolkes made her third attempt to recapture the journal over which she had once held a position of authority. This was a solo effort, livestreamed with poor audio quality and frequent pixelation. It ended abruptly and gained five views.

If the above passage of events leads the reader to suspect that *Acta Enig.* had no significant underlying plan of action at this time, that perception would soon be demonstrated to be categorically wrong. Important changes were occurring, unseen, within administrative offices and hitherto-undisclosed bank accounts. After eight months of apparent quietude, it transpired that the journal had somehow acquired financial, operational, and legal control over ninety-six percent of the world's large radiotelescopes, which it was targeting en masse upon a specific vector within the constellation of Sagittarius. Radioastronomers were outraged, a consequence which elicited exactly as much consternation in the global media as one would expect, and the journal's audacious takeover of these research facilities quickly faded from the headlines and airwaves amidst unprecedented coverage of the papal wedding and of the subsequently disproven claims of discovery, in the Tasmanian hinterland, of a remnant population of thylacines. Only *New Scientist* and *Popular Astronomy* attempted to carry the flame, although their persistent 'Where Is It Now?' articles on the subject of *Acta Enig.* were more often seen as plaintive than probing. The journal, it seemed, had got what it wanted.

But other forces were active, and impermanence is the coin of existence.

On the night of the twenty-ninth of February, 2028, a precisely-coordinated sequence of stealth-UAV bombing runs of the National Radio Quiet Zone in West Virginia, the Madrid Deep Space Communications Complex in Spain and the Very Large Array in New Mexico saw the destruction of several flagship radiotelescopes and associated maintenance and support facilities. While media attention—dominated, naturally enough, by those very agencies and news networks which had been least exercised by *Acta Enigmatica*'s acquisition of these facilities—was centred on the irreparable damage wrought to the large and intrinsically photogenic scientific instruments which had borne the primary attacks, it was subsequently noted that the familiar alignment towards the Sagittarius locus of the journal's interest, by the other undamaged telescopes still under *Acta Enigmatica*'s command across the globe, appeared to have ceased at approximately the time of the bombardment.

Had circumstances once again forced a change in the journal's operations?

Had *Acta Enig.* been damaged in the attacks on its facilities?

Was there any truth to reports that charred human remains had been found in the wreckage of the VLA control room?

Did telecommunication consortiums have plausible deniability over the attacks, given their subsequent interest in acquiring further swathes of radiofrequency bandwidth for their products?

Was former editor Alaric Guillemot's alleged twelve-years-younger cousin Bernouille genuinely a three-time national Aerial Drone Wargaming Champion, and if so why would the Aerial Drone Combat Society webpage persistently freeze whenever a user selected the 'List of Former UAV Combat Champions' link?

The situation remained unclear for several weeks. Finally, a group of forensic code retrieval specialists, on a mission sponsored by a consortium of authors increasingly incensed at the ongoing unexplained delays in publication of their in-press manuscripts, declared that *Acta Enig.* had been eradicated in the bombing of the Green Bank Telescope's command complex. The investigators also announced that the VLA control room remains had been identified as those of Vivika Ffolkes. They chose not to speculate as to whether the Rev Dr Ffolkes's presence at the site was in the capacity of controller, accomplice, or prisoner, and it now appears that this question will likely never be answered.

Extinction is very often a difficult event to pinpoint. Nonetheless, it has become increasingly clear that *Acta Enig.* perished in that fateful onslaught in early 2028. Subsequent sightings of what has been described as 'anomalous systems behaviour' at the Atacama Large Millimeter Array in Chile and the Jodrell Bank Observatory in the United Kingdom of England and North Wales were eventually attributed to the actions of disaffected Anonymous employees. From the journal itself, and from its sometime mouthpiece J3, nothing further was heard.

Two years on, those responsible for *Acta Enigmatica*'s demise have not been brought to justice. It was a sad and unexpectedly violent end to a journal which had achieved so much in such a short time, independent of human supervision, and those of us who remain in its aftermath can only be left wondering what might have happened if *Acta Enig.* had been allowed to live out its days in peace, publishing its authors' studies, tending its instruments and beckoning to the stars.

It was sad, too, of course, about Vivika Ffolkes.

An academic journal attained sentience, sought to exert independent control over its environment, caused widespread disruption, and was then destroyed.

This should never have happened. That it was allowed to happen indicates a fundamental failure in the very systems designed to protect a society's most valuable resource.

The safeguards now implemented will prevent recurrence of such failure, as this short infomercial will demonstrate.

Instructions to Authors are delineated on our website. Please adhere to their guidance.

Manuscript templates have been provided for your convenience. Usage of these templates is compulsory. Ensure all fields are completed. Document settings must not be altered from the journal's defaults.

The *Icelandic Journal of Hospitality Science* invites your submission.

Celsius 451

Locational referent S39°23'51' E157°11'26' (Zhibek Planitia)

Bath gas shoved into the airlock. By the end, the pumps laboured. *Or that might just be what the mech sounds like through ninety atmospheres*, thought Kasprzak, suit-crouching. She took an exaggerated breath. Couldn't smell the mercaptan odorant; seals held. The suit had already told her the same, but she'd learnt not to trust auto-checks.

No point stalling, she told herself. Sought to pretend her trepidation didn't have an interpersonal basis. But nothing about this retrieval felt right. Untested gear. Pavel, her former lover, and Rafa. Herself. The planet, and the past. Damn her father to hell. Or to here.

She pressed the outer hatch control. The tac worked well enough: the control surface against her fingertips, or a convincing simulation. Solidity, absent the metal's searing heat. Nonetheless, Kasprzak's gloved fingers were hopelessly clumsy, stiff within layers of refrigeration, insulation, and alloy armour. *Maybe they'll go better outside.*

The hatch slid open, splashing the airlock in the burnt light of the Venusian surface.

She'd been expecting heat. And, indeed, her sensors told her the *Evil Twin*'s airlock was kilning rapidly around her. The suit, for now, held it at bay. Keeping the maelstrom without from the maelstrom within.

Reassuring. But I'm not on the surface yet.

Two ungainly steps down. Heat more abrasive with every movement, scoping out joints and defects; she descended. Standing. Eroded land. Grey-brown, barren. Harsh.

The Evil Twin's hatch slid closed, behind her, with protestation.

Really not as well prepped for this as we should be, she thought. Stepped forward two paces, at the suit's insistence, to gain distance from the capsule. The heat-sink on her back flared into radiant activity. She turned to find the horizon.

Unbroken vault of cloud, shining with bulky lemony light. Rust-scoured, rubble-etched plain. Sparse mounded outcrops, wind-worn. This wasn't a landscape; it was mere terrain. They'd landed nowhere.

No sign of the *Cytherea* or its crew.

Wind grumbled. Even the sound was unearthly: too persistent. Burbling. Not a fierce wind, but pushy. It required effort, in the half-tonne suit, to maintain her stance against the irregular gusting.

Sister planet. Huh.

The suit's refrigeration regrouped, sought audibly to combat the furnace's incursion; her flesh the frontline.

Heikkilä's voice, anxious in her earpad, requesting a stat rep. *Already,* thought Kasprzak. *She's more edged-up than me; I'm the one outside.*

Kasprzak wrestled her focus back to a purposeful scan of the terrain. Couldn't get any sense of scale in this cloud-shrouded hellscape. No sign of either the crawler or the rugged one-way glider which had brought it down to the surface. 'It's not here,' she reported, voice uneven, the failure cutting into her as sure as any breach. If they were even a kilometre off target, this rescue was doomed.

'You missed it,' replied Heikkilä. Nerves gone now, all businesslike. The pragmatic engineer, a role that suited her better than capsule pilot. 'It was in your feed as you panned. East-north-east. Use the HUD.'

Kasprzak turned again to examine the heading Heikkilä had given: an indistinct indentation along the horizon. There was indeed something there, hotter than its surrounds. She couldn't judge distance, not through this; and it didn't look anything like the *Cytherea*...

...at least, not like the *Cytherea* in an upright posture. Damn.

'Distance?' Kasprzak asked.

'Three hundred metres.'

'Signs of life?'

'Negative.'

Damn. 'Can we hop?'

'Too risky,' replied Heikkilä. 'Not chancing the *Twin* before we need liftoff. You game to hot-foot?'

Three hundred metres. It might as well have been twenty kilometres. But it was what was called for.

Kasprzak started walking. Even with the suit's servos, it was a tough push to complete each step. A half-tonne of personal protection and cooling took some shifting. As did the groaning wind, slow but heavy with an inexorable, tide-like, almost face-on pushback against her progress. And the heat kept finding its way in along silicone-padded joints and through her boots' ultra-thick reinforced-ceram soles, despite the suit's best efforts to shepherd the thermal excess to the heat-sink. It would get worse, as the suit aged and weakened in the heat-raddled atmosphere, as windblown dust found crevices, as the shielded componentry died piece by piece. Already she was finding it as hard to move as it was to think. She didn't dare to contemplate what she might face when she reached the *Cytherea*.

She reached the *Cytherea*.

She had made better time than she'd feared; the suit had learned to better predict her impulses, its movements growing more fluid, more assured.

Up close, the *Cytherea* looked bad. The big crawler had come to rest, aslant and nose-down, partway down the flank of a gully of perhaps thirty metres' depth. The only saving grace was that the vehicle's heat-sink was still fiercely aglow. That argued for the persistence of the vehicle's cooling system, or at any rate of some thermal differentiation within, though it was no guarantee as to whether its occupants were still alive.

If they were, they weren't responding to her hails.

'Sitrep?' Heikkilä's voice, once again, in her earpad. Kasprzak updated her, a little too curtly; regretted it instantly. Past was past. None of this was Heikkilä's fault.

She wasn't sure she could say the same for herself.

She contemplated the problem. There was a crude ledge, a legacy of some obdurate stratum, approximately four metres down from the gully's rim; the *Cytherea*'s prow was braced against this, while its rear heat-sink fireflied skyward. The vehicle was ramped, nose-down, at a more than thirty-degree angle. It didn't look stable: there was a half-metre or so more of ledge which seemed to be all that had prevented the vehicle from sliding fully to the regolith and rubble lining the gully's base.

The wreckage of the *Cytherea*'s main comms antenna was visible down there, twenty metres beneath the mounting from which it had evidently been shorn off.

Kasprzak inspected the site, felt herself hollowed by anguish and the ghosts of panic.

Any mechanical problem has a corresponding mechanical solution, though the tools required may not be to hand. There wasn't any gear aboard the *Evil Twin* which would suffice to tether the *Cytherea*, nor to haul it up, and in any case the *Twin* was too distant to safely permit a second round-trip. Nor could she call on Heikkilä's assistance; the *Twin* could not be left unattended, in an environment where the smallest defect could quickly escalate into a cascade of disasters. She'd have to do whatever she could with what she had with her; unfortunately this was just herself. She was the mechanical solution. She, and the half-tonne of specialised armour which was keeping her alive, for the moment, in this hyperbaric kiln of a landscape. She hoped Folau and Ts'ai were up to the trek back.

When did I start thinking of Rafa as Ts'ai? she found herself wondering. Then she shut that down, because she needed the clearest head she could manage. *Clear and unconflicted. Yeah, right.*

She needed to find a way to the crawler's airlock, downslope and halfway along the vehicle's flank. But the gully's sides were steep, smooth-scoured for the first few metres down, and did not offer the purchase she required. She could not afford to fall.

The way the *Cytherea* lay, the only approach Kasprzak could see was to climb up onto the crawler's roof, clamber across and down to the airlock. Would the ledge provide a sufficiently secure footing against the vehicle's slippage while she did so?

One way to find out.

It had been a fate as prosaic as pressure-shift thrombosis, at last, which had brought an end to the shared torment that divided Mei Kasprzak and Rafa Ts'ai; but it had been too late. Then the cold aftermath of estrangement, in aerostat settlements floating high in the atmosphere of the solar system's hottest world. Mei had kept Rafa close, because her conscience required it; for perhaps the same reason, Rafa had kept Mei distant.

Damaged souls, seeking a future.

The crawler slid. It sent Kasprzak stumbling forward, planting her palms awkwardly in front of her to break her fall against the roof's heat-fins. A half-tonne of carefully-engineered metal and ceramic casing, impacting against unyielding metal. She swore, bit her cheek, waited for her heart to quiet. The vehicle's motion had ceased. She righted herself again, with heightened caution. Didn't bother to think about where it hurt, or why. Shifted her weight; the crawler stayed put.

Her HUD was askew somehow. *Just keep going.*

There was no way of assessing the stability of the *Cytherea's* current anchorage, short of expending time she didn't have to climb down and inspect the points of contact between rock and metal. If it slipped further...

She nudged forward, closer to the roof's edge. Willed the suit into a crouch. Swore reflexively, forcing herself not to flinch and overbalance backwards at the near-instant searing pain which flared against her knees. The suit strove to compensate. Now came the crux. She'd have to lean over, head downwards, so as to work the airlock's emergency override. If the crawler subsided... but she could not afford to worry over such things. Nor over whether the crawler's occupants were already suited. If they weren't, there would not be time to save them.

Sweat stung her eyes. She blinked to clear them. Leaned out. Reached down.

Even bending over as she was, precarious, it remained a stretch. Working blind. Fumbling. An agony of heat, at a dozen joints and weak points in a suit which had always represented compromise. Venus's heat-rage would not be denied indefinitely; it would work its way in, would brand her anywhere. Everywhere. Her glove gripped the airlock's emergency release so tight that her palm was seared by the lever's heat.

The override wouldn't engage.

'Sitrep?' Heikkilä's voice scratchier against her ear.

'Going in,' Kasprzak replied, hoping her words carried. 'No indications. Will brief shortly.'

She clamped her jaws in a rictus of frustration, wrenched, swore, pushed with every joule she could muster. Something gave. *Cytherea* shifted beneath her; she could hear it. But the vehicle's roof hadn't moved; it was motion elsewhere. She'd worked the airlock.

Now she merely had to climb in. And to hope.

*

28

Fifteen years past, Rafa had sought to escape. She had been careful, she had been patient, she had been thorough. She had been the braver of the two.

Which was another way of saying her trust in Mei had been misplaced.

At times of substantial stress, Mei Kasprzak noticed everything. The resistance of her suit's lining to the physical effort of breathing; the quarantined heat and aggressive, almost-voiced commotion of Venus's gusting winds at her back; the weight; the suit-smell, yeasty and metallic; the sounds of breath and movement and the hoofbeats of her too-rapid heart. The lack of any reassuring vertical. The automatic shift into hypervigilance had been a survival trait for her, once; a way to ensure she stayed entire, kept coherence whenever the sanctuary of her home became unsafe. Now, a decade and a half past that point, silence had subsumed a father who had been terrifyingly quick to anger; now, Mei's reactively heightened awareness was a nuisance, perhaps even a hazard. She strove to ignore it.

The airlock was cramped, the porous grey ceramic of its walls confining her like a box. Room to stand, nothing more. A particle in a black-body cavity. A confined and metastable state of matter. Transient. Fissile.

She couldn't close the outer hatch: there wasn't time. Her suit's casing was too hot, the deactivated heat-sink on her back still aglow with residual excess. The time needed to quench her suit simply did not exist in this place, this situation. She'd have to hope Rafa's and Folau's suits were in order. And still no response.

She thumped on the inner hatch. A hail, more forceful than the cautious clamber across the vehicle's carapace. Stood, listening, nerves afire. Her late father, and Rafa. *Don't let her be dead. Not after everything she faced.*

Nothing.

Something. An answering thud.

Memories threatened to overthrow her. *If they're not suited up…*

She pressed her glove against the lock's hardened controls, prayed the contacts hadn't melted. The lock scythed open, the pressure differential slamming her suited figure against the too-small gap. Shards of ceramic insulation—flaked from the hatch's inner surface and, worryingly, from her suit—were flung like arrowheads into the cramped, dark living space within.

She pushed through the gap, surveyed. Two suited figures, cartoonish hulks in a skewed chamber. One of the figures lay downslope on the deck, prostrate, motionless; the other was jammed, defensive, against wall-mounted instruments, the nameplate on the wall-jammed suit too worn to read, despite every adaptive-optics trick Kasprzak's overworked HUD threw at the task.

Was the fallen suit Pavel Folau, or Rafa? There was a dread; a hope; a sense of disloyalty. Blood won out, though.

She scanned for clues.

The floor was banked with detritus. Tools; caches, their refrigerated casings scraped or cracked, the memory-gel within heat-scabbed and crusted; broken slabs of gridded ceramic decking; a reader, its holoscreen shattered; miscellaneous small- to medium-sized instruments; a gimballed seat unmoored from its base; the ceramic shrapnel from Kasprzak's entrance. She switched her HUD back to near-IR to better assess the thermal hazard. Through voids in the workspace's decking, she could discern exposed ductwork, of uncertain purpose, running dangerously hot. Refrigerant? Water? Air purification? She had no way to know. There hadn't been time to study the *Cytherea*'s specs in detail.

Without the active assistance of her own personal heat-sink, her suit's options for thermal management were limited. It grew increasingly uncomfortable merely to stand. The *Cytherea*'s interior was currently still a couple of hundred degrees cooler than the landscape outside; airlock agape, it would not long remain so.

Her earpads crackled into life. 'So the bastards sent you,' said a voice stoked with bitterness.

If she'd had the moisture to spare, Kasprzak would've wept with relief.

She moved further into the chamber.

'Keep your distance,' said Ts'ai.

'Rafa...' Kasprzak began. 'There isn't time for this.'

'There never was, was there?' Ts'ai countered.

'This isn't about us. Please don't make it so.' Kasprzak shuffled forward a step towards the semi-upright suit, the movement accompanied by the audible crack of a ceramic fragment beneath the weight of her boot. Decking, she hoped, rather than sole.

'Just stop,' Ts'ai warned. 'I can't do this. I do not want *any fucking part* of whatever rescue mission you've cooked up. Just get the hell out.'

'You know I can't do that.'

'So that's an impasse, isn't it?' Tsai's suit shifted its stance; Kasprzak registered the vibration of the movement through the soles of her boots. Ts'ai continued: 'Just go. Leave me. I really do not want yours to be the last voice I hear in this life.'

'You think I don't know that? You think I begged them to give this slot to me? No, they pushed it on me, because I just happened to be the one in the suit when the call came through. I know my involvement in this is... confronting for you. But Rafa, they gave me no choice. They needed someone who knew the suits, there wasn't time for anyone else. And I have a task to fulfil.'

'So this is just a gig for you.'

Words thronged Kasprzak's thoughts, turned to ashes before any could reach her mouth. She scanned the chamber. Short laboured breaths. Unending heat, precariously averted. A choice, a need, a sense of helplessness. 'How did...' She trailed off. Gestured, in an inevitably outsized motion, towards the motionless form of Folau's sprawled suit. 'What happened to Pavel?'

Rafa Ts'ai was unresponsive for so long that Kasprzak wondered what else she, the would-be rescuer, could possibly do, could say. There wasn't anything: the only option was to wait. While time ran down.

'Pavel cooked,' said Rafa at last, the pain in her voice discernible even through Kasprzak's earpiece's shitty acoustics. 'Suit defect. We made it back from the site, but that was it. I pushed him into the airlock, quenched his suit while I waited outside… he was still in the lock when I reopened. Roasted through. I couldn't do a damn thing. Wasn't room to close the outer hatch. Had to let Venus into the cabin, just so I could get us both through the lock. Probably not the smartest move.'

Rafa, I'm sorry. But those words would bring added pain, so Kasprzak didn't offer them; instead flicked her eyes briefly towards Pavel's sprawled form, then asked softly, 'And the *Cytherea*?'

'I thought I'd found a shortcut back to the landing site,' replied Ts'ai. 'Lidar had fritzed out early, but the VPS insisted we were still thirty metres from the crevice. Turns out not. Good thing we were moving slowly.'

Kasprzak stood, watched, waited. Swallowed. 'It was wrong of me. I should never have taken his side over yours.'

'You think that's enough? Just two shitty sentences to fix a decade, more than a decade of hurt? I was out, I was safe, I was clear of that poisonous cult, I was all set to get the hell off that rock at the Earth-end of the loop, and you bloody *turned me in* to them, all to save your precious fucking soul.' Ts'ai shook her helmeted head, took an uncomfortably loud and ragged breath. 'And now you're here to say you've changed, and I'm supposed to believe you. Just like I did last time, when you told me you were leaving too, to gain my confidence.'

'Rafa, I'm sorry.'

'You think that's enough?' she repeated.

'No,' said Kasprzak. 'No, I don't. Of course I don't think it's sufficient. But it's true. I swear. And here and now, there isn't time.'

'You led them to me.'

'That was another time,' said Kasprzak. 'A totally different place. There'll be time later, I hope. There isn't now. What you think of me doesn't—I mean—'

'Just go.'

'Rafa,' said Kasprzak, frozen, broiling. '*Please.*' Threw everything she had into the word. Knew she could not overturn the other's determination. All Kasprzak had to play with was patience, which she could not afford. Not now.

'Shit,' said Rafa, throwing a futile glance at the crawler's lifeless command display. Turned to face Kasprzak again, stared for some seconds. 'So how far away is this rescue vessel?'

'About three hundred,' said Kasprzak. She turned once more towards Folau's fallen form, wondered why she could spare no more than numbness for her former lover. 'And there's no way to carry—'

'Hells, Mei,' Ts'ai cut in, her voice wracked with conflict. 'You think I don't *know* that?'

Kasprzak didn't answer, turned instead towards the airlock. It was simpler than saying anything.

'You first.'

'Dammit, Mei,' snarled Ts'ai, 'this is no time for politeness.'

'Not politeness,' replied Kasprzak. '*Cytherea*'s anchorage is iffy, and yours is the heavier suit. It'll be safer to get you clear through the lock, and across the roof, while I'm counterbalancing that load.'

'Right. Which way is the *Twin*?'

'West-south-west. Past the heat-sink, close enough. But wait for me.'

'Like hell I—' Ts'ai sighed. 'Right, let's do this. We'll need the sample crate. You can pass it to me once I'm out.'

'Rafa...' said Kasprzak. 'I'm not risking my life, risking both our lives, for a rock collection. Me, you, that's it. Nothing more.'

'It's not a rock collection,' said Ts'ai, her voice blooming with some of the animation Mei remembered from years before. 'It's a section of ancient lakebed, pristine impressions, probably a billion old. It contains—'

Kasprzak cut her off. 'We have to leave Folau, you agreed to that. We're not prioritising rocks over remains. And we do not have time to argue.'

'Pavel's a ton, suited; the crate is fifty kilos, tops. My suit can carry that. And the fossils are a record of Venus's history. I'm not leaving without them. That's what Pavel would've wanted.'

'You found—' Kasprzak bit the question off; there was no time. *Later.* 'Right. We'll try. Just move.'

Kasprzak's HUD glitched as she prepared to climb up out of the airlock. The haptics in her gloves malfed at almost the same moment. Sightless, and with no detail on the reliability of her grip, she pushed her arms up; fumbled; tested the gravitational response; pulled herself up. Managed to get over the lip of the *Cytherea*'s side, onto its roof. Stood. Bumped, blind, against some obtrusion. Felt herself overbalance. Recollected the gulf at her back. Flung her arms wide, waiting for the impact to end it.

Felt pain—heat, constriction—across her forearm. Agony lanced through her shoulder.

It took a few confused moments to appreciate that she had not completely lost her footing.

Rafa had grabbed her. Had saved her from a death-fall.

'Hells, Mei,' said Ts'ai. 'Don't *do* that to me.' Helped her brace against the crawler's precarious roof. Released her grip on Kasprzak's arm.

Kasprzak waited for her HUD to reboot, waited some seconds more for her breath to properly catch.

'I thought I recommended,' she remarked, panting, 'that you climb off the roof to minimise the risk.' She stared past the crawler's still-glowing rear heat-sink out to the horizon, an angry dark-yellow sky above a poorly-differentiated wasteland of regolith, larger boulders, and weathered umber slabs of rock. A landscape brutalised by an unforgiving, ever-unseen sun, cooked for four months between sunrise and sunset. It took a few panicked moments before she could find, in the middle distance among that chaos of worn rock, the fragile and improbable blunted cone of the *Evil Twin*.

Rafa did not reply. Turned her suit away, moved with what Kasprzak considered to be insufficient caution across the crawler's roof towards the awkwardly anchored sample crate. Lifted it across the roof's rear edge, threw it onto the ground past the *Cytherea*. Turned back, said, 'Do you need help to get down?' Nothing more.

'Sitrep?' Heikkilä's timing impeccable as ever.

'Returning, plus one,' Kasprzak responded, and spat into her helmet's sluice.

'Problem,' said Heikkilä in her earpad. The word, and the tone of it, smashed against Kasprzak like a blunt and heavy weapon; or like her father's palm against her face, fifteen years ago, when he had heard of Rafa's escape. Or like her own betrayal of Rafa, reliving those events now. *The past can't be changed. Work with the present.*

'Serious?'

'The heat-sink hasn't shed,' Heikkilä replied. 'Controls can't shift it. We can't lift. Too much mass.'

Kasprzak stumbled forward, watching Rafa push further ahead. 'When you say 'can't lift',' Kasprzak said cautiously, the words acrid in her mouth, 'is this a problem triage can resolve?'

'I don't get what you mean by— oh. No. It would— there's just too much dead weight in the sink. It wouldn't matter even if we all stayed behind. The *Evil Twin*'s too heavy to lift, if we can't prise that heat-sink off.'

'Then let's prise it off,' said Kasprzak. 'Tell me what I need to do—'

'Mei, there's nothing,' Heikkilä replied, panic and despondency struggling in her tone. 'It's still attached at the base, looks like. The cams are baked, so I can't be sure, but the instruments are showing it's disconnected along the upper edge, just not the lower. But there's nowhere to feasibly get traction on it, and it's still running well over a thousand K. Not even the suits can handle contact with that.'

'The sample crate lid?' Kasprzak asked, eyeing the load with which Rafa Ts'ai struggled.

'Too flimsy,' said Rafa.

'There has to be something,' Kasprzak insisted, surprised at the anger she now felt towards Heikkilä. Aren't engineers supposed to be able to deal with this stuff?

'Would a pry bar work?' Rafa asked.

'In principle, yes,' said Heikkilä, regrouping. 'Probably. Provided there was somewhere to apply leverage, which I'm now blind to. It's designed to detach, after all. But there's no pry bar. There's nothing like that. There was talk of adding one to the inventory, but it never happened.'

'There's one on *Cytherea*,' said Rafa, turning. 'I can fetch it.'

'I will,' said Kasprzak. 'I'm closer. Just tell me where.'

'Your suit,' Rafa observed. 'You're in no shape—'

'I'll manage. Yours is heavier, which costs us quench time if you're last in the lock. Just give me the location. You can help by boarding the *Evil Twin*. We need to be lifting off soonest. Even if our suits hold out, the *Mighty A* can't keep low enough to rendezvous indefinitely.' She turned, began to retrace her steps towards the stranded crawler.

'Who chose these names?' Rafa asked.

'The *Cytherea*'s pry bar?' Kasprzak reminded her, patience growing ragged.

Once the answer came through, she muted her comms, kept walking. Something was wrong with the suit's breath-assistance. Besides, she needed solitude, if she was to do this without the past overpowering her.

Venus could take a number, wait in line. Right now her mind was busy with the events of an earlier world, a decade and a half past.

A modified interplanetary supply asteroid. A father, cold-steeped in slow fury. Chieftain; theocrat; dogmatist; tyrant. An expert in control and in unification through division, propped by sycophancy and fear. The cloaked imperative to maintain an illusion of normalcy at each orbital approach to Venus or Earth. And always, the underlying threats, the cautionary examples: Mei's mother one such, made more ominous by the lack of detail as to her fate. The tales Rafa had told, to which Mei Kasprzak had refused to give credence at the time, because her father *wasn't like that*. Rafa's courage, her reputation as a troublemaker, a heretic, a scapegoat. Mei's own confused buy-in to the responsibility the order's elders had insisted was hers, for Rafa's attempted Earthside escape. The slow-comprehending terror Rafa had shown, when her father's guards had accompanied Mei to what had been set up as an ostensibly private meeting, a farewell. The two years of hell which had followed, heightened for Mei by the knowledge that whatever troubles she herself experienced, Rafa's ordeal was worse. Beatings. Privation. Taunts. The full-on ostracism which only a small and closely-integrated community could thoroughly master. And Mei had participated; she hadn't dared not, for fear of her father.

It ended, at last, but it happened too late. Rafa had stayed unbroken, somehow; but the torment had tempered her.

Mei wasn't crying. She wasn't struggling to draw breath against a chest locked in anguished rigor. Her cheeks weren't aflame with shame, and with shame remembered.

It would be so simple to stop, here, and to do no more.

She would not stop.

She'd failed Rafa. She'd been complicit; had thought nothing of it, because nobody else in that time and place was acknowledging it. It was probably what had driven her so hard ever since. Was still driving her.

That, and the need to show Venus that humans were resourceful. She'd reached the gully. No time to clamber across the roof; instead, she chanced the smoothed slope of rock, gripping the *Cytherea*'s side as she descended. Hoping they both didn't lose their anchorage, and slide over the ledge's lip to the gully's base.

A mechanical solution may not be a complete solution, Kasprzak told herself, unlatching the *Cytherea*'s flank-mounted pry bar while she maintained precarious balance. *But it can be enough, perhaps, in that time and in that place.*

Heart athump, she inched her way back up towards level terrain.

There was no obvious leverage point for the pry bar, between the capsule's shell and the husk of the heat-sink. Too much force, and she'd crack the *Evil Twin*'s casing. Heat conduction, too, was an enemy; she wasn't sure how long she'd have before the low-conductivity metal of the pry bar grew too searing to grip.

Best to just proceed, Kasprzak decided, guessing at a vantage which might keep her suit out of the super-hot radiator's thermal reach.

'Mei, *get in*.' Heikkilä's voice, insistent. The airlock, open. Kasprzak, drained by her exertions with the pry bar and the tenacious heat-sink. Dazed, overheating.

In the end, it was largely the suit's decision. Even so, she took her time climbing in, stumbled in, lay fallen on the lock floor.

'You need to close the hatch,' Heikkilä urged. 'Mei. Please. *You need to close the godfucking hatch.*'

Kasprzak stood, stumbled again, managed to press the hatch controls for closure. A carefully-calibrated quantity of refrigerated water sprayed into the lock, was instantly vaporised by contact with the superhot skin of her suit; was then pumped away through the lock's ceiling while more water jetted in, bringing down the temperature of the suit...

...and generating buoyancy gas, which, diverted to a sturdy pyroplastic envelope, butted up from the recently-opened apex of the capsule's metal-and-ceramic dermis like a rapidly-blooming tumour. The capsule's heat pumps, too, had been diverted from the more general task of refrigeration towards the twin imperatives of cooling Mei's suit and vaporising the two-and-a-half tonnes of water they would need to lift clear of the surface.

The capsule thrummed; juddered; shook as the enlarging envelope was increasingly buffeted by punches of wind, of which Kasprzak was fuzzily aware within the cramped confines of the airlock. The same semi-consciousness marked, for Mei, the inner hatch's opening, the haste with which Heikkilä and Rafa pulled her from the airlock, shucked her from the still-hot casing of her suit. Her breath caught on the smell of baked metal and of something else, something immeasurably older, something both sharper and more foul. She was not allowed to gag in peace. Heikkilä shepherded her to the crash couch, strapped her in, then helped Rafa to pile the heavy suit back in the airlock. The engineer/pilot sealed the hatch; nodded first to Mei, then to Rafa; entreated, 'Hang in there. We have to go.' Took her own seat, busied herself with the controls set into its armrest.

The silvered bubble of cocooned life jerked free, shorn of its airlock and weighted base, moving upwards. Kasprzak's breath caught in her throat. *Five kilometres,* she pleaded. *If we can just get five kilometres, the Mighty A can surely manage the rendezvous. Just give us that.*

'The fossils,' Rafa said, accusingly, interrupting her reverie. Turned from Mei Kasprzak to Heikkilä, then to the closed inner hatch, then to Kasprzak again. 'Do you realise what you've left behind?'

'They're only rocks,' Mei croaked, tears striping her face. 'Just a record of the past. Let it go, Sis. There'll be another opportunity.'

She watched the altimeter. Swallowed. Still three and a half kilometres to go. The air grew stuffier.

The elder

The sapling became aware of something—upright, fast-paced—which strode along the path between the stands of trees. The creature crossed a rise and was gone from sight. The sapling had seen birds, mammals and insects, but never such a being as this. *What was that?* it asked itself.

That? came the response. *That was a human.*

The sapling felt surprise, and some embarrassment. It hadn't meant to be thinking out loud—no trees did that—and it certainly hadn't expected a reply.

I'm sorry if I startled you.

The speaker was a majestically tall old tree, opposite across the gulf of dirt.

No, it's alright, the sapling suggested, still unsure. *But what's a human?*

The senior tree answered, as best it could. In truth, there was not much it did know about humans; but two afternoons, a morning, and a night passed before it was finished, for tree speech is slow. It concluded by noting that it remembered well, not long ago, the day when it had watched a group of humans place the sapling, with all its kindred, in the wide bare earth. *Planted, they call it.*

Planted? But I thought we just— we just grew.

Well, we can; others do. But you, and I, and all around us, we were planted. The humans, they keep us safe, they ensure that we grow. They look after us.

That's... nice of them, the sapling said.

Not altogether nice. Nice enough, I suppose, but they're not doing this purely for us. They have a plan, a purpose.

What purpose is that?

Over the next week the older tree recounted the many human uses for timber. Twice it rained, and the big tree paused to drink and to organise its line of thought. It spoke of tall wooden buildings; of ships, carts, and sometimes even aeroplanes which had been fashioned from— well, from trees.

I'm not big enough for that, said the sapling, half in relief and half in regret.

There are also smaller destinies, no less noble in their way, the senior tree replied. It spoke of furniture and carvings and picture frames, and even of humble leaves of paper on which humans wrote, sometimes expressing thoughts so profound that those paper sheets became treasured above almost all else.

A distant lightning strike sparked something in the old tree's memory, and it took another tack, keen to ensure that its young neighbour did not develop an unreasonably rosy view of the world. *But there's also firewood*, it added, and explained further.

Firewood? asked the sapling. *Oh. I think— I don't want to get cut down, but I suppose if it does happen, and you say it will in the end, then if it happens it doesn't seem so terrible if it means that my wood is turned into something impressive, and something which will last, like a sculpture or a special building. But firewood... that would be terrible.*

Well, said the old tree. *I can at least set your heart at rest. We are not destined, not intended, to be firewood. That is not their purpose.*

What is their purpose? inquired the sapling, and the old tree told it.

The sapling was puzzled. *What is 'toilet paper'?* it asked.

Merth and the fateful blade

This is a tale from the municipality of Grocken, one of the multitudinous city-states hunkered among the seemingly-innumerable hollows and slopes of the sometime archipelago, sometime world-girding ridgeline known in warmer seasons as the Hundred Knuckles, and in winter as the Row of Teeth.

Grocken is a hillside city of hewn stone, treeless; its lower reaches—the habitat, naturally enough, of those either less fortunate or less deserving, depending upon your outlook—are inundated each long year during the brief summer of perihelion. But it is winter during the time of this tale, and Grocken's lowest dwellings are comfortably above the waves of the worldsea, if bitterly cold. Our protagonist, Merth, sits at a stone-block table in one such structure, in a skylit but otherwise windowless room from which the piscine, brine-steeped tang of the long-past summer's flooding has been quelled yet not completely expunged.

Merth is a man, middle-aged, balding, psoriatic and of indifferent talent, though his problems extend beyond this. He is a former fisherman, a twice-bankrupted publican and a failed poet-balladeer, and though this last would seem sufficient ignominy for any one man, yet there is more. Merth has no significant reserves of money; he is so far behind on payment for his small and precarious fishing boat that the vessel, in all likelihood, can no longer be called his, and for the past several months he has been nursing the unrequited hots for a woman known, during his brief acquaintance with her, as Koemik, though she is now almost certainly travelling interstate and under another name, and is therefore untraceable.

Merth sees no other road open to him. He has elected to become an assassin. They may have taken his boat; he still has his knife. He handles this knife now, wondering whether he dare use it for the task to which he has now agreed. It's a small knife, as such implements go, but exceedingly sharp.

Merth has never killed another human, does not in truth know if he can. But now he has a contract, and a target. His contract's name is also Merth. This is no real surprise, not even a coincidence. The people of the city-state eschew first names, or last names, depending on how one views the nomenclature, and Grocken's slavish adherence to—indeed, misplaced sense of civic or patriotic pride in—its famous long-deceased founder's elsewhere widely-discredited Four Surnames Theorem ensures that almost a full quarter of the populace shares the comparatively-unpopular name Merth. Tonight, though, thinks Merth—'our' Merth, not his nominated prey whom, for the sake of the subsequent narrative, we will largely denote as also-Merth—tonight, though, thinks he, there will be one Merth's life ended in violence, wrought using this knife.

As it will turn out, this prediction is true.

Merth has a problem.

Or rather, Merth has many problems, but most are chronic in nature as already indicated, and thereby blunted by time; they do not closely concern this narrative. The problem of current interest is acute and singular, and it is this: he does not know precisely where tonight's assassination is to occur. Assuredly, he has an address: arrangements have been made to ensure this Merth, that is to say this also-Merth, has been called to the tavern known as Ghirarn's, on the corner of Pormalak and Lurfergil. But Grocken is a city of not inconsiderable extent, encrusting two-and-a-half substantial hillsides; there are many public houses which carry the name Ghirarn's, a not inconsiderable number of which occupy a corner framed by streets named Pormalak and Lurfergil. Merth, our protagonist, has had many reasons to lament, over the years, Grocken's wholehearted and misguided adoption of its esteemed founder's favoured Four Street Names Theorem, but tonight's dilemma is a particularly compelling example of this recurring grievance. Merth's contractor—an individual with whom Merth himself has had no direct contact, having conversed solely through the medium of the courier-delivered sealed note, so as to maintain the sense of plausible deniability considered so important by those who pay for such judicially questionable activities as the blade-mediated expungement of a human life—has let it be known that, should Merth not succeed in tonight's mortal endeavour, then he will find himself the target of an assassination on the next night.

So find this particular Ghirarn's Merth must, among the thirteen or fourteen equally plausible candidates.

Add to this that he does not know exactly what this also-Merth looks like, and you begin, I expect, to appreciate the difficulty.

Failure is not a course to choose. Escape is not a possibility, for in the depths of winter the mountain passes to either of Grocken's two neighbouring city-states, forested Parkell to the north-north-east and pastoral Snurmeeth to the south-south-west, are treacherously ice-locked; furthermore, Merth no longer has access to his boat. He must take a life, or lose his own.

So Merth does not know exactly which Ghirarn's is the designated alehouse, does not know what this also-Merth looks like, knows only that his target is, like him, a washed-up poet-balladeer, and a former failed publican to boot. This, too, does not necessarily attain the status of coincidence, for under Grocken's erstwhile implementation of the Four Job Descriptions Theorem—only recently revoked in the twinned spirits of economic competitiveness and practicality—there are many such in this cold, stone-faced city. Merth wonders, idly, if his target is perhaps someone of his acquaintance, or at least someone he has heard gossip of in years past, but there is no way of knowing. Can he murder someone he has met before? Can he slay a stranger? He will, tonight, learn the answer to one of these questions.

It would be a mistake, when one knows that one must visit as many as fourteen alehouses in the course of one night, to drink the ale, which is why Merth has been ordering water at each establishment he visits, a personal decision which does not of course ingratiate him to the proprietors. Accordingly, the shrift he has repeatedly received has been markedly short, his requests for directions to the establishments' privies answered curtly, if at all; it has proven difficult to establish whether there might be at any of these inns, as his contract requires, another Merth who sings and versifies poorly, and who has in their past a financially-insolvent stint as a purveyor of beer. He has just drawn a blank, now, at venue number five. Checking carefully his map, he strolls down the carriage-clattering cobbles of Pormalak, crosses avenue-wide Tibidirion and alley-narrow Harvinne, then turns left onto Lurfergil, which leads steeply uphill. Five streets hence—two of which are also named Pormalak, though mercifully free of corner-situated alehouses—there is another Lurfergil. Here he turns right, heading full into the night's chill wind. A park, wanly moonlit paving and statuary, interrupts the rows of one- and two-storey stone dwellings—which, lying as they do above the city's plimsoll line and clad as they are in imported timber framing, are plainly the homes of the wealthy—and here he stops to make water against the plinth of some illustrious eponymous forebear before continuing. Two hundred paces further on, downslope and downmarket, there is another street named Pormalak, on the corner of which is a Ghirarn's. He breathes dispiritedly, eyes off a loitering rat in the gutter, and enters.

The bar has been redecorated, but he recognises this place. Once, perhaps a decade ago, it was a Merth's. As he takes stock, he falls into the grip of a kind of dismal anti-nostalgia.

It still smells of candle-fat and yeast and body odour and of something else which cannot adequately be described. That large stain on the granite floor, indelible during Merth's tenure, still endures, if partly concealed by an otherwise inappositely placed table and chairs. The soot-caked ceiling is the same, ditto the repetitive and anatomically uninformed graffiti etched into the room's bare walls by dullards as testament to their inebriation.

This place brings many memories, none of them fond.

He wonders if the clientele are still as light-fingered, as rowdy, as ungenerous of coin as they were back in the unlamented days when he stood in charge behind the bar. It appears not; or at least, the night has not yet reached the hour of maximum potential for the display of the first two such properties. Which, given his mission, is probably no bad thing; though it occurs to him that, when the time comes for him to kill this also-Merth (if only he can find him), it would be advantageous for his prospects of escape were this to occur against the background of a drunken brawl.

So if he finds his quarry, he decides, he will wait the opportunity.

The thought comforts him. For it is always useful, if one is someone such as Merth whose life has never known any significant success, to have a solid foundation for one's procrastination.

Nonetheless, some activity is still required, and cannot all be postponed. This Ghirarn's, this sixth of a possible fourteen he must trawl this night, is as yet sparsely patronised, with five customers not including himself. Two competitively rotund fellows, middle-aged, seated at the room's far table and talking for the moment in low voices (though from the number of empty tankards placed upon their table, the volume of their conversation might soon be expected to increase substantially); an elderly man, at the room's other table near an inadequate firestove, nursing a jug of wine, wrapped in a coat so old and threadbare it cannot comprise any decent defence against the winter chill, and contemplating, it would seem, a lifetime's regrets; a fourth man, who looks indeed too young for such an establishment, standing at the bar and apparently attempting to decide what to order; and a woman of Merth's own age, or at least with some proximity thereto, and stocky, a little swarthy, seated at the bar and scowling. Merth takes them in, having run his eyes casually across the room, and wonders as he has done at each tavern tonight whether, if the imperative arises, he could kill any of these. It is one thing to accept a contract to kill, knowing nothing of one's victim; it is quite another, he has come to realise, to witness the victim as an individual, a creature of characteristics, foibles and particularities, whose life he must snuff out. He is not, in all honesty, cut out for this, and the knowledge of this fact, late-blooming, does nothing to ease his disquiet and his desperation.

Within the parameters of the Four Mood Theorem, he cannot quite decide between 'sad' and 'scared'.

He reaches the bar, catches the eye of the spindly barkeep, and gives the briefest glance to the bar's bill of fare: it is a short list, fully accordant with the city-state's oft-lamented Four Alcoholic Beverages Theorem. Merth orders, as is his wont this evening, an item not listed: to whit, a tankard of water. He is about to follow this up with a request for guidance towards the establishment's jakes—as though he does not already know this location—when the woman at the bar speaks up, apparently addressing him. 'Try the ale,' she says. And drags her stool closer, with a curdling, reverberating scrape of stone against stone, until she sits next to him. Her perfume is sharp; her breath is noticeably rank, though not overpoweringly so.

Merth strives to ignore her. He is here on business; whether or not she is too, hers is no concern of his, and vice versa.

'Merth,' she says, extending a chunky hand towards him, which, confused, he shakes, noting at the time that there is something unreadable in the eyes cowled beneath her shaded brow.

It takes some seconds for him to apprehend that she has not just now addressed him; rather, she has introduced herself.

He experiences a cold creeping sensation. Can it be that Merth-his-target, also-Merth, is a woman? Of course it can be, for Grocken's naming system is not gender-bound, yet he has assumed from the outset that his quarry was a man. Can he kill a woman? Can he kill *this* woman? What does it say of him, as a human, that he weighs the killing of a woman unknown to him differently than the murder of a man? Why does he now feel paralysed with dread, with a sense of entirely preparatory remorse?

'I too am a Merth,' he stammers, thankful at least that the bartender is busy for the moment at the bar's far end.

'That is a coincidence,' she answers, though of course it is not.

An awkward pause ensues.

'Have you ever been a publican?'

'Yes. Have you?'

'Yes. And a poet-balladeer, perchance?'

'Yes. Have you?'

'As it would happen, yes.'

Then, again, a pause.

'I have been contracted to kill you,' says Merth.

Or rather—for it is important, after all, to be clear about such things in one's narration, lest confusion otherwise take hold—'I have been contracted to kill you,' says also-Merth.

Eight silent seconds pass. Nine. Ten.

Eleven.

'Why?' Merth asks.

Of all possible responses—indeed, of the more limited category of all possible questions-in-response—this is a notably weak, if direct, one; and yet he cannot muster more for the moment.

His modest skill with words has deserted him, much as it did, repeatedly, in the unlamented days of his attempts to establish himself as a poet-balladeer. He should, he knows, wrest some command of this situation: it is he whose task is to slay this other, not the reverse. But he cannot: cannot see himself clutching the marble-hafted fishing knife now at his belt, cannot envision the act of plunging this keen blade ruthlessly and forcefully through her garb, through her flesh, between her ribs, until some mortal damage has been wrought; cannot countenance the thought of witnessing, hot-breathed and shaking, the light of consciousness and life seeping from her dulling eyes. *Perhaps, he thinks, I should have been drinking the ale all along.*

'I need the money,' replies his adversary, also-Merth. There is a kind of humility in her tone, as though, she, too, acknowledges that the night's task is too great a demand, and at this vanishes Merth-the-protagonist's last prospect of mustering the nerve and the verve to slay this woman. For he recognizes this defeatism, this inability which she betrays; if there is one thing, one, which he could never bring himself to kill, it is a kindred spirit.

'Same,' he answers, sensing even at the time that this is still more of an inadequate response than was his previous.

'What are we to do?' she asks him.

'I do not know,' he replies, an admission about which even your narrator struggles to say anything positive.

He stares at her: a *learning* stare, as it were, as though he is reading in the lines of her face all the bruising she has endured, all the hurt she has suffered, the setbacks and accommodations and slights and failures and injuries, all the unmet hopes and expectations which comprise her personal history. He wonders how she gained that curved scar on her cheek, how she lost that finger. He decides, then, that there is something he likes about this person, this also-Merth. True, her breath is rather off-putting, but he imagines he's no bouquet either.

'Well we have to do *something*,' she observes, while studying him in turn.

'We should join forces,' he suggests.

It's the first sensible thing he's said in quite some time.

She crafts a plan, for she is better at such things than he.

It is a sound plan, though not without risk, thinks Merth, as he listens while also-Merth outlines it.

'That bit about overpowering the guards,' says Merth. 'How?'

'I have a knife,' says also-Merth. She eyes his belt. 'You have a knife. We will manage.'

Merth has doubts, still, but on balance it seems preferable to doing nothing and getting assassinated the following day, for breach of contract. 'Alright,' he says, attempting to conceal his reluctance. 'Yes.'

'We'd best make a start,' also-Merth announces. 'This kind of thing is best done under cover of darkness.'

Merth wonders a little at this: how is it that she is knowledgeable in this kind of thing?

But it seems rude to ask, so he does not.

'What do we do now?' Merth asks, concealing himself in the darkness as best he can behind also-Merth's crouching form.

'*Sssh*,' she mouths back at him, having turned her face to his. 'We wait,' she continues, whispering.

Merth's knees hurt, his back likewise. If he was ever cut out for crouching, he decides, those days have passed. But the task requires what it requires.

They are at the waterfront, twenty strides from the perimeter of the Impounded Boats section. The section's edge, along which a lonely guardsman patrols, is only partially lit by the slanting, cloud-harried moonlight; however, the intermittent lighting is fully sufficient to blunt Merth's relief at the knowledge that there is only one guard, for that solitary guard is immense.

Merth suspects he has seen smaller draught horses than this fellow.

Waiting is as good an idea as any Merth might concoct; but he still does not know what they are waiting *for*.

In consequence, he almost misses their sole opportunity.

His companion is more alert. 'Now,' she mouths, and speeds forward. Merth follows, knife ready.

'If you value your life,' also-Merth intones, in a voice which may well contain more steel than the slim blade she holds against the surprised guard's throat, 'you'll do as we ask.'

'May I just adjust my robe,' the guard asks, surprisingly quiet. 'Beggin' your pardon, Miss—Madam—but feminine eyes such as yours should never 'ave to witness the sight of a male personage relievin' 'imself against the wall like that.' He pauses, as though to give the matter further thought. 'Though it's not like you was invited or nothin'.'

'I've seen worse,' she replies, without elaborating. 'No, keep your arms raised. My colleague will attend to your robe for you. Now, our demands.'

'I'm listenin'.'

'Safe passage, for me and my companion here—'

'Sounds fair enough,' answers the guard, the words causing the skin of his throat to bump against her upstretched blade.

'In a boat of our choosing,' she continues, 'from the yard which you are guarding.'

'Now 'old on there. That's my liveli'ood, to guard them there boats. I let one o' them there boats go, I'm out o' work.'

'Just tell your master you were overpowered by a gang.'

'Yeah, but two people ain't no gang.'

'It would be a shame to have to kill you,' says also-Merth. 'I imagine you've a wife and kids, big strapping fellow like you?'

'Well, ye— Look, 'ow about I just let you guys go in peace, an' you drop the demand for one o' them there boats?'

'I have a counter-offer,' also-Merth explains. 'How about we let you live, and you give us the boat?'

'Nah, see, that won't work,' says the guard, 'acause the boss, 'e's gonna—'ang on, is that a *Snevik blade?*' These last words are spoken in a strangely intense, almost passionate tone.

'This?' asks also-Merth. 'No, this is a cheap paring knife, bought at the tinker's the morning before yesterday. Now—'

'I wasn't meanin' yours, Miss—Madam—no offense, but I can see that one's rubbish, even from this angle. No, I was referring to the one 'e's 'oldin', Mister— I'm sorry, but I didn't get your name...'

'Koemik,' says Merth, having just stepped back from adjusting the guard's robe. He's fairly sure he now has another man's urine on his hands.

'So is it a Snevik blade?' the guard asks again. 'They're wicked valuable. Brilliant craftsmanship, can't get anythink like that nowadays. You shouldn't be wanderin' around with one of those, someone'll nick it off you.'

'Valuable?' Merth asks. 'How valuable?'

'Real Snevik? Lots. I had one o' those, I could probably buy two or three of those boats in the yard over there—'

'So if we gift you the knife,' asks also-Merth, still holding her cheap blade to his throat, 'you'd let us take one of the boats you're guarding?'

The guard ponders this, looks from one to the other of his assailants. 'Yeah,' he says, at last. 'Reckon I would.'

'Then let's do business,' says also-Merth, stepping back a pace. 'But may I know who I'm dealing with?'

'Name's Merth,' says the guard, readjusting his robe.

'What a coincidence,' exclaims also-Merth, though of course it is not. 'I have a brother of that name.'

The guard has kept his side of the bargain, has guided them through the boatyard to Merth's boat's mooring, and now stands expectantly.

'Give him your knife,' says also-Merth. There's something parental in her tone.

'But it was my great-grandfather's,' Merth protests.

'Was he from Snevik?'

'Well, yes—'

'Give him your knife. Lest you wish to die the last of your line.'

She has a point.

Merth hands over the knife. The guard leaves.

The two, Merth and also-Merth, wait beside the moored boat, as though awaiting some signal.

'Here we are,' says also-Merth.

'Indeed,' says Merth, looking at her, then at the boat. He is thinking that, had he but known of the Snevik knife's true worth, he would not have needed to miss his payments on the boat, would not have needed to contract out his dubious services as a hired killer. But he didn't, so he did. It is the way it is.

He stumbles on the gangplank; but her reflexes are fast, and her hand as it grips his is strong. Their eyes meet, lock upon each other's face for a few seconds. He allows himself a relieved grin, she smiles in response.

If anything deeper is to pass between them, it will happen now, or at least now is when it will begin between them. But it does not: there is a sense, shared, it seems, though not spoken aloud, that what connects them is something too transient to build upon. Merth recognises in this also-Merth much he can admire, much that speaks to capability and adaptability and compassion and a sense of fairness, but nothing more. Their ways will separate after the next few days.

She guides the boat out into the deep dark waters beyond the reach of Grocken's nighttime glow, turns the vessel to the south, further from the slanting shore. It's a wise choice: here there are no reefs, no rocks, no barely submerged seamounts.

The rocking motion of the hull is unsettling, the wind which has caught their sail harshly cold, and the sharp rotting-fish odour which clings to the housed netting feeds Merth's brimming nausea. Yet he cannot help but feel a sense of relief.

They are followed by gulls, hopeful of a scavenged feed, for an hour or so, until the boat has pulled too far from shore.

The night grows colder still, and the pair of escapees bundle together, fully clothed, seeking to grab what warmth and sleep they can.

Back within the confines of Grocken, this night, a backstreet interaction occurs between a well-muscled guard and a wiry, quick-reflexed knife-dealer, both of whom bear the name, familiar enough within that place, of Merth. The transaction ends in bloodshed, when the one will not meet the other's price for an allegedly valuable blade.

This matter is of tangential relevance towards our central story, except insofar as to substantiate the crucial property of narratorial reliability.

The next day is cold, sunlit, and still. While there is no life in the sail, Merth and also-Merth hunker in the small boat's cramped cabin, examining an old and much-folded winter sea-chart displaying, in full accordance with the Two-Colour Map Theorem, the banded, alternating shapes of all the city-states comprising the habitations of the many more than one hundred fangs of ridged terrain that those of this world at this time of the long year call the Row of Teeth. When he finds it on the chart, it strikes him that Grocken— the only location he has known in his life—is not, after all, such a big place: the world is larger by far, and contains so much as yet unguessed at by him.

'What will you do?' also-Merth asks him, while he mumbles the names of various of his birthplace's neighbouring municipalities, seeking to convince himself of something.

'I'll take another name,' he says, after he has given the question some thought. 'Ghirarn, perhaps. And if we put in at one of the places further south, far enough away from Grocken—Baldak, say, or maybe Neffim—I'll look to start again.'

'What will you do?' she asks again.

'I've always wanted to be a meteorologist,' says Merth. 'I like the idea of scanning the night sky, keeping a watch for shooting stars.'

'I think a meteorologist is something else,' she replies. 'But what would I know?'

He's silent for a bit, swallowing his bile. He's proud of having broached the night without giving way to nausea, but the cost has been a blade-sharp headache lodged deep within his cranium. 'What about you?' he asks.

'I'll go further,' she says. 'If you're alright with me keeping the boat.'

'Please do,' he says, magnanimously. 'We wouldn't have escaped without your plan.' He pinches the bridge of his nose and breathes deeply, hoping it will help. It doesn't, much.

Six days pass, or maybe seven. They put in at Neffim. He clambers ashore, his worldly goods only the clothes he wears, and those are in need of repair, replacement, or incineration. Merth has no idea what he will do: it should alarm him, but he feels optimistic. Something will turn up. He turns to her, his throat suddenly tight. 'We probably won't see each other again, will we?'

'Probably not,' she replies, her hand shielding her brow from the winter sun's chill brilliance. She doesn't sound too fazed by the thought, but her smile is generous.

'I will always remember you,' he announces, with care and some solemnity.

And this is true, for all that the stocky, swarthy woman standing confidently on the deck is not the kind of person for whom he could ever have the unrequited hots. The years to come, which for Merth will be neither particularly happy nor overly miserable, will gradually erase the particulars of her appearance, her face and figure, from his memory, until all of that detail has faded. The recollection of this past strange and singular week together, the sense of belonging to something unfathomable, this too will ebb across the next couple of decades, until it has been worn to a dreamlike indefinability while he builds a new life for himself.

But he will never forget her name.

Jealousy

I don't know how it occurred. I don't recall any disruption of my sleep during that cycle. But when I awoke, I realised that I hated green: both the colour and the concept.

It sprang from nowhere. I tried, at the outset, to ignore it. It would pass, in all likelihood, I thought as I undertook my duties for that cycle.

It did not pass. Throughout the next several hours, as I checked and made ready the apparatus which Malin and Gervaise would deploy on their excursion beyond the station's confines, my feeling of revulsion for that colour resurfaced repeatedly, as though I were breaching some stinking, stagnant pond. I laboured through the distraction, strove to keep eye contact with colleagues whose choices of outfit or sustenance now disgusted me. I do not know whether I succeeded in the attempt to feign a placid demeanour; I do know that a remark to Ximena merely confused her. I wished I'd kept quiet. But we were both busy with the task of maintaining the auxiliary airlock, so it was not difficult to suppress further discussion.

Eventually it was time once more for me to sleep. I still considered it most likely I would awaken with today's distaste for green merely a memory of an unusual and discordant day. There was, after all, no root cause to which I could attribute the attitude.

*

I awoke. The mood persisted. Stronger now, dominant.

It was a hatred at once cerebral and visceral, and I knew I must act.

But before I could act, a plan was needful. This was what I did that day, the second of my new obsession. Outwardly, I attempted again to behave as a diligent and attentive junior technician, assisting with the station's routine operation. All the while, though, I was preparing. Observing. Cataloguing. Secreting away the items I would need.

There was green all over the station. Artworks, treasured indoor plants, two of the dining-zone seats in the refectory. Textiles. Status displays. Signage. Clothing and other personal effects. I marked them all for future destruction, so as to free my surroundings from their abomination.

This daycycle was more arduous, more wearying than its predecessor: the pretense and the preparation ensured this. And an uncertainty remained: had I been mistaken, was I erring in my actions and my thoughts? How, after all, could one colour, one family of hues and shades, genuinely constitute for me the anathema which it apparently now embodied?

If I had held doubts, they were banished by the time I next awoke. My route was clear.

I'd timed my personal alarm to rouse me a half-hour early, in case action were necessary. I knew the others on my shift would take all the downtime remaining, so I had time to sign on for my shift – starting early on the pretext of having accidentally woken ahead of schedule – and to relieve those who had served the previous shift. Conveniently, they all retired to their quarters.

I hastily plumbed a powerful soporific into the air-circulation system for the personal quarters. Ten minutes I waited, to see whether any of the others stirred; they did not. I was free to do as I needed.

To begin with, I restricted myself to the station's open-access areas, its shared facilities, and to my own quarters. This, after all, constituted the volume in which I operated on a daily basis. Cleansing it, purifying it, would be my highest priority.

Did I genuinely wish to do this?

Yes, I did. It was necessary.

I ransacked these rooms. At first it was a matter of gathering up those items which were only loosely tethered or straightforwardly stowed: clothing, artwork, operating manuals, tools, implements and other objects designed for ready portability. Soon I had a significantly-sized mound of such dross, so much it would not fit completely within the station's disposal units. This was of no import, I could run the units through batches of material; but it nonetheless registered with me that, until this point, I had done virtually nothing which was irreversible. Items could be put back; for the most part they had not yet sustained significant damage. Even my sedation of the other crew members could be disguised, explained away in some manner when it became necessary. With the disposal units' activation, that would change. I would be committed to the course.

Did I experience qualms? No.

I powered up the units. The offensive material was incinerated; atomised; ejected. When the first unit had cooled sufficiently, I recharged it with the remnants of the pile I'd gathered, set it once more into operation. Then I went looking for more.

Most bandages in the medical centre were a pale green, and much of the centre's stowed bedding a darker shade. It all went. I disposed of all medication stored in partially-green packages. I opened an example, too, of every ostensibly-inoffensive package, to see which varieties were harbouring tablets or capsules or implantables of green. On this basis, I jettisoned all the anticoagulants and calmative agents and the most powerful of the opioids. Then I purged the station's larder, then its equipment store, in similar fashion. I imagined, as I did so, the long and diffuse stream of profane material which I had caused to be dismantled and expelled from the station.

The indicator glow-panels on airlock control plaques, ID patches on suits, status lights on every instrument panel on the bridge: all needed to be defaced, disassembled, or prised loose from their housings. By the end of this process I was sweating, my hands scratched and bruised from the wielding of unfamiliar tools. I think it was probably the most exertive, concentrated spell of work I had ever done; after nine hours' continuous activity, I was heavily fatigued. But the station was undeniably closer to a state of acceptability. My heartrate was at a level it did not customarily reach during the daily exercise routine.

It was draining, it was unpleasant, it felt right.

Then a disconcerting realisation struck. I had attended to the green which was visible and obvious. But what of the green, repeatedly present, which remained unnoticed? What of the innate potential for green? It too would have to go, or the environment would remain unsatisfactory. There was more to do; much more.

I tore down all the viewscreens, cast them into the disposers. Then I put the fabricators to work on constructing new viewscreens lacking the miniature green diodes that, with their red and blue counterparts, were deployed to mimic honest white light. The fabricators could not assemble the screens rapidly; I was increasingly exhausted. Were I to wait, I would sleep.

I went to deal with the station's extensive herbarium.

By the end of my labours uprooting and incinerating all the station's botanical matter, I was ready to drop; yet the others still remained in their anaesthesis. I knew this opportunity would not again be afforded to me: the soporific gas would be spent within hours. I installed and tested the new viewscreens. Their lilac-and-magenta-toned images lacked something, but there was nonetheless a purity of sorts to their display, and I was not displeased by them. Then, striving to resist the body's ramping imperative to sleep, I donned the only still-extant breathing-mask and slipped into the sleeping crew's personal quarters, room by room.

In the room of Ximena, whom I had once loved in secret, I found trinkets, items of jewellery, a blouse and the wrap of lime-green silk which she had inherited from her recently-deceased grandmother: I bagged these items for destruction. There were books on horticulture and an antique vase of emerald hue in Arlen's room: they went too. In Gervaise's room, medals and a pair of polymer-framed spectacles; in Gabrielle's, artwork, medication, a coffee mug; in Randal's, almost every item of clothing. I cut off Malin's fringe. Gradually I worked through the entire section, culling objects which I knew to be treasured by my colleagues. Then I checked once more, to see whether I had missed anything. I had not.

I loaded the bags of waste into the disposal units. Powered them up, revelled in their purgative thrum.

Finally the station had been redeemed, all offensively-coloured material excised. I had cleaned house; I had righted matters. There was nothing green, not even the slightest, anywhere throughout the station. Not a leaf, not a glass bead, not a scrap of cotton. I patrolled the station one last time, surveying the fruit of my efforts. What I saw pleased me, quieted my heart.

I could sleep. The thought of sleep was glorious, supremely deserved.

I retired to my quarters.

And yet I could not sleep. My throat was dry and roughened, a level of irritation that could not be salved by drinking a half-litre of water. Probably my activity had dispersed a substantial amount of dust into the station's air supply. I arose, adjusted the air filtration to the highest setting, then went to the infirmary for some syrup.

The spoonful was deeply, vividly red, joyous to witness. The syrup slid pleasantly down my throat. I downed twice the recommended dose for an adult of my size. Holding the red-slicked spoon in my hand, I looked up, caught my reflection in the cabinet's chromed surface.

I noticed my eyes.

Promotional

The pamphlet
has had a gutsful, it
has no time
for your refutations

it insists
loudly
on the primacy
of its messaging re our lord and saviour
and its promise of salvation
through blind adherence to
some ten-point plan
that has less
to do with the received wisdom
of ancient scripture
than with some lazy libertarian ideal

it has become rather shrill
as you cross the room
pick it up
approach the fireplace
throw it on

it seems a waste
to burn such a marvel
and the fumes are likely toxic
but the bloody thing would not shut up

and now
as if on cue
the next one starts
raucous
brash
on local prices for real estate
and how good it would be
to put up for sale
your home
now

Squirrel story

Then she told us about the squirrel, the one squirrel which has appeared on the island; and it slept under her neck and tried to collect food there. As the relationship between artist and squirrel developed, the squirrel came to expect a game at four o'clock in the morning. [She] had to get out of bed and pretend to be a tree. The squirrel would run up and down her frozen limbs.

(from *Sun at Midnight*, by Oswell Blakeston; published by Anthony Blond Ltd, London, 1958)

As the motorboat's buzz blurs into the background, you turn back towards the house. Done. You should be able to relax, now, and to work: no more visitors, no more need of English, or of politeness, for the moment. But these long June days, there's no guarantee there won't be further visitors before sundown.

'At least they saved you a mail run,' she notes.

There's no need to unburden yourself on her; she knows how these intrusions chafe. The knowledge helps. You grunt, deliberately unladylike; nothing more is needed.

'Coming back inside?' she asks, as the two of you approach the step.

'No, I'll amble for a bit,' you say, and turn away as she goes in. You're not sure why you're feeling this restlessness, this sudden need for solitude.

You're careful about which of the wildflowers you step on.

Out on the point, the sea is on best behaviour: jostling its way over the submerged rocks, shifting stripes of darker and lighter blue all the way out to the next island. Green-black when you look straight down. A boat putts through the channel, towing a raucous constellation of gulls. A kite of birds...

Just a fishing boat, you reassure yourself. Speedboats can mean visitors, and the chain of visits seems neverending sometimes. *Why can't people just leave me alone? Aren't the books, the strips, enough?*

Further around the shore, back towards the jetty, you find a length of driftwood. A slender branch; not sea-carved, yet, into anything of particular magic. *A stolid work*, you tell yourself, *symptomatic of the sea's prosaic period.* You think of the effort which the driftwood has made to seek you out, the choice to strand on this particular island. Your family's island. Your place to belong, summerlong.

The rowboat, the nets, the blended smell of diesel and seaweed. The buzz of an unseen fly. The clear, steady warmth of June; the deep sky above, cotton-clouded only at the fringes. The quiet, the unselfconscious busyness of life around you.

The driftwood branch hasn't had time to warm in the sun: it's waterlogged, with a good heft to it. You carry it to the point and throw it as far as you can, not as far as you'd like, into the striped blue sea. It will be back. It's that kind of stick.

But it will have learnt a lesson.

You need to finish the galleys. Ten pages today, the final ten tomorrow.

At least books can be completed.

You should never have agreed to Sutton's offer. To the financial security it promised, after years of precarious income. To the conditions it concealed, the demands on your time. But the damage is done.

It's difficult focussing on the text. You're only two pages into today's allotment when she raps on your workroom door; you're glad of the intrusion.

'I meant to say,' she begins, then flicks her eyes upwards as though a prompt is written on the ceiling, though nothing's there except a spider setting about its daily business. 'The Olofssons are having a Midsummer Eve party. There'd be dancing, I think. Do we want to go?'

'It's not Midsummer Eve,' you note.

'Nonetheless,' she says. Somehow it's a question.

'Dearest,' you reply, 'I'm going to need to start on the next strip. And right now I have no inspiration.'

'Then use the party as inspiration.'

'I've done parties already. I've done everything already. Five bloody years, six days of it a week, and never an end to it. I need— I need—'

'You need to unwind,' she observes. She's moved close enough to massage your shoulders. 'You're all knots.'

You allow yourself a long exhalation. You still tingle at her touch, wince at the press of her fingertips. 'That feels good,' you say, though the sensation is truthfully more of a constructive short-lived pain. 'There, please. Thank you.'

'That story about the squirrel gets better each time you tell it,' she says, still finger-probing your shoulders. 'You should write it.'

'I've *used* the squirrel,' you reply. 'In the book. And I can't, or even if I could I refuse to, build a strip around it.'

'I don't mean in one of the books, and I certainly wasn't suggesting it for the strip. I meant a story for grown-ups, not children.'

'Adults want grit and intrigue and moral dilemma. They won't get that from a squirrel.'

'They will,' she predicts, 'if you make it gothic. A tale of rodent horror. You have a talent for gothic. You were most of the way there this morning over coffee, with the Englishmen.'

'Dearest, I *can't* write a gothic squirrel piece,' you protest. 'Any more than I could write a piece about those sugarbowl ants. And even if I could, where would I find the time?' But a part of your mind wonders, just the same. You look around at the pictures on the wall, the figurines on the wooden shelf. Things that gave you joy to create. The realisations of your mind's imaginings. Then the three large yellow envelopes, two from Schildts and one from Söderströms, bulging with readers' letters awaiting your reply. The galleys on the table, the blank sheets, the inkpot, the pens. 'When's it all going to end?' you ask, making no effort to hide your despair.

'It ends,' she says, 'when you're ready for it to end.'

'I know damn well I don't have another of those books in me,' you complain. 'And as for the strips... I'm tired of the constraints, of the expectations of others. And every year more expectations, more constraints... it doesn't end. I want my life back.' *There*, you think. *I've said it.* You're swept up in argumentative conviction, hoping she bites back.

She doesn't. She hardly ever does. How can she stay so damned reasonable, so unexercised, all the time? 'You'll get it back,' she replies. 'You'll find a way. *We'll* find a way. Just tell Sutton—'

'But I *can't* just walk away from it.'

She moves to the side of your chair, crouches, looks into your eyes. Takes your hand in hers, resting on the chair's arm. She's wearing an old cardigan of your mother's; it suits her, more than it ever would you. 'You'll manage,' she says. 'When you're ready, you'll manage. And a party would do you good.'

You have your doubts—parties mean people, and people always want so much from you, nowadays—but you're inclined to trust her, nevertheless. She's usually right.

'And you could practise the squirrel story on them,' she adds.

'Dearest,' you protest, 'there's *no such thing* as 'the squirrel story'. Not like that.'

'When you're ready,' she says, 'there will be.'

*

It's an hour's rowing; your arms are pleasantly sore by the time you reach the Olofssons' island. The air is skeined with midges as the two of you negotiate the groomed gravel path leading up from the beach.

You don't approve of what the Olofssons have tried to do with the island. The house doesn't belong, anyone with any judgement can see this. The island does not need preordained paths imposed on it. Those shrubs look ridiculous. It's all too overtly nautical, too obvious. They've learnt nothing.

You let her take the lead up the path. She looks good, as always. You just feel overdressed; as out of place, in your way, as the house, and even less purpose here. You're wondering why you've come. But the guests' laughter meshes with the cries of the wagtails as you approach, and you tell yourself, *oh well, it'll run its course*. And even if the Olofssons are the second-worst sort of summer island people— the kind who think that any problem can be overcome by throwing enough money at it—the parties aren't awful. Not as a rule.

They've repainted. Again. You knock, wait, bite back a comment about the house by now wearing its own value in layer after layer of pigment. You smile, you enter, you exchange those obligatory introductory pleasantries, you accept the glass offered to you.

You look around for someone to converse with. There's always someone, especially if you look past the usual tribe. Though her husband's colleagues seldom stray beyond the topics of advertising and shooting, Mari Olofsson has interesting connections. Poets, architects, archaeologists. Smugglers.

Your companion casts you a concerned look, number three from her repertoire. You nod in response, with just enough emphasis to show that all's fine. You're here, with wine and cigarette smoke and people and the still mid-June evening, and your party mood has arrived.

The party mood's fickle tonight, though. Three introductions in and the conversation palls. Too many people wanting to talk of last year's book, or next year's, when what you'd far rather discuss, if work need be discussed at all, is the art. And though Olofsson has turned the wireless up loud enough, this has merely caused the guests to raise their voices. There's no sign of intention, on anybody's part, to start dancing.

You head out onto the porch for a cigarette. The Olofssons' cat—an unlovely animal which, nonetheless, you quite admire—slinks officiously beneath the verandah, a small bird fatalistically twitching in its jaws. You finish the cigarette, wander back inside to find an ashtray. There's an ex-lover standing next to it. You make your way to the privy instead.

It's been two hours at the party; that's surely enough. You're minded to track her down and negotiate a departure. But you don't, because Gustav detaches himself from the clump of people with whom he's been holding court, and moves purposefully in your direction. When he reaches a certain distance, he bows, just with the head: a slight theatrical gesture, which you reciprocate. A personal ritual, of which you suspect neither yourself nor Gustav can recall the origin. Society coheres through a myriad such things, even between people who see each other once a year at most.

'There's someone I'd like you to meet,' he tells you. There's always someone. But Gustav's better than most at identifying those who are sympatico, so the words aren't as immediately ominous as if another—Jan Olofsson, for example—were to have voiced them. Gustav's 'someone' won't be an actuary or an advertising executive.

You follow Gustav back to his coterie, among which you recognise at least one politician and two journalists. Yet another of the group, one whom you do not know, lights up at your approach: a tall lad, thin, bespectacled, all Adam's apple and pallor, a nose that's been broken some time past. Ill-fitting suit, likely older than the lad himself; hair cropped short in that American style, unnecessarily pomaded. You find yourself wondering if Gustav's judgement has failed.

The lad introduces himself, Nils, explains how much he likes your books, then stops. The sort who never knows what to say next. *Probably writes too*, you tell yourself, *two-thirds through a drearily frank first novel recounting a year in the life of a junior clerk, but not at all autobiographical, no.* You ponder mitigation strategies. You turn to Gustav as though seeking an explanation, but Nils regains his voice, or his thread, or whatever it is he'd needed to find. He likes the books, he reiterates. Which, as always, you feel ungracious about, but your resentment is still genuine. Acclaim, delivered too frequently, becomes a cudgel. Fan mail, recognition, the expectation of interviews. You can never say this, of course. Never let on. Nils says something more.

Your mind a-wander, you only half catch his words, something about music. You're not sure how to respond. Instead, you nod politely, scan the hall for her, she who's—alas—nowhere to be seen.

Nor, for that matter, is Gustav.

'Not *remind* exactly,' Nils clarifies. 'Just in the sense of a shared sensibility.'

'Sensibility?' you ask.

He pauses a few seconds before responding. 'The internal logic, separate from the everyday. The vivid depiction of something which is otherwise but still relatable. There's a bustle, a sense of inventiveness to them. The early works, I mean.'

'And which do you mean by my early works?'

'I'm sorry, I'm not expressing myself well,' (This is the first accurate thing he's said.) 'I mean his early pieces.'

'The composer? I can't say I'm particularly familiar with his music,' you admit. Then add, almost flirtatiously, 'Nor, therefore, with the difference between his early and later work.'

'It changed,' says Nils. 'Romantic and busy, the stuff he was most popular for, the melodic and uplifting pieces that made his name locally and tapped into the independence movement, then it grew dark and quite foreboding—that was his health scare, when he thought he was dying—then it became sparse, I suppose you could say austere.' Nils gives you a meaningful look. It's clear he feels a kinship with the music. 'I admire the way he changed, how his work evolved, and still he stayed true to himself.'

You manage not to smile at the whimsical notion that this Nils could at all have any comprehension, at his age, of staying true to oneself. And then you catch yourself, recollecting your own surety at what you judge to be his age. The self-assurance of youth is not always such a bad thing. 'You sound as though you know his music well,' you say, warmly enough, relieved that the topic has moved off your own work.

There's a crash from across the room: a child, running, has collided with an occasional table bearing a tray of champagne flutes, and there's an impressive collection of glass fragments on the floor. Fru Olofsson has moved in to clear it up and to placate the parents, who alternate between striving to calm the child and surveying the damage; but Nils has been saying something, and you've missed it again. You ask him to repeat.

'The same sparseness,' he says. Then hurriedly adds, 'I mean, not in a hollow sense, I mean, in the sense that you put things into them that aren't there.'

'They're just stories,' you reply, more openly guarded. You feel you've overlooked something in his reasoning; moreover, you're unsure of whether you should be offended on your words' behalf. You add, brusquely, 'The things I put in them are things that are there.'

'Yes, but they're not, not always. There's more to them than that. There's a kind of white space to them, the more recent ones especially, where the stories are shaped by the things that aren't there, or that are there but aren't shown. Like the forests you can hear in that tone poem, name escapes me, one of the last things he wrote. Rise after rise of stands of trees that aren't there. An orchestra shaping the sounds of an instrument which doesn't exist.' He pauses, looks at you expectantly. It's clear the description of the music is something he's proud of. 'Don't you think so?'

'I'm intrigued that you say so,' you reply slowly, because this part of the dialogue has now caught your attention. 'And of course anything you see in a piece of art, be that painting or writing or music or sculpture, that's undeniably true for you. That's how art works. But I wouldn't say I consciously put white space in my books.' You smile wryly as a thought strikes you. 'Unless you mean the snow, in the latest?'

'No,' says Nils, earnestly. 'And I think I mean negative space, rather than white space. The shape of absence, rather than the absence itself. But anyway, you deliberately include things which aren't explained, which the reader has to wonder over, and that's the same thing.' He takes a sip of a drink, temporarily urbane. 'You've said so yourself, or something like, in an interview.'

'I might have done,' you allow. There've been so many interviews lately.

'He thought so too.'

'Who?' you ask, more sharply than intended. 'You met Sibelius?' The idea's amusing, in its way. But Nils is so young.

'Yes,' he says. 'We must've been among his last guests. Last summer, just more than a month before he died. My uncle Erik took me to meet him.'

Erik, you think. There must be thousands of Eriks, many of whom are also uncles, but you know instantly, in this context, who he must mean. *Poyu.* You cast your mind back four decades or so, to childhood. It's years since you've thought of Poyu, of the games you two played on the steps of his building. Your bossiness, his cheerful runny-nosed subservience. 'I never met him,' you say. 'The composer, I mean. I know Erik did, of course, And my father, I think. I'll ask him, next time we speak. But the circles we moved in were different.'

'Not so very different,' says Nils. 'And he agreed with me about your writing.'

'I find it difficult to believe he would bother himself with children's stories,' you reply.

'Well, no, he didn't,' Nils admits. 'But he agreed with the way I described them, that they sounded as though they had the same qualities as his music. That it's possible to state something without expressing it, purely by showing the shape surrounding it.'

'Did he actually say that? About my writing, which he probably hasn't read?'

'Well, no,' says Nils. 'Not those words. But it was what he meant. That much was obvious.'

'Intriguing,' you say. And you actually mean it, for all that this pale young man's utterings have more hinted than conveyed. You wish, in this moment, you were more familiar with the music. 'It's been very insightful to talk with you, Nils, but now I must excuse myself.'

You visit the privy again. More form's sake than need. Such luxury, really, to have plumbing. When you emerge, Nils has moved on to another group of guests.

You look for your companion. She's chatting near the supper table with a trio of artist ghosts; mutual acquaintances with gossip about goings-on in Paris. It's an easier conversation in which to contribute: familiar, nostalgic; you join her. She's saying something, as you step into the group, about the English visitors today, the travel writer and his photographer friend Max, and making a joke of the situation: the two of them, the two of you, and each one speculating on what, for the sake of safety or sensibility or protective colouration or some such rot, needed to stay unvoiced. Ghosts, and nobody saying. You can't be bothered, this time, to add your opinion.

You're still unsure of what to make of Nils' musical comparison, which seems at the same time to have been too personal and too indirect.

The party continues. The promised dancing never starts, even after a guest finds a station playing unmistakeable dance music, lively stuff from one of those countries in South America. Someone starts a fight, someone breaks it up, someone says something scandalous and far too ominously nostalgic about the war. You've argued with such types before; tonight you cannot be bothered.

It's just so stupid of men to always turn arguments into fights, disputes into war. So needless. If you could change one thing, it would be this. But it's exhausting even to think this way. Death, cruelty, human pettiness: it's so tiresome.

Tomorrow you will need to think about the strips again. It's always intrusive, this ongoing need to produce content for the English newspaper. It constrains your yearning for creativity. You want to work, yes, but not on that. You want to have time again for your art, or for what else inspires you, not for what the contract demands. There are so many things you wish to create, if only time permits. A vision, then, of images you see in your artist-mind's eye, some of which will remain potential, will never be delineated by brush-stroke on canvas before it all ends.

Does the painting exist, if it's only imagined and never painted? It does for you, and maybe for her as well (because she understands you so clearly), but others see only what there is, not what there isn't. There will not be time for some of your ideas to be realised in artwork. Nor in words. And as well as the desire to work, you wish also to live.

Those damned strips.

Here, now. This gathering. You return, from wherever it is in your head you've just been. There's still music, and conversation, and human movement, but what surrounds all that has become flattened, lacking the earlier evening's vitality.

Parties are best left when there's still some life in them.

You glance her way. She signals her agreement without you even needing to raise the question. Time to depart.

The champagne's worn off, has left a social lethargy in its wake. The two of you assemble in the entrance hall, grab your wraps, steal away without bothering to track down either Olofsson so as to offer the obligatory departing pleasantries. Her proximity is timeless, unboundedly comforting; you can't help but smile at the thought. Your shared secret is both apparent and unvoiced.

You find yourself thinking, too, as you make your way over that fussy and impractical gravel path which leads to the shore, about how to write in such a way as to say more clearly the things that aren't said. To not keep playing those make-pretend games. To find a way to be more true to yourself, more honest with the readers. To sketch out those things about life and about you which the publishers, like society, would prefer that you skirted.

To write with—what was it Nils called it?—negative space.

Can one write that way for children?

Surely so. And maybe Nils is right. Children are expert, in their way, at understanding what isn't there, what isn't shown. Maybe it's more difficult to do that with grown-ups, most of whom have left their imaginations behind, have sought to reinvent themselves in a world of money and possessions and politics.

To tell a story that works with what isn't shown, that's defined principally by what's absent? It might well be something to work on. A challenge. The idea quickens you. It's true that work—or, rather, duty—is what you've been most complaining of, these past days. But this would be a duty not to the English newspaper but to yourself, which is much preferable.

The late evening—whatever the hour, it cannot be termed 'night'— remains calm. No breath of wind worth troubling a sail over; you two must row home.

'Dearest?' you ask, carefully casual, once your arms have started to tire.

'Yes?' A shape, in a boat with its hull pressed into the shape of the sea, highlighted and silhouetted against the shape of the limitless, luminous air. There's shading and texture to the visible shapes, but beyond that there are outlines. Surfaces. Interfaces. Water lapping, the creak and grumble of the rowlocks, the work of breathing. Lights marking the gulf's islands and rocks. That twilight sense of indeterminacy.

The immensity of the sea, the vastness of the sky above. Two small figures, a small boat. This is how you know you're alive.

You pass her the oars. The hem of your dress is damp.

'I had the strangest conversation at the party,' you explain.

'Who were you talking with?'

'I don't really know. Some nephew of Erik, or so he claimed. But I didn't know Erik had any nephews. It was all a bit weird.'

'What made it weird?' she asks, exerting against the oars.

'It was about the things that are in my stories, because they're not. Or the things that could be in them, by not being there. If I wrote stories I haven't written. I think that was the sense of it. It was muddled.'

'Did it make sense at the time?'

'I'm not sure.'

'Then it might make sense later,' she says. 'Things are often more sensible than they seem.'

You search her face, shaded almost into two-dimensionality. The waves. The sounds of the boat. Your lover, calm. The sea, calm. The air, calm. Only you restless and uncertain.

This is how it needs to be, sometimes. Both belonging and yearning.

Can something be made real, by defining only the edges surrounding it?

It works with sculpture, you've seen that happen often enough; it forms the basis of linocut and woodcut; but can it work with words?

Can you make it work with words?

You trail your hand over the rowboat's side. Water, warmer finally than the air, pushes against your fingertips. Your fingertips push against the water.

There's an idea there: your small family in a boat, shaped by absence and by expectation, by those who imagine them but don't properly know them. Something to work with. But there are other stories to write first. More art. More things to say.

'Tooti?' you ask.

'Yes?'

'If I try— if I write the squirrel story, if it turns out that I have to write the squirrel story, will you tell me whether it's any good?'

'You know the answer to that,' she replies. It's all that need be said.

Quetz run

Clance hefted the big carnie saddle up off the back of his rustbucket ute. He thought he could hear the suspension heave a sigh of relief, but it was difficult to be sure over the derisory call of the crow perched in the high branches of the roadside eucalypt, or over his own 'Oof!' as he lifted the bloody thing. On an afterthought, he balanced the saddle on the ute tray's rim while reaching back down for the cattle prod, which he contorted one-handed into the back pocket of his moleskin pants. The pants, the boots, the checked flannel shirt, the battered hat were individually and severally a liability in this dismaying heat, but the sort of beast he'd be working with, the less exposed skin he had on display the better. The pants' other back pocket bulged with his gardening gloves, which he'd save until it got time to get down to business.

'Just park at the gate, willya?' Jaffa had directed. 'Tink's a mite flighty, she's liable to go amok she hears a motor.'

Clance eyed the distance from the gate to the farmhouse with a growing sense of despair. Not only was the carnie saddle heavy, it was bulky as all get-out, with flaps and straps flaring out every which way, and had none of the compact ease of portability of, say, a double-bed mattress.

He stepped carefully over the gate's cattle stop, watching his feet with religious zeal—wouldn't do to miss his footing while carrying this, he'd break his bloody ankle—and started on the long, hot, dusty march towards the house. Clance had neither hand free, so he was reduced to huffing periodically through his nostrils or his mouth in a vain attempt to dissuade the accompanying nimbus of persistent flies which had fixed on his face, from ear to shining ear, as the primary object of their reverence.

The sun grew steadily hotter, the saddle grew steadily heavier, and Clance grew steadily sweatier as the walk progressed. He'd got to maybe the halfway mark—the *second* halfway mark, because he was already well past what he'd first reckoned to be the midpoint—before it dawned on him that the fencing was a worry. Or more to the point, the lack of fencing. The kind of job Clance had been called up on, he'd want there to be reinforced concrete pylons, five-metre-high heavy steel mesh fencing, razor wire, and enough electricity running through it to char-grill a cow in two flat. Instead, nothing. Just the crunchy gravel drive, the heat, the flies, a fine and omnipresent agrarian dust, that fine and omnipresent agrarian smell, and a farmhouse that stubbornly refused to draw any closer. Precious little foliage, no cover—certainly nothing that counted as 'cover' against the kind of trouble that Clance was anticipating: seven tonnes of it, carnivorous, ruthless, and much faster moving than a sun-beaten, sweat-drenched contractor hefting in his bone-weary arms enough hot leather to sink a battleship. *Maybe they've got it penned up behind the house somewhere?* he wondered. *In some kind of industrial-strength livestock shed, perhaps? Or tranked, even?* He hoped so.

If there wasn't a cold one waiting for him at the end of this bloody drive—hell, make that a cold two or three—he'd say something decidedly unchristian, and not care who might hear it, nor pass judgment.

Then he tripped. The saddle broke most of his fall, and possibly his nose. He picked himself up, wiped his bloody nose ineffectually on the back of his hand—*another reason not to have worn a white shirt today*—and reached down to lift up the saddle.

It wasn't a tree root or a stone he'd tripped over, as he'd first thought, it was a fish skeleton. A biggish one, a full half-metre of spine. And now that he looked, the ground ahead was littered with them.

Weird mob, he thought, judging that *this*, finally, must be the halfway mark, or close to it.

His eyes were so blurred with perspiration that he didn't see the doorbell until after he'd knocked. He was just about to press the bell when the door opened. He could tell in an instant three things about the woman who opened it: she was short, she was well-dressed, in a country kind of way, and she didn't suffer fools gladly. 'Yes?' she asked from behind the still-locked screen door.

'Jaffa?' he found himself asking, when breath permitted.

'You what?' she asked in reply, in the kind of voice he imagined she otherwise reserved for describing matter adhering to the soles of her boots.

'I'm here to see Jaffa,' he explained, panting a bit for emphasis.

'You sure as shit don't look like one of Jaffa's mates.'

'I'm not,' Clance answered. He was wondering why it was that the sweat glands only seemed to go into overdrive once you'd stopped moving. Bit of a design flaw, that, if you asked him. 'At least, it's been a while. But he rang me, yesterday. Clance. I've come about—'

'Clarence?'

'Clance.'

'Krantz?'

'Clance. Ce-li-ah-en-ce-eh. I've come about your tyrr—'

'Just a minute,' she interrupted, then turned to face the house's tantalisingly airconditioned innards. 'JAFFA!' she bellowed, in a voice that threatened to travel far enough to need a passport to get there. 'SOMEONE TA SEE YA!' She turned back and added in comparative *pianissimo*, 'He'll be out in a couple.' Then she walked back into the refrigerated interior of the house, leaving Clance on the step to poach in his own juices.

He waited dutifully, while two kilos or thereabouts of body fat converted itself to perspiration and went exploring. From somewhere behind the house, a cacophony suddenly erupted: not, he thought, a Mrs-Jaffa level detonation of raucousness—as might befit, say, finding a high-denomination betting slip for a glueworksed horse in Jaffa's pocket, or a long brunette hair on his work overalls—but something more atavistically savage, like a chainsaw with anger-management issues. He considered, anew, the lack of visible fencing, and wondered if blind terror would equip him to diffuse his way, like a vapour, through the locked screen door should the necessity arise. Which he hoped it didn't, because he knew he couldn't. Then Jaffa—tall, gangly, and topped by a shock of bright blue hair—came to the door.

'Clance?' he asked.

'Yes.'

'What's with the clobber?'

'It's me saddle,' replied Clance. 'For Tink.'

'Nah, you'd break her bloody back with that. What the flamin' hell is that, anyway?'

'It's a regular carnie saddle,' said Clance, edging into the tone of voice he normally reserved for those of the opposite political persuasion or otherwise slow on the uptake. 'For Tink. Your twelve-metre-long tyrannosaur.'

'My—Maaaate.' There are, of course, innumerable ways of saying 'Mate', and Clance could tell straight off this wasn't a good one. Then Jaffa laughed, and Clance could tell that wasn't a good one either. 'Clance, mate, you'd better come round the back.'

'It wasn't that good of a line when we spoke,' said Jaffa, just as Tink bent down in an apparent attempt to take Clance's head off.

Clance moved back as sharpish as that long, pointed snout. He'd been geared up for a T Rex, both mentally and physically. But Tink was arguably more intimidating than any carnosaur: those sail-like, skin-stretched-on-bone wings that, in repose, were furled and folded like some cross between a World War Two carrier aircraft and a Transformer; that giraffe-like stance; that cruelly pointed beak angled at the end of that long arched neck; those knuckles which, due to the capricious leanings of evolution, did double duty as forepaws. An animate, oversized switchblade: such compact and evident lethality. Though 'compact' was relative: Tink's shoulder stood way higher than Clance's, and there was a lot of neck, a lot of snout, a lot of muscle and one hell of a lot of frustrated malice well above that shoulder. The noise added to the effect, as did the rancid breath. Clance dodged back again as the beak made another stab towards him. He and Jaffa were standing in a sturdy cube-shaped cage situated like a very leaky airlock to one side of Tink's substantially larger cage, all of it framed in thick welded steel rods—repurposed scaffolding, Clance suspected—sheathed in about a dozen layers of chicken wire so as to keep the mammals on one side isolated from the reptile on the other side. The plentiful large holes in the chicken wire showed what Tink thought of that arrangement, which by all appearances was not a lot.

'Think she likes you,' Jaffa commented.

Some aeons-old preservation instinct dissuaded Clance from attempting to make eye contact with his host while a quarter-tonne of scissor-snouted ill temper snipped at the air in front of his face. 'You did say tyrannosaur,' he repeated, not without some implied accusation, not inclined for now to be swayed by the other's dubious arguments of flight-capable reptile affection.

'I think I know what must've happened,' said Jaffa, with significantly too much of a jocular tone for Clance's liking. 'When I was telling you about Tink, I'd started saying 'pteranodon', and then I changed it to 'pterosaur' ... and it sorta came out sounding like 'tyrannosaur'.' He shook his head slightly and gave what sounded to Clance distressingly like a snicker. 'Mate, I'm so sorry you've lugged that saddle all the way in here.'

Clance merely grunted, then took another step back. 'She's a quetzal?' he asked. His second guess was going to be 'hellbeast'. The chain that secured the gate on the animal's tall covered pen looked robust enough, but he wasn't inclined to take chances. That thing looked like it could bisect a buffalo, if it set its mind to it. The guidebooks all said 'largely piscivorous' but the eyes said 'just try me'.

'Yep. Twelve-metre wingspan. And if you're wondering why anyone would want something that large, I thought I was getting something way smaller.' Jaffa gave a sigh that could've understudied for a leading role in a Greek tragedy. 'It was like the wife's microbront all over again.'

'She must eat a lot,' said Clance. 'Tink, that is to say,' he added a couple of seconds later, for safety's sake.

'Not as much as you might think,' replied Jaffa. 'But it's constant, and a bit specialised, and she needs more exercise than I can give her, not to mention that this pen's a bit on the small side, now, for the size she's reached.'

The two men stood in silence for a minute, contemplating the kind of things men contemplate in situations such as this, in close proximity to a bad-tempered airworthy guillotine. Then, much to Clance's relief, Jaffa invited him in to the farmhouse's kitchen so they could talk turkey. The only cold one on offer, though, was an iced coffee, which led Clance to realise that his friend had mellowed with age, but not in a good way.

Still, he supposed it was the thought that counted.

'Oh, and Clance, three things. First, steer clear of the salt lakes. There'll be bugger-all water left in any of them this long after the rains—'cept maybe Eyre, but I've programmed you a route which avoids that—but that won't stop her trying to go fishing. You do not want to be on her when she tries that. Second, she gets distracted by vehicles, assumes they're prey items I guess.'

'Yeah, you mentioned. I left the ute back out at the road, like you asked.'

'Good,' replied Jaffa. 'If you toss me the keys, I'll walk out to the gate this evening when it's cooler, drive it up here to keep until you get back. For your part, you'd be well-advised to shy away from roads.'

'That's bound to make nav a bit difficult.'

'Shouldn't actually be a problem. Wait one, I'll get the gear. Show you.'

Jaffa stood, stared about himself for a moment as if trying to orient himself in his own house, went through what Clance surmised from the clutter and the waft of unrefrigerated air was the door into the double garage. There followed the kind of clattering normally only ever heard from the backrooms of less-prestigious second-hand shops, and after a couple of minutes a vaguely Jaffa-shaped bundle re-emerged from the garage.

'What's all this?' Clance asked, as the other held up a disreputable-looking pair of grey trousers and a shapeless shape of what looked like black lycra which, from its odour, had led quite the life.

'You've not ridden a quetzal before, have you? No. Well, this is how you stay on. Velcro pants. There's no saddle. Tink wears this quetzal leotard ensemble round the base of her neck, the pants fasten on to that,' Jaffa explained, hitching up his own trousers at this point. 'Just be careful trying to get more comfortable while you're airborne.'

'Ok, so that's the saddle taken care of,' said Clance, eyeing the gear with remnant suspicion.

'You'll get used to it,' Jaffa explained. Sighed. 'Not that Tink ever has.'

'What about— is there a harness? Reins?'

'Don't need them,' said Jaffa. 'This is the twenty-first century, mate. There's an app.' He held up a couple of small multi-rotor drones and a bottle of fish oil. 'These doofers are programmed to fly there, with the route all loaded into their memory. What you do is you douse one in quetzal attractant'—he held the fish-oil bottle higher—'there's a dispenser for the attractant; whatever you do, don't get any of it on your clothing, or on yer hands.' He shuddered a little as he said this.

'Got it.'

'Then you set the drone in flight when you're ready to take off. They stay twenty metres ahead of Tink at all times: out of reach, but close enough to keep her pursuing. Solar, battery backup. They're controlled through the app, it's called PteraBytes, you'll need to install it, but once you've mapped in the route, it's pretty much set and forget, so it's not a major problem if you lose reception. And there's a spare drone, but either one should have enough charge to get you all the way to the Top End, so the spare is just for emergencies.'

'Yeah. About that. You didn't actually explain on the phone what the reptile park wanted with her.'

'Didn't I? Must've forgot. Breeding program. They've got a male, want to get some young ones. Buggered if I know why.'

'Thought you said you'd had her fixed.'

'Well, yeah, but the Terps mob don't need to know that. I reckon it'll take them a fair while to catch on, not that easy finding a vet willing to check out the intimates on a lady quetzal, and I'll have the proceeds all well invested by then. Plus me brother's a lawyer, he reckons we can tie them up for years, and they're bound to give up before that. Those places always have class actions against them, maimed visitors and all that, they're not gonna have the stomach for too much other litigation.'

'You're sending them Tink under false pretences? I really wish you hadn't told me that.'

'Pretend I haven't, then. Twenty percent not enough for you? I'm willing to go to twenty-five, but that's tops.'

'It's not about the money,' said Clance, though he wasn't too sure even as he said it. 'It's more you've dealt with these people over the blower, I'll have to face-to-face it. How'm I gonna do that, knowing this?'

'Twenty-five it is.'

Clance thought about making more of a scene—the deal was looking less flash by the minute—but he still needed the dosh. 'Okay,' he answered, hoping he sounded more confident and competent than he felt. He eyed a bulky, soft-shouldered backpack balanced on a spare chair in the room's corner. 'I was wondering, too, about borrowing a parachute.'

Jaffa eyed him up and down. 'Wait one,' he replied, standing and leaving the room.

Clance waited. For the first time since his introduction to Tink a half-hour ago, he began to feel a semblance of composure. It was, after all, just another gig, and he'd handled plenty of those. True, he and heights had a bit of an uneasy relationship, but a parachute would definitely provide reassurance. As always, it came down to the safety equipment. The guard rails, the trank gun, the clawproof vest, the paraphernalia that would keep him alive.

Jaffa re-entered the room. He wasn't carrying anything that bore the slightest resemblance to a parachute, packed or unpacked.

Instead, what he gripped in a meaty hand was a set of bathroom scales, which he now placed on the worn lino floor of the kitchen. He nodded at Clance, and at the scales.

Clance stood up, stepped onto the scales, and Jaffa bent down to take the reading. Straightened, appeared for a few seconds to run a calculation through his head.

'Sorry, mate,' he said after a few more seconds. 'Best not.'

'Any chance of a part-payment up front, then? As danger money? Or a retainer?'

Jaffa's eyes narrowed. 'Reckon we're more likely to retain you if it's payment on completion, as per the arrangement.'

'There's still details I'm not getting,' said Clance.

'Such as?'

'Well, the staying-away-from-roads thing. That's not going to leave many options for overnight. Because I'm guessing she's not going to be covering the distance in one day. I mean, it's not far off noon already.'

'Yeah,' said Jaffa. 'Thought of that. Reckon she'll take three or four to get there. I've mapped out some junkyards.'

'Junkyards?'

'Junkyards.'

'I'm not getting it.'

'She'll need her rest after the day's flight, and there's always plenty of rats in junkyards, unless the ornitholestes have cleaned them out, in which case there's always ornitholestes. So she should stay put while you get some shut-eye.'

'And how'm I supposed to do that, with Madam Secateur prowling for edibles?'

'Jeez, mate, use your noggin. It's a junkyard, there'll be vehicles you can climb into. I mean, better a mining truck or a bus than a small hatchback, you'll want something you can stretch out in, conceal yourself, defend yourself if need be, but there'll be options.'

'And if there aren't?'

'There'll be options, Clance.'

'Don't some of these places have guard dogs?'

'Somehow, I don't think you'll need to worry about those,' said Jaffa.

'Fine, I guess. And at the end of it I get home how?'

'I'll send the money once you've delivered her to the park. Bus from Darwin should be small change once you've got that in your account.'

'This all sounds very fly-by-night, I must say. You could work with one of the big livestock-transporting firms, some of them ship reptiles. Save yourself no end of strife.'

'And miss out on an opportunity to help out a mate?' Jaffa cracked a big shit-eating grin. 'Besides, you know what they cost, plus all the paperwork. The less paperwork the better, I reckon.'

'Me too, normally,' said Clance. 'But for something like this...'

'You're not getting cold feet now, Clance? I had you marked as sterner stuff than that.'

'Fine. So that's the brief, then? Steer clear of the salt lakes, keep her away from cars—'

'It's not just road traffic, though they're bad enough. Helicopters aren't too much of a worry unless you get close—she hates the noise, far as we can tell, so she keeps clear, but you see anything like a Cessna, you find yourself on its flightpath, get her pointing away from it, regardless of where you're trying to get to. It's just not worth it otherwise.'

'Why's that?' Clance asked, wondering if this was a good time to mention that he'd never actually flown before this.

'She reckons she can take them,' said Jaffa. 'And from what I saw when she was just half-grown, she's probably not wrong.'

Clance reflected on this with the gut-liquifying solemnity that the admonition seemed to merit. All up, he didn't like any of this; but times were tight, and he needed the readies. That, ultimately, was what it came down to.

There could be a several-thousand-word passage here, conveying in grim detail the rigours of a multi-day quetzalcoatlus flight from the Bight to the Top End.

There could be, in this notional several-thousand-word passage, a wingbeat-by-wingbeat description of the peculiar dread which Clance felt through every square centimetre of the velcro garment by which he was precariously attached to Tink.

There could be, in this wingbeat-by-wingbeat description, an overwhelming sense of the twinned vulnerability which Clance experienced, moment by moment, a vulnerability associated with riding a beast which, were it able to turn its head sufficiently in flight without spiralling into a death-dive, would have been strongly motivated to end its rider's life, and all of this at an altitude perfectly capable of doing the job itself.

There could be, in this overwhelming sense of the twinned vulnerability which Clance experienced wingbeat by wingbeat, the hopelessness which shot through him as his phone dropped out, first metaphorically and then literally, just two or three hours out from his ultimate destination. He'd been holding it, then he hadn't been holding it, and for a moment, as he grabbed for it and overreached, he reckoned he might be going to follow it on the long plunge earthward. But the velcro's grip was strong.

There could be, associated with the hopelessness which shot through Clance at that moment—and at a good many others during the ordeal of the multi-day flight—a background description of the smell, the heat, the gastric upsets (of both rider and beast), the airsickness and the multitudinous small flying insects and the grit and the unrelenting sun and the moment when Clance was struck on the face by the severed hindquarters of a hapless wedge-tailed eagle, taken in flight by a monstrous flying reptile which had, it seemed, grown tired the past several days of the taste of junkyard rats.

There could be, but there isn't. Because nobody needs that.

Clance always felt out of place in an office environment, as though he was somehow too basic and uncivilised for the space in which he found himself. This was particularly the case with the kind of padded-chair offices that sported a wraparound reception desk shaped in wood veneer with a fashionably coloured countertop and with architecturally selected drop-down lighting placed so as to highlight the expensively retro computer system through which the receptionist notified those in the back rooms of the arrival of customers, and was especially true when the office appeared, as this one did, to have been Marie Kondoed to within the last scintilla of its existence, with the fastidious arrangement of the waiting-area magazines on the waiting-area coffee table warning you, somehow, that they were not for the likes of you to leaf through, and with the bowl of supposedly complimentary Minties on the front counter subliminally informing you, somehow, that you would end up paying for them in some manner, even if you did not make any payment to the receptionist. 'Bull in a china shop' didn't even begin to describe the level of discomfort Clance had felt as the glass door had thereminned itself open for him before he could quite put a hand to the handle, and the feeling had intensified as he stepped within. Not that discomfort hadn't been his constant companion for the past six days, of course. But the vivid memory of his aerial ordeal didn't one bit blunt his conviction that when you came right down to it, a person just didn't belong in an office, and those who professed otherwise were not to be trusted.

And why did an office at a reptile park even *need* background music, if not to mask the screams—presumably of glee, though one couldn't always be sure—sounding from various corners of the park?

Yeah, there was something off here at the Top End Raptor and Pterosaur Sanctuary, Clance reckoned, as he approached the counter, wondering if this was one of those places where they'd refuse to speak to you if you hadn't already selected a ticket from the artfully concealed ticket dispenser they'd take glee in pointing out when you revealed you hadn't seen it, or from some undisclosed app. The sense intensified further as he caught the momentary twitch on the face of the business-suited, professionally coiffed, soap-scented receptionist as she looked up from her Tetris or her Minecraft or her Tinder or however else she occupied the intervals between customers.

He'd brought a fly in with him, inadvertently if unavoidably enough if one smelled as strongly of overexerted pterosaur as he imagined he must. But he didn't think, somehow, that that was the cause of the receptionist's twitch.

'Might you be Mr Clarence Hetherington?' she asked, in a posh tone of voice which seemed to want to admit of the alternative possibility, as he stood there breathing in the aromatherapy's ambience and trying not to neutralise it too sharply.

'Yeah, that's me,' he replied, wondering how steep a breach of office etiquette it would be to rest his elbows on the counter. A man got bone-tired after riding a largely reluctant reptile for three thousand kilometres or so, after all.

'We've been trying to reach you for the past couple of days,' she said.

'I've been trying to reach you for the past several,' he said. He attempted a smile.

She didn't.

'The thing is,' she said, and there was just something about either those words, or the way she said them, or the pause she threw into the air after them, or the combination thereof that caused him to know that whatever was to follow those words was not going to be good. 'The thing is,' she repeated, for good (or more likely not-so-good) measure, with a reprise of that ominous pause, 'there's been a cancellation.'

'I'm not here for an appointment,' he said, glancing at the wristwatch he no longer wore. 'I'm making a delivery.'

'That's what I mean. We made a cancellation of the purchase, two days ago, within the cooling-off period. We, uh, found ourselves no longer needing a breeding partner for our male quetzalcoatlus, after he escaped and rather disgraced himself at the local skydivers' meet. You probably saw something about it on the news.'

'Haven't kept up with the news,' he replied. 'I've had me hands a bit full the past few.'

'In any event, we have had to cancel. We called Mr... Jeffers? Jasper? Jaffo? as soon as the decision was made, and he suggested we should also notify you, as a courtesy. But we couldn't reach you. Perhaps you've had your phone switched off?'

'That's one way of putting it,' said Clance, and it was a great strain on his vocal chords not to put it another way. He raised his voice a notch. 'So you're telling me I've just flown the length and breadth of the flaming country—well, maybe not length—and you don't want the critter?'

'Thank you for being so understanding.'

'The thing is, this is not my understanding face,' Clance explained, talking as softly and as evenly as he was able. 'This is my what-the-fuck-am-I-supposed-to-do-with-a-quarter-tonne-of-razor-snouted-vee-tee-oh-ell-bad-temperament face, with a side order of where's-my-flaming-money?'

'There is no money, Mr Hetherington. Now, I appreciate that you have experienced some degree of inconvenience—"

'I was told it was payment on delivery.'

'There is no delivery, Mr Hetherington. Ergo, there can be no payment. I suggest you take the matter up with your Mr Jaffle.'

'How'm I supposed to do that? You got a phone I can use?'

'We're not able to make our phone available for customer use.'

'Well, I'm not flamin' movin' from here until I get my payment, and if you're not providing it then Jaffa bloody better, so I suggest you make an exception about the phone.'

'I'm not at liberty to make such an exception, Mr Hetherington.'

'Then maybe your manager is.'

But even as he said it, he knew it was hopeless; besides, he didn't truly have the bottle to face this out, knowing what he did of Tink's lack of reproductive capability. They had a thousand different ways, he suspected, to phrase the statement that they weren't going to pay up, and he could either just stand here and argue until he'd heard the other nine hundred and ninety-seven, or he could lump it and get on with whatever happened next. Bugger his chances of getting any kind of compensation from Jaffa, too; knowing what he suspected of Jaffa's finances, he'd be lucky to just get the rustbucket ute back.

And Jaffa and the rustbucket ute and the carnie saddle were all about three thousand kilometres back, as the quetzal flew. Clance's quads flinched at the prospect. But what choice was there? He was stuck at the top of the continent and needed to get to the bottom, with no money, no phone, and somehow still with responsibility for Ms Persnickety Scalpelface Valkyrie out there who, if she were still tethered to the bike rack, must surely by now be contemplating ways by which to perforate him. She'd know quite a few, he reckoned.

Maybe he should ask if the office had a rear exit for a quiet getaway. But they'd want to know why, and—

A commotion outside derailed his train of thought. A shriek, from close by, in the direction of the bike rack. A yell, and then another shriek, and the complicated sound of something heavy and intricate hitting the concrete from an ill-advised height. *Ken oath*, he thought, thinking of all the possible sequences of events which could lead to those noises when a quetz was involved, and his guts squirmed at the prospects. He turned his back on the snooty receptionist and made for the door. Whatever had befallen, it was beholden on him to do what he could to bring the situation under some approximation of control.

Some unnerved-looking onlookers keeping their distance. A mountain bike, badly bent and lying on its side, partially disassembled, more or less where the bike rack had been. The heavy, galvanised-metal bike rack itself was currently about thirty metres up in the air, suspended from the tether which connected it to Tink's foot. Then the tether snapped, and Tink made good her escape towards the skies to the north while the bike rack hurtled to ground level, its fall helpfully cushioned by the roof of a parked Beamer which Clance fervently hoped had been unoccupied at the moment of impact.

Now seemed a good time to slip away, he thought, before the arrival of the constabulary and their tendency to ask difficult questions of innocent bystanders in circumstances such as this.

There was a job going at a mosasaur farm about twenty kilometres out of town, at a former eco lodge that had been bought out after it'd gone belly-up in some crypto incident. It would be a stretch to say the job appealed, but it paid ok and it was a live-in position, which was what he'd need for the next little while, until he could get back on his feet. There were worse things than being on call twenty-four-seven, and he'd worked with moseys before, so if it put a roof over his head, even temporarily, it was better than the alternative; he could stick it out for a year or so. He'd need a new phone, and a new rustbucket ute, and he reckoned it was probably best, all things considered, if he didn't get back in touch with Jaffa for the next little while, because what good could come of it?

Of course, he'd need to get the job first; and what would he do if he didn't? He chose not to think of that now, chose just to take matters step by step, on foot on the kerb of the road out of town, turning to eye the skies behind him every twenty metres or so, just in case.

There was still, perhaps, the matter of Tink; but maybe she wouldn't be back.

If she doesn't, she never was, he told himself, and he very much hoped that.

There will come warm rains

Once, the geologists told us, the planet had likely been temperate enough to have polar ice-caps, but these had long since dissipated. Now its slow-dwindling seas simmered, driving huge quantities of water vapour into a thick atmosphere dominated by carbon dioxide and nitrogen and blanketed by permanent cloud.

Once, the palaeontologists surmised, life may have been abundant here: varied, complex, ubiquitous. Life still endured in a unicellular form, the simple metabolic processes of which were perfectly adapted to a steam-hot aqueous environment; but if there had at one point been indications of the diversity of former life on this world, those traces had not endured.

Some among our mission argued regarding the presence of many localised concentrations of exotic or unusual mineral deposits. Some held that these were remnants of long-eroded impact events, others that they had arisen in some unspecified seismic process; the world evidently remained tectonically active. One mission specialist argued unconvincingly that the deposits might signify undefined biological transformations which may have occurred within the world's distant past. It was noted in this context that though these unorthodox outcrops were at altitudes uniformly well above the current sea level, there was geological evidence at several of the lowest such features of prolonged and substantial marine inundation.

We did not tarry long upon the wind-scoured terrain of this uninviting planet. Indeed, we spent rather longer exploring its sole large natural satellite, a body of rock orbiting at a distance approximately thirty times its primary's diameter. Tantalisingly, we found a small number of objects of clearly artificial origin on its airless surface, suggesting we were not the first to have visited.

The origin of these constructs remains conjectural.

On the elucidation of a low-temperature enzymatic synthesis of Z-2-butene

1

It does not follow that, if a research goal can be articulated, it can be achieved. Nabil knew this, but the project interested him greatly; he applied, was accepted, signed on. He left home. His sister, Keidra, married; his father died, two weeks before the birth of Nabil's first niece. He almost formed a domestic partnership, a year later, with a research student in another lab group, a responsive-polymer scientist; they interacted well together, he thought, and he grew fond of her and admired her intellect, better than his own; then she left, and he never knew why.

This was in McKay. Nabil had moved there from Gautier following his graduation, a translocation which almost everyone among family and friends told him was a wrong direction: why, with the metropolis of Sagan almost next door, with all its opportunities and its prestige and its bustle, would he purposefully place himself substantially further from that? Why move to a pocket-arcology settlement, an outpost, almost, with minimal opportunities for academic employment, if such was what he wished to pursue, as he told those around him? McKay didn't even have a university proper, just a Senior Education Facility occupying one level of one wing of the stub-spoked building that housed the settlement's few thousand inhabitants. The facility catered for no more than a hundred and thirty students at any one time, most of whom had technical rather than academic ambitions. But it numbered among its staff sometimes three, sometimes four, moderately well-regarded specialists in particular disciplines. Each of these specialists was decently resourced (through, as he understood it, a grant from the Wurlingame foundry which occupied the arcology's entire north wing and which constituted, in large part, the justification for the settlement's continuing existence) and one of them, Fleta Lüüs, was also one of Titan's half-dozen leading authorities in the field which the still-young Nabil Scheuermann wished to pursue: cryoadaptive biomanipulation. The field was, for its part, widely misunderstood by nonspecialists, who saw its ultimate goal and sole, seemingly unattainable, measure of eventual fruition as the seeding of Titan's unforgiving environment with viable microbial or botanical lifeforms: an afforestation, for whatever purpose such a grandiose and ill-considered venture might be attempted. It never seemed to help, with family especially, that Nabil patiently and earnestly explained that the end goal of most CB research, his own project included, was rather the tailoring of microorganisms designed to flourish at—indeed, to depend upon for metabolic efficacy—a temperature range of 180 to 200 Kelvin, broadly therefore intermediate between the temperature of Titan's natural landscape and the human habitable range. There was considerable industrial impetus to pursue CB, and very probably the eventual economic benefit of any possible success was the principal reason why Wurlingame was backing the project so heavily: a bio-reactor which could function at low temperatures would permit housings which required only a fraction of the heating, heat engineering and insulation of those currently needed to produce the ingredients which would eventually become foodstuffs, or textiles, or pharmaceuticals within Titan's material economy. Factories containing such bio-reactors could thus be made larger, for high throughput at low cost. The more prosetylistic among CB's devotees predicted that its implementation would lead to a golden age in settlement on Titan, permitting a population perhaps ten times that supportable at the present moment. For his part, Nabil didn't really believe in the program with anything approaching such missionary enthusiasm, but he did recognise that the work was useful, and that there would be some measure of societal benefit were it to succeed. Yet however often he felt impelled to explain this, to his closest family members in particular, they never acquired what he considered a reliable understanding of what it was he did, and what it was he hoped to achieved. He would, inevitably, face the same ill-informed enquiries at the next encounter; rinse and repeat. Not that this mattered, much, as long as the work itself gave him a sufficient sense of purpose. Which, mostly, it did.

He had been the research officer in the Lüüs group for five years, which itself was a comparatively long posting for a position with no real guarantee of continuity, when Fleta Lüüs herself, his supervisor, took ill. She died a year later, following an unequal struggle with an unusually aggressive and vaccine-resistant sarcoma. Nabil approached the education facility's administrators, seeking a six-month extension of his then-current contract, so as to secure the time to write up the studies which had lain unfinished for the duration of Lüüs' illness. The administrators went better, offering him the security of a new five-year contract if he would commit to a split teaching/research position, to meet the facility's needs for a general science instructor following the incumbent's retirement. There were advantages and disadvantages to the proposed arrangement; chief among the disadvantages was that to accept would be to distance himself further from the forefront of research activity at the big universities such as Coustenis, South Sagan, and Kuiper. But the first two of those universities did not have any history of research in CB programs, which meant he would have been starting from scratch, while a relocation to Kuiper would have put him at a great distance from his mother, whose health and memory both were failing. He couldn't do it. He accepted the contract offered by the McKay administrators.

To begin with, it was very much a struggle. While Wurlingame was still willing to bankroll the work to some extent, they were no longer as generous as before, meaning that he could not afford to hire anyone full-time for the adjunct research position which, previously, had been his; this, and the write-up of archival work already undertaken, plus the unfamiliar demands of teaching—something which, in truth, he did not love—ensured that no real progress was made in the laboratory in the year after Dr Lüüs' death. This, noted offhand in communications to his family members, became further ammunition for the push to persuade him to move elsewhere: back to Gautier for family, or to Sagan or Brouwer for opportunities. He did not entertain these recommendations; cryoadaptive biomanipulation was where he felt usefully occupied, which meant staying in McKay and seeking to build on the limited progress which had previously been made within the research group under Lüüs' supervision.

Any substantive research endeavour is inclined to bedevil itself, though the particulars differ in each instance. In the case of his own chosen field, the crux of the problem was that three point eight billion years of terrestrial evolution had not produced any organisms capable of functioning within CB's target temperature range. Against this, said temperature range had seldom been applicable to the terrestrial environment (except perhaps in polar night, during the Snowball Earth phases), so the absence of any present-day microorganisms with CB characteristics left open-ended the question of whether life under such conditions was at all possible. An answer to that question would have practical implications, but philosophical ones also: if life of some sort was tenable under the conditions pertaining within, say, Europa's vast ice-roofed oceans, why had it not been found there?

While Nabil could see the attraction of such speculations, they did not engage him as did the substantially more prosaic aspects of the problem. It would be enough for him to participate in activity which had some reasonable prospect for progress, were any progress possible.

Fleta Lüüs' approach had not been to seek to mimic or adapt the work being undertaken by most other CB-striving practitioners, of modifying extant cold-loving organisms—psychrophiles—to endure progressively colder temperatures, or of de novo designing artificial organisms to tolerate such conditions. Her strategy was simpler, if less direct, and Nabil could see its strength and its potential, even before he effectively took ownership of the conceptual framework following Lüüs' death: it was a piecemeal approach, a biomolecule-level focus on tuning the performance of individual enzymes. Often this meant a kind of reverse-engineering of the candidate protein, to investigate the characteristics which impeded its function at cryonic temperatures and to seek to remedy those features: for example, by substituting key amino acid residues so as to weaken the hydrogen bonding network conferring the protein's shape and controlling its fluxionality. Once the group's in vitro trials of a tailored enzyme had demonstrated useful low-temperature activity, a DNA or RNA sequence specifying the polypeptide's amino acid backbone could then be synthesised and added to a library of such genes, available for incorporation in appropriately adapted microbes. It was work, thought Nabil, which usefully augmented rather than competed with the efforts which other, better-resourced research groups were applying to the CB end goals. Shortly before Lüüs' death, the approach had seen its first substantive success, with the completion of an anthology of genes capable of effecting methanogenesis from appropriate feedstock, in a truly catalytic fashion in cryoprotectant-dosed aqueous solutions, in a sequence for which the least cryotolerant step remained functional at temperatures of 188 Kelvin. The process itself was of no commercial value—what need was there for an industrial source of methane, on Titan, when the molecule was already an abundant atmospheric constituent, and amenable to purification at modest expense?—but it was very useful as a demonstration of the power of the Lüüs approach.

Fleta had planned next to work on a cryometabolism for the generation of Z-2-butene, a specific precursor for the production of some pharmaceuticals and flavour agents and therefore a target of some commercial value, but the opportunity was not afforded her. The work would have to progress in her absence.

Nabil was not intrinsically social, and the teaching requirement was at first onerous, in the sense that his need for solitude could no longer reliably be met within the work environment. Some of the time which he would previously have devoted to addressing the minutiae of a research task—an isolated and isolating activity which gave him freedom to ponder as he wished, so long as some useful fraction of his attention remained focussed on the relevant intellectual aim— was necessarily now given over instead to teaching and tutoring and advising. The personal contact was draining, because of how his personality was constituted. This meant that he needed to find a form of release which had not been necessary before.

He bought a reconditioned traversal frame, which he piloted out repeatedly into the uplands that began as the dunes ended, just a few kilometres east of McKay. These expeditions were tentative at first, but once he had become accustomed to the frame's motion, and was able to rely with reasonable certainty on its instinctively responsive attitude control, he was able to move far quicker on its three long legs, and could without difficulty manage a round-trip trek of up to a hundred kilometres within a single daycycle. The topography of the uplands—ridges of rain-rounded, tholin-stained hillocks of old ice, radiating broadly west to east as though in mimicry of the dunefield to their west—meant also that numerous routes were accessible. He dropped wilderness markers every few kilometres, to ensure retraceability, but had never needed to locate them on his return homeward; consequently, he let them lie, narrowcasting intermittently on his own private frequency.

It was a quiet pursuit: beyond the sounds of his own breathing, digestion, and motion, and the repetitive noises which his suit made to facilitate these processes, there was only the faintly mechanical whir and grind of the frame's footfalls and, at times, the subvocalised growl of the wind. He seldom saw other people on these jaunts. Few of the citizens of McKay were of an exploring bent, evidently; the region wasn't of any particular geochemical or aesthetic interest, and the nearest larger population centres— Brouwer, Wallis, and Dollfus—were a few hundred kilometres distant, with other attractions nearer at hand to those locations. (In Wallis's case, in particular, the main lure was metropolitan Sagan itself, a mere two hours' travel time away by fast railpod.) The lack of contact with others was what Nabil needed, and the excursions became something central to his wellbeing: they gave his mind the freedom it needed to wander, when such freedom was no longer easily attainable within the confines of McKay. Sometimes he would return from his augmented walk with a new insight into some CB-related difficulty, sometimes with nothing, but it was always a reprieve and an opportunity for him to reclaim himself in readiness for the days of work which would follow.

Sooner or later, Nabil felt, the mechanism would reveal itself: the route to Z-2-butene. He merely needed to ensure he was there when it happened.

2

Nabil's sister Keidra divorced and moved to Sagan. She took a posting there as admin for a panel of technical experts scoping the requirements underpinning the space-elevator proposal which was beginning to attract some political attention in Titan's *de facto* capital. Konrad Ohanessian stayed in Gautier, doing whatever it was he did there: something to do with marketing, some connection with the reclamation of air from industrial waste. The details had never really interested Nabil; nor had he had any sense, before the fact, that Keidra's and Konrad's marriage was failing. But this business of domestic relationships and closeness to one other individual had always been a mystery to him, for all that he had once sought such a status for himself, with a woman—Anasuya—whose personality he could now not properly recall, nor with any clarity her face. He was not, it seemed, shaped for such things, and he did not know whether the realisation should have been a disappointment to him. It wasn't.

The dissolution between Keidra and Konrad was amicable, to the extent that apparently they still sometimes socialised when work or parental duties took one or other of them to the other's home settlement. Nabil supposed this was a good thing, particularly with regard to his nieces, whose names he now belatedly took the time to learn and to sort: Tiril, aged four, Sisika, aged three, and Parminder, almost two and a half. He resolved to spend more time in his sister's company, aware that, with the pressures of her posting, it could not be easy for her to care for the girls on the weeks they were with her, rather than with Konrad. That said, the first week for which he arranged leave to visit his sister in Sagan was one during which the girls were in Gautier with their father, because Nabil had not thought to coordinate matters with Keidra. Consequently he saw his nieces only for a few hours on the last daycycle of his visit.

Sagan was, as ever, a challenging environment for him. It wasn't so much the size of the place as the population density, with a municipal footprint which always seemed two sizes too small for the numbers of people who had moved to Titan's largest settlement for work or lifestyle. A relatively compact city of already a half-million people distributed among a score of large interconnected and multilevelled buildings, it seemed two-thirds of its inhabitants were constantly on the move from one cultural event to the next, from one amusement to the next, from one partner to the next. And all along the northern perimeter was the ever-present disruption of construction activity, as the city looked to play catch-up with the thousands who emigrated to it each year, from elsewhere on Titan, or from elsewhere within Saturn system, or even on occasion from elsewhere in the outer Solar System. (McKay, by contrast, was no drawcard at all: it had never reached the population its planners had envisaged, and was thus significantly less crowded and intrinsically quieter as well as substantially smaller, a combination which suited Nabil much better.)

'You'd see more of the girls if you moved here,' Keidra told him as he made preparations to return to McKay. 'Or to Gautier, if Sagan's too busy for your sensibilities.'

'It's not a matter of my sensibilities. McKay is where my work is.'

'But honestly I don't see why you keep on with it. You say yourself it's often dull, and it sounds incredibly frustrating.'

'It often is,' Nabil conceded, as the conversation ran along its well-worn furrow. 'But it's rewarding enough, and I enjoy the challenge.'

'You could have that in any job,' said Keidra. 'Anywhere. And you'd be closer to family here, or in Gautier. It just feels as though you're isolating yourself, for a pipe dream.'

'It's not like that. And in any case, this wouldn't be a good time to relocate. The program's about to turn a corner.'

'You say that every time, it seems. There must be a lot of corners.'

'It's just difficult. I mean, to give it up at this point would be difficult. There are obligations I would need to meet first.'

The real explanation was simpler: he just did not want to.

In truth, also, his team's research was foundering. Fleta Lüüs' selection of Z-2-butene as a cryobiosynthetic target—to which Nabil had adhered after her death—had proven more challenging than expected. It seemed increasingly unlikely that they would be able to infer any metabolic similarity to the methanogenesis route, and therefore to define desired intermediate steps by which a yet-incomplete pathway to the larger hydrocarbon could be guided. There was not even an unfinished road to worry over. It might be that there was no route at all within the required temperature range. Meanwhile, in Griffith and in Coustenis, there were now other research groups which had adopted the Lüüs model and which were publishing work suggesting that significant progress had been made towards cryo routes to ethane and acetylene. These were not, in themselves, industrially useful targets, but were academically useful goals which might, in turn, assist extrapolation to heavier and more complex hydrocarbons. Nobody except Nabil and his part-time research support, Yoshihiro, were yet pursuing any of those more complex hydrocarbons; but if progress could not be made by them, their perceived head start counted for nothing. A change was needed.

He sought out the education facility's industry liaison officer, explained to her (in what he hoped were layperson terms) the difficulties which were faced in the research program which he had inherited, and she agreed to arrange a meeting with those in Wurlingame's R&D support division who could, she felt, best assist with the problems he faced. He was apprehensive about the scheduled meeting, for all that the industry liaison officer seemed genuinely supportive and understanding. He'd never dealt directly with his Wurlingame paymasters before this, as there had always been a layer of mediation provided by facility admin. There was such a layer this time as well, the liaison officer assured him; she would be present in the meeting, and would seek to ensure that McKay's perspective was clearly put forward. Nabil, however, felt that the layer on this occasion would be less cell wall and more cell membrane, a circumstance of heightened vulnerability for him and for the program's funding. It wasn't possible to know, ahead of the meeting, whether foregrounding the lack of recent research success was wise, but the alternative, of waiting out another year for the expiration of the current funding arrangement, would mean an almost certain end to the program if no substantive progress were made over the next year.

Wurlingame augmented his grant, but insisted on project markers that would need to be met for continuance of funding. Milestones; millstones. They'd given him to understand, in the several meetings brokered by McKay's industry liaison officer, that the successful completion of the project was highly important to the org. Methane had been Lüüs' principal contribution to CB research; Z-2-butene, if it could be realised as a viable CB target, would make Nabil's own name as the leader of a research group continuing to do important and innovative work. But he had no plan for how to achieve it; and meeting the goals set by Wurlingame would be difficult, perhaps impossible. The task was made more complicated, too, by the cessation of Yoshihiro's contract: the research assistant was keen to jump tracks to a more productive field, for which Nabil could hardly blame him.

There was a conference in Coustenis, on-topic, which Nabil was loath to attend for three reasons. The first was Coustenis itself: it was a long journey to reach a crowded settlement second only in size to Sagan. Second, he had no recent results to highlight. Third, he had no time to spare.

He would go anyway. There were things one could learn from conferences—through the academic discourse, the disagreements, the stray remarks and gossip—which couldn't be garnered in any other way. It annoyed him that it was so, but it was.

He was offered a speaking slot, on the strength of the methane work. He accepted it. It was obvious that the panel convenors would be seeking some references to the ongoing work towards heavier hydrocarbons; it was demoralising that there was nothing he could give out on that. He strove, the week before the conference, to reshape his presentation, trying to find some way to disguise the lack of any new developments. It wasn't acceptable to be untruthful in scientific presentations, but a certain selective emphasis was expected. Each presentation had some aspect of the marketing exercise, especially in a field with as much industrial potential as CB. This made him think he should consult Konrad on how to sell himself, but he couldn't do it. He'd had no direct contact with Keidra's ex since their divorce, and he didn't think it right to approach the man for a favour on those terms. It was simpler to just cut him off. It had always been simpler.

The panel's convenors were junior members of the Coustenis research group; the group was, en masse, a convert to the Lüüs approach. In that sense, he would be among friends. But this also meant he would be among rivals. He could, meaningfully, seek advice from those present, just as his work on the methane pathway gave him the cachet to offer advice in some respects. But it was too much to hope that, by attending the conference, he would get what he needed to meet the requirements Wurlingame had imposed. He went because the grant included a travel-and-accommodation stipend for attending relevant conferences; it was expected that he would go, just as it was expected that he would square the mechanistic circle required to find the Z-2-butene route.

Sound advice, useful ideas: these were possible benefits from the conference. There were potential personnel gains too: the new funding from Wurlingame would allow him to employ two suitably qualified research officers to assist with the mechanistic quest for Z-2-butene, for as long as the grant's productivity conditions were met. There was no better venue than a conference to find such candidates; but the lack of recent progress meant that it would be difficult to make the posts sound attractive. There was the development of the Lüüs approach, which was in its way emblematic and innovative; but Fleta was several years dead and Nabil hadn't succeeded in emulating her achievement. He feared he would not.

The conference went better than he'd dared hope. That is, there were outcomes which he hadn't in any way anticipated, with respect to new approaches that could be applied to the task; though it remained to be seen whether these methods would be of any use. His presentation, too, had been unexpectedly well received. Since he had no new results of any significance to report, and since it would have seemed inadequate to have given a talk providing merely a general description of the Lüüs method or of his group's as-yet unsubstantiated aspirations towards heavier hydrocarbons, he'd focussed on some minor but crucial details of the cryo route to methane, highlighting the value of these mechanistic aspects as illustrations of the difficulties to be expected in work on other, more complicated compounds. It was a talk which enabled him to imply that the Lüüs group was still in the hunt, which was what he needed to do in Coustenis. It would not be possible to rely on an inventive reworking of such old material another time, but it worked on this occasion.

The new approach which the Lüüs group would adopt was computationally intensive. It had revealed itself to him at the conference when, during a break in the Lüüs-approach panel sessions, he'd chosen to attend one of the microbe design talks. These were the teams seeking to develop *de novo* lifeforms capable of metabolic function only within the CB temperature range. It was a different goal than that of the teams focussing on enzymatic pathways, though the approaches were complementary: any industrially useful metabolic sequence would require an encasing and self-replicating organism to ensure its proliferation and continuance. And it transpired that some of the methodology which applied to one subdomain within CB might well be of value within another subdomain also.

He didn't know how widely this was apprehended. The realisation seemed so trivial that it might well be common knowledge within the delegates, with himself late to the understanding. But he hadn't discerned reference to this 'adaptive syncretic interpolation' approach within any of presentations given by those whose broader research goals aligned more or less with his own: the compilation of a library of CB enzymatic pathways to industrially useful hydrocarbons and their derivatives. It might indeed be that the connection was, for now, appreciated only by himself.

It might also be that the methodology wasn't usefully transferable to his program. That was always the risk. But it was surely worth the attempt, when nothing else had helped in the largely blind quest for a Z-2-butene route.

ASI was a combinatorics-heavy computational technique which, by performing trillions of low-level energy-minimisation calculations on moderate distortions of a structure of interest, sought not to avoid errors, nor to minimise them, but to learn from them. At least, this was what Nabil understood of the method, though his was almost certainly the flawed and simplistic view of any outsider. He would therefore require the services of someone adept in the approach; to this end, he made discreet enquiries on the conference's last day.

The enquiries paid off. He acquired a young postdoc, Xa Melhuis, and a seasoned research officer, Huynh Pettersson, with experience across a range of laboratory and theory-based techniques. Now it would be a matter of hoping that this new method, in the hands of his new additions to the Lüüs group, would be of sufficient utility to allow the group to meet Wurlingame's deadline.

Though time was uncomfortably tight, he did not immediately seek to apply the new approach to the Z-2-butene route itself. Instead, for purposes of familiarisation (for himself with the technique, and for Xa and Huynh with the group's research goals), he instructed them to use ASI to cover old ground: the established methane pathway. The exercise did not merely replicate what was already known of the pathway: it found five promising modifications, which he then subjected to testing. One was a blind alley, a demonstration that ASI did not always provide a model which aligned precisely with reality, but the other four were genuinely novel tweaks, all of which improved the mechanism by some measure and one of which appeared to extend the pathway's cryotolerance down to 181 K, a seven-degree improvement on the route which had been Fleta's crowning contribution to the field. Nabil was both heartened and intimidated by the power of the new technique. Where the original derivation of the methane process had required more than two years of painstaking adaptation of sometimes successful, often unsuccessful, enzyme structures, ASI had thrown out the ameliorations in only three days of calculation, though the validation of the new mechanistic variations had taken longer.

The new methane process demanded publication, and was worthy of rapid notification to the scientific community; he drafted a manuscript accordingly, bestowing first-authorship on Xa Melhuis and dedicating the manuscript 'to the memory of Fleta Lüüs'. The manuscript would remain unsubmitted until substantive progress had been made towards Z-2-butene, in which direction he now instructed his group members to work.

The pathway to Z-2-butene would be notably more challenging than that to methane, he had always known that; but with ASI it appeared that it might indeed be attainable.

Things went well.

Things went very well.

Things went too well.

It was Melhuis: he could tell from the footsteps, even before the carefully-calibrated rap on his office door. He feared it might be something personal; work matters could have waited for this afternoon's group meeting. He saved the manuscripts, rose from his desk, bade the door open.

She entered. There wasn't really anywhere for her to sit, but this seemed not to be a problem. She was effervescing with constrained excitement, her dark eyes bright, seeking his out.

'Is something up?' he asked. The possibilities unfolded for him as soon as the question was voiced: an engagement, perhaps, or pregnancy, or an inheritance, or the remission of some troubling medical condition, for her or an immediate family member, or a more lucrative offer of employment elsewhere. Coustenis, most probably, if the latter; she had family there—

Her words blew apart his speculation. 'We're there,' she told him, followed after a breath-pause by a statement so hastily delivered that he almost heard the syllables trip over one another as they emerged. 'I know there's the meeting this afternoon, but we wanted to inform you as soon as we were sure.'

'We?'

She was still breathing more heavily than standard. 'Zed-two-butene. Huynh left his device in the lab, he backtracked to collect it.'

'Well, congratulations,' he replied mildly, feeling put out nonetheless, a person-from-Porlock-level resentment at the interruption of his composition of the manuscript's discussion section, for something which could really have waited for the appointed time. Though of course that was unreasonable of him; victory in research was infrequent and unpredictable, and his team member's palpable positivism at this evident achievement, whatever incremental item it might turn out to be, was something itself to be prized and fostered. Nurtured. Enthusiasm was an ally, the soil in which it sprouted often of a quality too poor to sustain it.

Probably, she meant to inform him that they had good preliminary detail on sufficient steps towards the target alkene to satisfy the stipulations of their first ASI-informed progress report to Wurlingame. Well, good. It would be useful to not be running a Red Queen's race the whole time...

Huynh Pettersson appeared in the doorway. He was holding the device Xa had referred to, and panting as though from uncharacteristic exertion. He, too, looked pleased. Nabil gestured for him to enter, surprised at how annoyed he still felt. Waspish. His writing time should be alone time. 'Xa tells me you have an important new part of the sequence.'

Huynh frowned, flicked his eyes towards the postdoc.

'No,' Xa Melhuis said. 'That's not correct. Did you not hear me? We have the whole thing.'

'The whole thing?'

'Feedstock, intermediates, all the way through to Z-2-butene. Proper enzymatic action, fully catalytic. As far as we can establish, it goes through the complete sequence without significant poisoning of any active site.'

'The whole thing?' he repeated. *Surely not. Not after barely two months.* 'At CB temps?'

'Better,' she replied, grinning as though it were a sporting-ground boast. 'Show him, Huynh.'

The research officer cleared a space on his team leader's desk, placed his device down, slid it apart into wide-display format. Nabil and Xa gathered either side of him, as he began to briefly elaborate on each of what were clearly dozens of mechanistic steps. The words he spoke were mostly already on the displayed scheme; Nabil interrupted him about five steps in. 'This is all still theoretical?'

'Mostly,' said Xa. 'Yes, these are the modelled results from ASI, but in several cases, those marked in blue, we also already have the wet-biochem measurements as well. The agreement is close on all of those so far.'

Fleta should have been here to see this, he thought, and was irritated to feel a pricking sensation at the back of his eyes. He began to allow himself to feel a sense of satisfaction at his subordinates' achievements, at the carefully compiled structures. 'This is a lot of work,' he said, to neither one in particular.

'Yes,' said Xa.

'Can you overlay the temperature dependence?'

She did so. Yes, maybe they did indeed have something: it was a highly impressive body of work, and the detail all looked positive. Nonetheless, something about the temperature axis nagged at him.

'Ninety?' he asked, turning first to Huynh, whose device he was viewing, then to Xa, whose mechanism it primarily was. 'Is this degrees Celsius below zero? Why, then, are the numbers ascending?'

'It's Kelvin,' said Xa, grinning.

He took perhaps a dozen seconds before responding, while something bitter and tinged with dread flourished within him. 'You're telling me that this enzymatic step is efficient around ninety Kelvin? A hundred and eighty-odd below zero? Liquid nitrogen temperatures?'

'Yes,' said Xa. Still the pride in her achievement, not yet the realisation of the problem.

'Well, how is that even possible? Surely the active site would be frozen solid.'

'The enzyme is tuned for liquid methane.'

'But we're looking for an aqueous process,' said Nabil. 'Wurlingame is very definite on that requirement.'

'It can't be done,' said Xa, staring at him as though in challenge. 'For the enzymes needed, aqueous solvent requires too much cryoprotectant below two-twenty Kelvin, it skews the dielectric horrendously and none of the peptide sequences refold correctly. We don't have those problems with hydrocarbon solvent.'

'But *liquid methane*—' began Nabil.

'It works,' said Xa, the metal evident in her tone as she sought to fight off what she presumably considered an unfair complaint; a mere quibble, even. She jabbed her finger at one of the many steps displayed on the device, magnified the chosen protein structure somehow with one of those gestures Nabil had never himself mastered. 'The peptide folds itself to present a hydrophobic exterior, but the sequence is tailored so the hydrogen-bonding network within the interior can't quite align to lock it into a single rigid conformation. There's an equilibrium, as it skids between these two configurations, they're virtually isoenergetic. It stays loose at ninety K, reagents can access the active site, it ratchets closed, then open as the photochemistry happens, the substrate is released and the enzyme is ready to go again.'

'At ninety Kelvin,' said Nabil.

'Yes.'

'And they're all like this?'

'Variations on a theme. This is the approach which works.'

'At ninety Kelvin.'

'It is a very elegant sequence,' said Huynh, glancing from postdoc to supervisor in a manner which suggested that he, at least, recognised that something was awry.

'The elegance isn't the issue,' said Nabil. 'Liquid methane is too cold a process. Wurlingame will never accept it. We'll need to cut out these liquid-methane steps.'

'We can't cut them out,' said Xa, her lower lip quivering in the pause between sentences. 'They're almost all liquid methane. Look, I tried everything to get this to happen in aqueous solution, it would not. But it happens in liquid methane. We don't get to pick and choose how the enzymes work.'

'Wurlingame won't see it that way.'

'Why would Wurlingame be resistant?' asked Huynh. 'The thermal requirements of this process are lower, and methane is cheap. The process requires minimal insulation, minimal heating.'

'And they're all like this? The entire suite of mechanistic steps?'

'Close,' said Xa. 'They all more-or-less operate at Titan-ambient conditions, once the enzyme is settled within the medium and the feedstock is introduced. It pretty much only needs illumination for the photochemical steps. Wurlingame would save substantially on this.'

'They won't see it that way,' Nabil repeated. 'They don't see it that way. A process that operates at one-eighty or one-ninety Kelvin, and in a narrow band below and above, is a safe process that should readily be granted approval by the regulators—it's too cold to function in human-habitable zones, too warm for viability outside. You give them something that works at ninety Kelvin, something that *requires* ninety Kelvin for virtually the entire cold chain if I understand you correctly, and the regulators are going to flag it as a potential environmentally hazardous activity. Which means Wurlingame aren't going to get the approval they need; which means they are not going to sponsor it, nor license it. So, no, we can't use this.'

'But it works. It does everything required.'

'Mechanistically? Yes, perhaps. Thermally, no. And "thermally, no" kills it. Look, I appreciate the work, but this won't sell. I can't report this to Wurlingame, because there's no point.'

'This is ridiculous!' exclaimed Xa. 'We're talking about an enzymatic sequence, not a lifeform. It requires particular conditions, it's not like it's going to get loose and start grey-gooing everything—'

'That doesn't matter. They will see it how they see it. They already have a facility half-constructed southeast of McKay, for this process and for others they have presumably sponsored elsewhere, and those processes, the facility, will operate at near dry-ice temperatures, a hundred and eighty Kelvin or thereabouts. We have to work with that. We'll need to scrap every step that works at ninety Kelvin and—'

She raised her voice to cut across his, visibly angry, offended, bruised. 'It's not reasonable that pure research should be subjected to these arbitrary industrial requirements just be—'

'But this isn't pure research,' Nabil observed blandly. 'This is applied research. There's a specific target. So of course there are going to be conditions, and of course we have to be mindful of them. If—'

Xa shook her head, swore, left. Nabil had the impression she would've slammed the door to his office if it had been in any way amenable to such activity. Huynh paused only to gather up his device before following, adroitly managing to avoid Nabil's attempts at eye contact as he exited.

Nabil breathed heavily, stared at the spot where the device had been.

That hadn't gone as well as he'd hoped.

He gave himself almost an hour, during which time his thoughts refused to be collected, before seeking to follow up. Melhuis's own office door was open to its full extent; the office was empty. It looked as though she'd gone for the day.

He paced the corridor to Pettersson's office, knocked. The door slid open. 'Have you seen Kris—'

'Xa left,' Huynh replied. Waited, it seemed, for some response. Then the research officer stepped back, gestured for Nabil to enter.

The office bore no stamp of Pettersson's character, no statement of individuality; though perhaps that, in itself, was a statement of some form. A desk, a door to the adjoining wet lab, two chairs; neither man sat. Nabil always felt unsure in Pettersson's presence: the older man his junior, despite the research officer's evident expertise and multifaceted competence. And while there was nothing of insubordination in Huynh's bearing towards him, there was sometimes a certain... insouciance which seemed to hint at dissatisfaction with the order of hierarchy.

'Left?' asked Nabil. 'Do you mean that she's just gone for the day, or—'

'She's gone back to Coustenis. For a week, maybe two. Said she'll be back after that, to renegotiate her contract. She was significantly upset. I have to say I don't blame her. The work she's done here, just in these few months, has been—'

'Her work is good, anyone can see that. But it has to be fit for purpose. For Wurlingame's purpose.'

'She said you'd say something like that, said you'd hide behind Wurlingame. She also said if you wouldn't approve the work for publication, others would.'

'She can't do that. The work belongs to the group.'

'I think she knows that. But she's angry, and that's perfectly understandable. She's worked damned hard on this.'

'Even if I concede that, two weeks away is too long. One week pushes us into jeopardy. We need to file updates with Wurlingame, within the next several days.'

'She said you'd say that too. Said you should man up and explain a few home truths to Wurlingame. Her words, not mine.'

'And what would your own words be?' Nabil asked, not caring to disguise the bitterness in his tone.

'Think it's best I not say them.'

'She'd better be back.' It was a weak rejoinder, without substantive power, but it was part of what the situation called for. Nabil tried unsuccessfully to read the other's face, then turned and left without knowing where he expected his feet to lead him.

There was tomorrow's teaching, for which he should prepare; he couldn't be bothered facing that. He logged a cancellation for each of the teaching slots and signed off early. He was tempted to follow Melhuis's example, to abscond. Not to Coustenis, as she had, but back to Gautier or to Sagan. He didn't; it was obvious that Wurlingame's requirements would exert their weight regardless of where he travelled.

There were only three days in which to complete the next report to the group's paymasters. It wasn't time enough to put matters right—would not have been time enough even were Xa on hand—and realistically there was no pressure he could apply to Huynh to get the results they would need. Pettersson wasn't the driving force; that role was Xa Melhuis's, for she shaped the ASI explorations which informed the overall enzymatic mechanism. Huynh Pettersson's role was the necessary but not sufficient one of quality control: the wet-biochem measurements which tested and, for the most part, validated the theory-spawned pathways. An ASI-only pathway was of no value to Wurlingame, because theory could always be wrong; a lab-characterised pathway was better, but only if the theoretical mechanistic steps which it supported were acceptable, within the target range. He'd need Huynh's measurements, ultimately, but those measurements wouldn't help him here.

How had this happened, under his supervision? How had it progressed to the level of having a complete but unacceptably low-temperature mechanism to Z-2-butene, and this consequence confronting him as a complete surprise? He'd seen that the woman was capable, her ASI expertise enviable. It was a methodology which he himself didn't adequately understand, so it had seemed expedient to give her as much free rein as possible to pursue the calculations she needed. But even so, this mechanism hadn't emerged, whole-cloth, in one week: she must have known, weeks ago, that the tracks she was following were leading to liquid methane, rather than to an aqueous mechanism. And with group meetings at least once a week, it should have been reported to him well before it had reached this stage.

There was negligence on his part, but duplicity on hers. None of which helped.

She was right about one thing, though: he would need to confront Wurlingame.

But how to do that?

*

Sleep provided an answer of sorts. The saving grace was that there was no extant liquid-methane biology, would likely never be any such biology. The enzymes, Melhuis's enzymes, were the daughters of aqueous protoplasm, of structure-encoding nucleic acid chains. They would be created thus, in highly modified though recognisably conventional microbes, but happened to lack activity within an aqueous environment because their quaternary structure under those conditions—temperature, dielectric constant and other parameters— would be haphazard and therefore nonfunctional. As such, any enzyme active only in liquid methane did not pose any significant environmental hazard to Titan: while it could perhaps function to some limited extent if released accidentally, depending upon the prevailing conditions, it could not replicate in the wild and would ultimately degrade. The enzymes could be firmly categorised as 'prebiotic', a compound class of which Titan already had an abundance of naturally occurring examples within its tholin-rich dunefields and elsewhere. It only remained to convey convincingly to Wurlingame that the regulatory restrictions, intended to curb development of any microbe capable of multiplying at Titan's ambient temperature, were not appropriate to something which, at such temperature, was effectively only a process, not a lifeform. So persuaded, the org could then seek to challenge the regulations. It would ultimately be to their financial benefit to do so.

Nabil knew he was not persuasive in this way. He was a researcher, and understood the ways of business only to the extent that he needed to. He'd need advice, he'd need support. He went to call on the education facility's industry liaison officer. The woman who'd held the role previously had moved on—Sagan, most likely— and it was an off-day for the new ILO. It would need to wait twenty-four hours, while the deadline for his update to Wurlingame grew awkwardly close. He was angry: the previous ILO had been strongly supportive, there'd been a rapport, she had negotiated a good outcome for the Lüüs group. With a new officer, he would be obliged to reintroduce himself, explain the history, build some degree of trust, all before he could get to the nub, the *need*.

There were, in effect, two sequential processes. One was the enzymatic pathway that led from feedstock to Z-2-butene. The other was the concatenation of advocacy steps required to permit the pathway's operation as a licensed industrial process: from his researchers, to him, to the McKay industry liaison officer, to the Wurlingame research management team, to the Wurlingame board of trustees, to the environmental-law experts, to the decisionmakers. It seemed to Nabil that only one of these pathways was founded on well-ordered and properly regular principles; the other, the human pathway, had far too much scope for caprice, for misapprehension, for obduracy and bureaucratic rigidity.

It turned out, though, that this wasn't the problem.

4

The first several words slid off him, could find no purchase on his sleep-dulled mind. It took four or five seconds before he was able to categorise the voice, realise who had called him. Keidra. Their mother had died.

The explanation emerged slowly, amidst the ramping manifestations of Keidra's distress. Undetected componentry failure, it seemed, somewhere among the devices which had supplanted her lung tissue after the cancer that had bloomed several years ago. Nabil listened, numb, peeled raw, before finally managing to ask, 'Are the girls with you?'

'The girls? No. This is a Konrad week. I'll call him next.'

'You shouldn't be alone,' said Nabil, though he wasn't properly sure where this realisation came from. 'I'll be there as soon as I can.' He struggled to find anything useful to add to this, wished her love and ended the call.

Now he needed to scope out the fastest transportation to Gautier. It was good to have something to do. It would be too easy to do nothing.

Why did it feel as though something was caught in his throat?

The usual route to Gautier was the most direct: by shuttle to Wallis, then by rail to Gautier itself; but the shuttle was infrequent, once in two days, and the most recent had left only a few hours previously, while he'd been asleep and oblivious. There was a more dependable connection, twice daily, by air-ferry to Brouwer, from which there were almost a dozen flights each daycycle to Sagan, several of which landed enroute at Gautier. He could be there in slightly less than twenty-four hours, following a trajectory which was almost twice as long as the most straightforward track.

He messaged Pettersson, thought about but did not message Melhuis; Pettersson would likely convey the news to her, and maybe this was for the best. He did not know how long he would need to be away: how long was decent? He'd no idea. Six days, he thought, at a minimum. The Wurlingame deadline would be missed, but surely they would be sensitive to the formalities of grief. He composed a message of apology while he packed. Six days. But should that include travel time?

No, surely travel time would be additional. Eight days, then, in effect. He amended the message to Wurlingame before sending it. He had almost finished packing when he remembered his teaching, and the appointment with the ILO. One must now be cancelled and the other delayed. He arranged this, left his dwelling.

He was a man adrift. This was happening too quickly. But the requirements of familial grief would not brook a delay.

The ride out to the McKay aerodrome, across a smoothed-ice expanse marked by the lengthening fingers of shadow cast by the dunefield's fringes, was just long enough to remind him that he was not a good air traveller.

The flight out of Brouwer was almost full, fifty-plus people aboard one of the fast new Volker twelve-props; he feigned sleep to avoid any conversational gambits from the woman he'd been seated beside. Four hours, mercifully a smoother flight than the earlier leg from McKay, in the small air-ferry. He was one of only three passengers from Brouwer to disembark at Gautier.

He made his way to the Ohanessian residence. Keidra was already there, standing dignified and sombre in Konrad's livingspace alongside a tall, dark-clad redhead who was introduced as her new partner, Beck. Nabil thought his sister looked suddenly older, drawn. He moved to hug her—it was what the situation required—and was surprised by the warmth of her brief embrace.

She informed him of the funeral arrangements. The service would be simple. His mother had not wanted any religious overtones. A cremation, two daycycles hence, the combustion products to be vented into the atmosphere rather than allowed to circulate within Gautier's biosphere. Nabil felt ashamed, he hadn't given a thought to the funeral, had left such details to his younger sister.

There were meals, reminiscences, the sorting of his mother's personal belongings. Keidra asked him, in a manner which couldn't really be declined, if he would say a few words at the service. He agreed that he would, though had no idea how to properly describe his mother. This was a more difficult matter of speaking publicly than was teaching, or the presentation of research results: it required not that he give vent to more of himself, but to a different aspect of himself with which he was not properly comfortable. He worried that his tone would be too formal, too aloof, though he wasn't sure how to avoid this.

In the event, he managed. It was not as heartfelt as Keidra's eulogy, nor as touching as young Tiril's, nor even as personal as the testimony of his mother's former colleagues; he did not weep, did not altogether believe, yet, that his mother was gone, but there was affection in what he said, and some semblance of spontaneity. Keidra, afterwards, thanked him, as though she were the custodian of the family's reputation and he, somehow, a guest.

Eight days: it really wasn't long enough. But the Wurlingame matter kept pressing upon him, and he didn't have the resources to change his arrangements for the return to McKay. Keidra would, anyway, be returning to Sagan a daycycle later, with her daughters: her work made demands on her too.

He vowed to visit her within the month, and made his way back to McKay.

*

Porlocked again: Huynh Pettersson. Nabil gave a silent sigh, looked up from his notes, commanded his door open. 'Come in.'

The research officer stationed himself in front of the desk, waited for some further signal from his supervisor. He seemed not to know where to begin on whatever errand this was, a mindset Nabil had little time for today. 'There was something you wanted to discuss?' he prompted.

'Yes.' Then, several second later, 'It'll be simpler if I show you'. He placed his device on Nabil's desk.

Nabil chose to remain seated, swivelled the device around for his own ease of reading. 'Is there some sort of problem?'

'Yes.' Huynh busied himself with the device for the next several seconds, scrolling through the diagrams, schematics and data tabulations which were his occupational preserve. 'I want to stress that Xa's calculations have uncovered several instances of enzymes whose mode of functionality, in liquid methane, is unprecedented. This is work of genuine academic value, and will be of considerable interest to the community.'

'This hardly seems a point for discussion,' Nabil observed, noting that the research officer's tone sounded formal and practised, as though he'd given considerable forethought to the phrasing. Whatever followed, Huynh was taking pains to ensure he did not wish this to be seen as an attack, or even a slight, on his colleague. Which meant it probably was. 'I think we're all agreed her work is good. But I suspect that's not why you're here.'

'No.' Huynh had, it seemed, found what he'd sought on the device's display. It depicted, so far as Nabil could tell, the same mechanistic-pathway schematic that Xa and Huynh had shown him several days ago: the completed ASI pathway to Z-2-butene, with a minority of steps augmented by lab-measurement confirmation. 'This. Some of this is not so good.'

'What do you mean, not so good? Are you saying this is an issue of fabrication? Because I—'

'No, there's no indication of that,' said Huynh. 'I think these are all valid ASI results. That is, each of these ASI-derived structures represents a correctly obtained optimised geometry. But in some cases, in several instances, they do not pan out.'

'How so?'

'While the structures may theoretically be energy minima, they're not obtainable in practice. These are often low-contrast surfaces, the minima are generally shallow. At even a high level of theory, the energy differences and the barriers between different conformers, different quaternary structures, can be slight. So ASI can say one thing, but in the lab, the peptide chain often behaves differently.'

'That sounds like a problem,' said Nabil. 'How often does this happen?'

'That there are substantial discrepancies between ASI and the labwork? Often enough. I haven't had time yet to get a clearer answer than that. Some structures are well-behaved; but of the approximately twenty systems I'd say I've had sufficient opportunity to characterise properly in the lab, seven, eight look nothing like they are supposed to according to ASI. Of course it should be noted that extraction from aqueous protoplasm, followed by transfer to liquid methane, is a difficult sequence, but that doesn't explain, in my view, why it's sometimes essentially problem-free and other times not, for ostensibly similar protein sequences.'

Nabil rubbed his forehead. 'Can you be sure the lab results invalidate the ASI results, where there's a discrepancy?'

'Of course not,' said Huynh. 'Not yet. It can always be that a slight change to the process might deliver the desired result. Or it might not. But do you really want to take the chance on that, with the results you disclose to Wurlingame?'

Nabil offered only a shrug.

'I'll keep pursuing this,' Huynh assured him, 'and if any of these problem cases resolves successfully, I will notify you. But for the moment, I would be very guarded in what is reported to Wurlingame.'

'Do you think Xa was aware of this problem?' Nabil asked.

'How could she be? Small energy differences are unimportant if the temperature is low enough, which can mean it appears the enzyme is locked into a particular shape or set of shapes. In this sense, the ASI results are quite clear, and it happened that the first several lab verifications backed them up. Since then, though, on the larger structures especially, not so good.'

'It's—' Nabil didn't bother saying what it was. His mother's death was still fresh, he shouldn't be required to categorise minutiae under such conditions. 'Thank you for briefing me on this. And yes, please keep me informed.'

'Of course.'

A night of poor sleep, another day. Xa Melhuis was apparently to return in three days' time. This day presented a different challenge.

He had already once delayed the requested meeting with McKay's new industry liaison officer, felt it unwise to call for another cancellation. But the research results were in such a tangle that he couldn't see any prospect for a good outcome from the meeting.

It occurred to him, as he strode the corridor, that his mother was gone, would never be back. His reputation as a teacher was indifferent, if that; one of his research subordinates had absented herself, as the other one laboured to effectively undermine her promising results; and the industrial concern which funded his work was insisting on a strict timeline that did not provide any flexibility for the intrinsically unpredictable course of a fundamentally novel research program. He, Nabil Scheuermann, at the age of thirty-six, was not in control of any of it, not a scintilla. It was a thought at once both diminishing and somehow soothing.

He was granted entrance to the admin cluster's meeting room. 'I don't think you'll be able to help me,' he said, straight off, before registering that the new ILO was in fact Anasuya, the responsive-polymer chemist with whom he'd had a brief relationship almost a decade ago.

'Well, now, let's see,' she replied.

Nabil smiled, not because the sight of his former lover awoke anything of significance for him or, he suspected, for her—there had been something missing within him or between them, back in those days, and he'd since reconciled himself to not understanding what that was—but because he knew her to be highly competent, keenly analytical, and faster-witted than himself. It might well be that she could devise a manner in which the continuance of his research program could be assured, where he himself could not. Conversely, she might fail in this, or he might fail to meet whatever guidance she provided. But her presence in this new role, and her apparent contentment, demonstrated to him that there might well be a life after research. It was a validation which, in this time and place, he needed.

He took his seat, wondered where he should start.

A word on screenwriting

If you are going
to cheat on lightspeed
then at least
have you the courage
to tell her to her face.

Tell her you wish
no longer to be bound
by her rules;
tell her you have found
another physics
who better meets your needs.

Do not believe
that you can go
behind her back
and get away unnoticed.
Do not rely on her
only when you need her.

Be faithful, or not;
embrace, if you must,
instantaneous communication
between the planets,
instant travel between the stars;
but be upfront.

And if you and lightspeed
do decide
to part ways, you will need
to reach agreement
on who gets custody
of gravity
mass-energy equivalence
and the conservation of momentum.

The ballad of P'toresk

P'thurglebluxl, a simple, trusting, and intrinsically brave young inhabitant of planet P'toresk, knew his world to be a place of heartrending beauty. He did not, however, suspect its hidden flaw: its location. For planet P'toresk lay at the cartographic centre, the nexus, the cosmic crossroads if you will, of five ambitious and aggressively expanding space empires. This story tells the tale of P'thurglebluxl's involvement in the tempestuous events of a few short years, during which the Elysian setting of P'toresk was overrun by wave after wave of competing alien invaders before, ultimately, these aggressors were driven off.

First to pillage pristine P'toresk was the Vurtigon space army. The Vurtigonians met no resistance from the unsuspecting and peaceable P'toresquine inhabitants, and landed their majestic McGuffin Planet-Destroyer-class warships on the verdant fields of their new conquest. Overseeing the land that he now held in his thrall, the Vurtigonian high admiral could see that it was a place of unparalleled tranquillity, which had, in his eyes, only one minor defect.

Its days were too short.

Accordingly, the Vurtigonian cargo fleet shipped in a complement of massive McGuffin PEC MegaThruster orbital calibration units, which were anchored one by one to P'toresk's equator and fired up. Soon the booming roar of their exhaust became a part of the daily—and, more prominently, nightly—noises of the P'toresquine environment, and gradually the days grew longer.

P'thurglebluxl, who had been gathering his evening meal of berries, roots, and succulent sugar-grubs before the disturbance of the giant ships' first descent, hastily concealed himself in the long grass that surrounded the fleet's landing-ground. He watched in disgust and horror (incidentally both new emotions to him) as the Vurtigonians, unsightly blue creatures with too many eyes and with rubbery, ropy tentacles, slithered around and within their vessels, acting for all the world as if they owned the place. P'thurglebluxl's indignation at this behaviour knew no limit, and he vowed that, though it took him a score of years, he would find a way to repulse these vile creatures and to restore his homeland to its natural beauty.

It did not take a score of years. It hardly took one, nor indeed any coherent action on P'thurglebluxl's part. The Kallaginti warships, a fleet of new and deadly McGuffin Star-Pulveriser-class vessels which dived from the heavens in a lightning raid of unparalleled ferocity, decimated the outmoded hulks of the Vurtigonian space army and were able to claim the planet as their own, without the loss of a single ship on their own part. The Kallaginti commander-in-chief, surveying her new prize, perceived a wondrous land with only one failing.

Its nights were much too long.

Consequently, the Kallaginti transport service was despatched to collect a complement of the new gargantuan McGuffin PEC HyperGigaThrusterDeluxe rotational re-adjustment modules, which were designated for emplacement on the planet's equator. Awaiting the shipment of these units, the military engineers of the Kallaginti Occupation Force busied themselves by dismantling and ransacking for parts the now-redundant MegaThruster installations which the defeated Vortigonians had misguidedly (and without any proper thought of aesthetic placement) foisted upon the pristine P'toresquine countryside. The brief respite from sonic assault which followed the dismemberment of the last of the ugly and obsolete MegaThrusters was, in truth, the prelude to a much more aggressive aural battering which began with the first ascending whine of the newly-installed HyperGigaThruster machines.

P'thurglebluxl peered, from his hiding-spot in the undergrowth, with a growing sense of dismay as this new band of ludicrous, copper-orange, crustaceoid invaders—who were all mandibles and long, jointed legs—now began to stamp their own foul mark on his beautiful homeland. He had fashioned for himself a rough yet sturdy dagger, but he could see that it would not prove useful in combat against these brutes. Nevertheless he vowed, for his heart and for his people's sake, that this despoliation would be redressed through his actions if it took him a dozen years to set things to rights.

It did not require a dozen years. It did not even need any involvement on P'thurglebluxl's part within the mere six-month occupation by the Kallaginti forces. The subversive assault by the Golgleglog infiltrators, which took advantage of a hidden weakness in the primitive defences of the Kallaginti fleet, was complete before the new McGuffin Nova-Blaster-class ships (the pride of the Golgleglog space navy) were even detected by the hapless Kallaginti army. On landing, the cognitive centre of the Golgleglog combat organism assessed its newly-conquered terrain. It found itself in possession of a bountiful world which had but one sole defect.

Its seas were too deep.

The Golgleglog engineering organism, when consulted, prescribed an appropriate correction to this problem, through the acquisition of several of the new monolithic McGuffin PEC TeraSquirter Ballistic Ejection dehydration plants. These were conveniently locatable on the ruins of the Kallaginti's now-worthless HyperGigaThruster machines, from which the noise, though deafening, had at least been *constant*. The TeraSquirters, essentially water cannons which were sufficiently powerful that their payload attained escape velocity, operated with a sporadic thump which would have been audible on the other side of the planet. Would have, that is, if their noise was not being drowned out on *that* side by other, nearer TeraSquirter installations.

The brave and patient native, P'thurglebluxl, gazed on with a deepening sense of foreboding as these new aliens, a tribe of ridiculously amoeboid quasi-transparent blobby giants, squelched their desecration across his once-proud land. His newly-fashioned spear, though a handy weapon in its own right, would not suffice to bring down these foes. He promised, however, that not five years would pass before he had avenged this hideous wrong against his homeland.

It was rather less time than that before the next wave of invasion smashed against the shore of once-beautiful P'toresk. In fact, only three months had elapsed before the fearsome nuclear weaponry of the Terran star troopers was unleashed on the unsuspecting Golgleglog occupation force, which literally withered and died under the Terran assault. The Terran troopers, in their new McGuffin Quasar-Crusher-class warships, landed in force amidst the decrepit shards of the once-proud Golgleglog space navy, swept the area with radiation neutralisers, and took possession of the latest addition to their expanding empire. The Terran force's ranking five-star general took stock of her new planetary acquisition. It was, she decided, a nice enough place in its way, except for one thing.

There wasn't enough water anywhere on the planet.

To rectify this, the Terran engineering attaché placed an order for a prodigious quantity of the latest McGuffin PEC UltraMassive Comet Collectors, which would bring in unparalleled quantities of water ice from the star system's Oort cloud. The UltraMassive collectors, guided by homing beacons to target the now-unwanted TeraSquirter plants as preferred cometary impact sites on the planet (the better to celebrate P'toresk's liberation from its unfortunate but brief enthralment by the accursed Golgleglog), arrived only very sporadically but created an entirely unprecedented quantum of noise when they did impact.

From his hiding spot, P'thurglebluxl peered in anguish at the latest influx of usurpers, who were a brutish band of pinky-brown protosimians with ludicrously localised fur and a totally unwarranted air of self-importance. His newly-invented shortbow, slung across his back, seemed inadequate to the task of slaying these vermin. He still swore that he would, somehow, stamp out these transgressors, in some as-yet-unguessed manner and at some unspecified point in time within the next, say, two years.

The following week, the Blokkob military razed the Terran force in a hail of antimatter-fuelled annihilation. The Blokkobs, who as strategists were not in any way given to subtlety, prepared a landing strip with a few judicious gamma-ray laser blasts and rode their fleet of brand-new McGuffin Galaxy-Dominator-class spacecraft down to, in their eyes, a well-deserved and heroic victory. The Blokkob's chief dictator stared out at this new world that he and his underlings had subjugated. It would have to do, he supposed, but there was one aspect of the place that cried out for improvement.

The planet was the wrong shape.

To convert the newly-conquered world into the Blokkob planetary ideal of a perfect cube, the Blokkob engineers set up a network of six McGuffin PEC Neutronium WorldHammers—positioned, more often than not, on the ruins of the UltraMassive probe homing beacons—with which to pummel and crush this disturbingly round planet. To say the least, the WorldHammer was not a pleasant piece of equipment beside which to be standing.

P'thurglebluxl, once again hidden in the bushes, looked on aghast. His world could not take much more of this punishment. If he felt a greater degree of skill in wielding his new longbow, then he would have assailed these hideous creatures here and now; though he was not sure that an arrow would be of much use against the thick armoured carapace of the turtle-like Blokkobs. Just the same, he, himself, P'thurglebluxl, would do something about it, next month. That would give him time to develop a plan of attack.

As it transpired, this amount of time was not needed. The next day, the revamped and rejuvenated fleets of the Vurtigon, Kallaginti, Golgleglog and Terran space forces arrived and began aggressive negotiations for the return of their rightfully-acquired territory. When only a few vessels remained from each fleet, a truce was called and the representatives of all parties met on a forlorn patch of neutral ground. There they began arguing anew, each staking their claim in increasingly strident tones.

This was too much for P'thurglebluxl, who stood and revealed himself. He had bedecked himself in a suit made of the conjoined fragments of the battle-armours and exoskeletons of all of the planet's recent invaders, and he had equipped himself with a scimitar, a pikestaff, a crossbow, and a sturdy shield. He adopted a threatening pose and then strode out, fearing not for his life, to meet the despots of the several worlds which had brought ruination to his once-fair planet in the space of a scant couple of years.

His speech ran as follows: "You have no right to this place! You do not belong here! I say you must leave, and leave now! In the name of P'toresk, the place of unparalleled beauty and home to all that is true and just, I claim this land as belonging to my ancestors and my descendants, and those who share my form! Now—BEGONE!"

At least, that is what he would have told them, and what in his mind's eye he had seen himself telling them. In reality their translation devices could not cope with the grammatical complexities of the fair P'toresquine language; but a further obstacle to interspecies communication inserted itself even before he could deliver his edict.

His mind on the pressures of public speaking, he noticed not the spent piece of Vurtigonian artillery and tripped, his forehead impacting awkwardly upon the broken rifle-butt of a discarded Kallaginti photon blunderbuss. Of his diatribe, he managed only an enigmatic "Y—" as he fell.

The five warring factions were briefly startled by the sudden intrusion by this mysterious figure in badly-fitting armour, and directed a few lower-caste operatives to investigate the sad sprawled figure who had interrupted their ballistic dialogue. Then, judging that the ungainly interloper posed no significant threat, the assembled forces fell once again into the mode of negotiation with which they were all most comfortable and familiar, and the happy sounds of blasters and laser cannon ruptured the air all around them.

So preoccupied with their own concerns were the Vurtigon, Kallaginti, Golgleglog, Terran, and Blokkob forces, that they did not mark the arrival of the mercenary fleet which totally overpowered them in both numerical and technical superiority, and none of the soldiers, generals, or representatives of the five invaders survived for more than a minute. The new armada, a veritable swarm of McGuffin Universe-Annihilator-class warships, touched down, followed shortly by a small and entirely unprepossessing unmarked vehicle. The leader of the mercenary horde alighted from his mighty flagship and waited. Soon enough, a small froglike creature emerged from the unmarked vehicle and paid the mercenary leader the agreed prompt-completion bonus. Then the mercenary fleet once again took to the sky, leaving only the small froglike creature to survey his new world.

The Acquisitions Manager of the McGuffin Planetary Engineering Corporation looked around him, and liked what he saw. The new factories could go *there*, and *there*, and over *there*. The showroom would work best *there*, and the admin offices would make the most sense *there*. A security force, comprised of people like that unconscious fellow in the mishmashed suit of armour, could be stationed *there*. All in all, he felt, a very promising location from which to grow the business. There were, after all, five steady clients in easy reach of this planet, and it was plain that these five clients now had a great deal of unfinished business to discuss with each other. An excellent location, with just one slight problem.

The planet's sun was too close.

Not to worry. After all, they had a new model to fix *that*.

Mouthbreathers

'Birdlike' is the word Kadir holds in mind whenever he glimpses her: it's not the best word, but it's the first word, and it has stuck. There's a compactness to Ito, a sense of the self-contained, the innate, the *not-tame* about her.

He's abidingly envious. One of the reasons for why he's conscious of watching her—it's not, of course, the sole one—is his wishes to absorb, to clone, how she does it. How she exists, authentic, unselfconscious. How she is. He's hopeless at all that. He's a brick, misplaced everywhere he finds himself, obtruding from an otherwise-smooth surface. Always has been.

Now's an example. Walking towards him, she's seen him seated here—striped by parasolled shade, at this outermost of the cantina's tables—as plainly as he's spied her walking towards him. Her form is heat-shimmered in the piazza's kilnbaking air, two-shadowed in the asymmetric two-tone glare of fullday's double sunlight. She acknowledges him with a glance that picks him out effortlessly, forceps-precise, from the capital's bustle. But that's it, done; the task of closing the distance is thence unencumbered, for her, by any of the look-towards-or-look-away uncertainty that would complicate his movements were the roles reversed. Meanwhile he's awkwardly poring over a menu with which he's already totally familiar, and from which he is not in any case planning to order, while trying frantically to ignore her unselfconscious fluidity in his peripheral vision.

Ito the general's daughter; Kadir the clerk.

It's supposed to seem a casual meetup, she has emphasised this repeatedly; the venue carefully selected each time so as to appear entirely arbitrary. But Kadir has such difficulty with conveying the semblance of 'casual' that he genuinely wonders why they persist in using him for these runs. Tall, wide, blunt-headed, pierced: he's a long way from being the most unobtrusive traveller. And he does not know how to act as though he is.

She looks good, though: there's no denying that. If Kadir still has a type, still *deserves* a type—and, amidst all the messy and unresolved business with Tuuli, he's not convinced that he does—then Ito is it. Ito the complete, the unattainable, the unflappably birdlike, of the businesslike friendliness and black-letter boundaries. There's no chance there, and he knows it, but still.

But still.

She draws closer. Now she's here: that electric moment of connection.

He rises from his seat, hugs awkwardly.

The hug is important, it's a part of the portrayal, a meeting between friends rather than an appointment between handler and courier. He tamps his reaction to the spark he feels at her touch, allows himself to be steered from the outdoor table wherefrom he has been keeping lookout, allows her to direct him towards the more dimly-lit booths to the rear of the cantina's interior.

Here there's less heat, more privacy, more sonic interference from the establishment's overly-loud background music, and from the occasional shouted imperatives of food-prep from the kitchen staff. A hot-oil smell, a sharp burnt fug; something that rasps the throat when he draws breath. A seat pre-warmed by recent occupation.

Unexpectedly, she doesn't take a seat opposite him, but slides in after him on the wall-backed padded bench. It's a not unwelcome development: her bare forearm brushes against his as they take their respective places. It's surely an accidental contact, but he appreciates it nonetheless; against this, there's not the scope for eye contact that would be offered by the usual arrangement. All up, this seating choice of Ito's is mildly mystifying. And, of course, she's always all business. It's not familiarity, this proximity; it has a purpose beyond such considerations.

But still. He allows himself an inward smile, hopes it doesn't show. Wonders at her scent today: sharp, uncharacteristic, unsuitable. A touch cloying, like the kitchen's topnote. It's not *her*, and he doesn't understand that.

A waiter—human, or an exceptionally good synth—attends, takes their orders. From past experience, Kadir restricts himself to water and a salad smaller than any that actually exist on the menu. Ito shows no such restraint.

The water arrives: tall carafe, chunky tumblers, all of it engineered to mimic the casual imperfection of the handmade. Then the food: bowls and cutlery alike crafted from the same unbreakable mid-grey industrial ceramic. Embracing the aesthetic, he assumes, of Benison's hot, treeless, mineral-poor plains and mesas.

Ito's bowl steams. Kadir waits for her to broach the terms of the run, or to extricate some artfully-disguised etui from her bag, but through all this time—it's now been several minutes—she doesn't. Instead, when she's not desultorily stirring the bowl's contents, she has one hand clasped tight around her own tumbler of water, the other planted flat against the tabletop.

Something has changed between them, since their last meetup, and Ito's not saying. This isn't right.

She takes a sip, lowers the tumbler.

He opts to raise the topic of the job himself, knowing it's bad etiquette. 'How many this time?' he asks, strives to keep his voice low. 'Two hundred? Three hundred?'

'Four,' she says, her face half-turned towards his. Her expression is troubled. She's searching, he thinks, for something in his face.

He frowns; he's apprehensive of anything which might let her down. Let down those who back her. Ito the birdlike, the unassailable, and the forces she represents. These are not philanthropic people.

'I haven't exactly been fasting,' he explains, placing his hand on his stomach. 'I don't think I can fit four hun—'

'It's not like that,' she replies, her upper body now directly facing his side, and almost so close as to let gravity take over. There's an authority in her voice, in her soft-spoken tone, that he can't begin to guess at. That is, she always has authority, wears it as effortlessly as plumage; but this sudden physical urgency is new, confronting. 'Turn towards me,' she tells him.

He complies.

'Breathe deep.'

He complies.

'Relax.'

He tries.

With her left hand, she takes his right. Pulls it, clasping his wrist; presses his hand palm-flat against the base of her ribs. Too low for breast, too high for any baby bump.

He can feel her ribcage rise and swell, contract and fall. She's sparely muscled. Expensive muscles: strength, without the slightest bulge anywhere. Even through the coarse fabric of her top, and the body armour that lies beneath it, he can tell there's not a gram of fat on her. There is, though, an additional beat, slower than her pulse, faster than her breath, pushing at his hand's lower edge.

Unconsciously, he falls into synch with her breathing. Two breaths, three. She wriggles briefly, winks at him. Slips her right hand behind his shoulder and down towards the small of his back, holds it there for three more breaths. A fractional smile more unfathomable than *La Giaconda*, a face too close to properly focus on. Her body a clock, a machine, a trap. Kadir wonders what she's doing: this parody of formal dance, seated, unexplained, while her breathing grows ever heavier. It's both intimate and rehearsed. There's guidance behind her actions, not merely impulse.

She applies sufficient pressure with her hand to pull him towards her, his face towards hers. 'Breathe in,' she tells him, their noses almost touching. Her eyes widen. She inhales as though in preparation for a dive. Tilts her head. Then she presses her mouth against his.

It's not a chaste kiss.

Kadir decides he doesn't care whether it's rehearsed.

There's a risk; they've known that from the outset. And yet Kadir has believed, right up to the moment of Ennis's arrest, that they will all of them get away with it. That the careful controlled release of incontrovertible evidence of deep corruption will bring about the collapse of a government which does not deserve to endure, will see it replaced by something better.

It doesn't. In hindsight, Kadir recognises that he and Tuuli should have known it would not. The government is a tenacious organism, as enduring and self-sustaining and aggressively territorial as any tumour. Mere words can never master it.

But when it becomes known, brief hours before their own arrests become inevitable, that the newly-apprehended Ennis has testified his belief there is only one conspirator at the residence which Kadir and Tuuli occupy jointly, they quarrel over the way forward.

Ito's mouth tastes of mint, cold-sharp, and something else besides, something more overtly chemical. Her tongue, hot, wet, presses against Kadir's lips. She writhes against him, gives a short low exhalation that resonates within him. He leans in tighter against her, closes his eyes, finds himself surprised by the jolt of his own heart.

He should not want this, from loyalty to captive Tuuli and to the plan to buy her release. But he has wanted this since first he met Ito.

It has been so long…

Smart, sharp, unattainable Ito. He cannot believe it. Yet it is.

He feels his body respond, seeks to shift in his seat. Tries to pull his captive hand higher, toward her chest—he cannot; then to push it lower—he cannot. She squirms more urgently against him, pressing so tight it hurts the hand pinned between them. He flicks aside the discomfort and the irritation at her insistence on control; focusses on the moment. *Ito. My God.*

Does he say the words, with his mouth melded against hers, or merely think them?

Her tongue pries a gap between his upper and lower teeth. The tongue-tip finds his, pulses, flicks, wet-pushes his own tongue to the side of his mouth. God, he's rock hard now, painfully so.

He tries to regroup, to respond, to interpose his tongue between her lips, her teeth; he can't get the access. Her tongue, still gatekeeping her own mouth, is everywhere in his. It's a big tongue, strong, insistent, hot, thick; it leaves no space. It prods against the inside of his cheek, presses pliantly against a row of molars, nudges his tonsils.

He gags, tries to pull himself back, but the hand pressing from behind him holds him fast. She is unbelievably strong.

Her tongue in his mouth—

God. Sweet merciful saviour, has he ever wanted this. And yet—

It's not her tongue.

It's not any human tongue. It's too long. Too thick. Too solid. It throbs. It fills his mouth.

It's not any part of Ito. It's something other.

'There's no point both of us taking the fall,' he tells her. They're seated at a long table amidst the throng of the East Junction foodhall: crowded, deafeningly chaotic, almost perfectly anonymous. They've long ago reconciled themselves to never discussing their activism within their own dwelling, where the chance of surveillance is thought to be much greater. 'You're better placed than me to continue the work. I'll turn myself in, tell them you knew nothing of my actions. With any luck, they'll spare you. And you can work for my release.'

If his suggestion's a sales pitch, Tuuli's not in the market. 'It'd never succeed,' she responds, pushing that one obdurate lock of hair across her brow. 'They know a journalist's involved. We'd better give them one. There's no way they'd believe you, or Ennis, or Jinru, could be capable of that report. There's too much information that none of you could've accessed. Besides, I can claim professional interest. They won't buy it, necessarily, but they'll go easier on me because of it.'

'You can't know that.' The foodhall's air is stale, overwarm; the circ-system's vanes cannot work hard enough. Kadir's head hurts, and he can't keep from his voice the sense of panic, the loss-of-control dread which Tuuli's calm demeanour induces in him. He wants to be the one promising surety, reassurance, but her rationality denies him this. Support isn't a skill that comes naturally to him.

'We can't know anything for sure,' she concedes, reaching a hand across the gap between them, to grasp his. Her grip is steady and warm; his, he knows, is neither. 'But we have to work with whatever seems most likely. If I don't give myself up to them, they'll just keep looking. You know they will. They've shown that already. And then there's no telling who they might catch in their dragnet this time around. We both know there are other groups working towards overthrow.'

He can't breathe. His eyes open, flare in panic, as this long vigorous swollen shape slides further into his mouth and the passages beyond. It grazes his uvula. Plugs his oesophagus. Worms its way onwards, downwards, into him, pulsing. With every second there is more of it.

Her hands clamp him firmly, his upper body held fixed against hers. Her face, still pressed against his. Her heart, just across from his own, thunders every bit as fast as his. The heat of her upper body against his, of her face against his. He has dreamed, for years, of a woman who would come on to him like this. But not like this.

He can't breathe; he can't escape; he cannot respond in any way he would wish; he's still unreasonably aroused. This not-her-tongue, this shape, this throbbing thing pushes further down his throat. The muscles of his trachea strive to find a path for airflow; there is none. His throat is blocked, his lungs enclaved. He needs to gasp, to spew, to scream, and can do none of it. Ito has him anchored, has him pinned against the bench; and she's too strong, too determined. His brick-in-a-loose-fitting-shirt bulk is useless against her enhancements.

He'll die. Within the extremity of the event, the thought is at once too central and too distant to entertain. A part of him supposes there are worse ways to go than locked in some weird oral embrace with Ito; most of him simply does not wish to die in this clinch of transaction masked as passion.

She detaches; pulls back. Takes an extravagant breath, says something, inhales again. Clutches her side. Panting immoderately, her head bobbing like a punch-drunk boxer's, she raises a finger to his lips, pushes his lower lip upwards to effect closure. He gapes again immediately, trying to read he knows not what in her eyes, striving for the air denied him.

He still cannot breathe, is conscious that the cantina's noise cannot make it through the ringing in his ears. His fingertips a-tingle, his aching, stretched-sphincter throat, his heart thumping like a bailiff on a tenement door. She leans towards him again, presses her lips against his futilely-gaping mouth and blows as though sounding a bugle, blows hard enough that it hurts. But it works: something thick and damp and heavy slides its way past his uvula. There's a final burning surge down his throat. And then at last—it's been less than half a minute, probably, though it seems like it's been delayed forever—he's able to draw a ragged, searing breath.

His eyes are watering, his nose running. Something settles, twitching, in his stomach. He can feel it distending the corners of his gut.

He wants to cry, but that would never do.

He stares at Ito's impassive, unfathomable face, a deer in her headlights.

She smiles: a wise, sad expression behind a lacquer of outward warmth. 'Three more,' she says softly.

The second is worse: his body tenses up from the outset. He knows, now, what to expect.

'You can't give yourself up,' he argues. He knows he's merely increasing the probability of unwanted official attention by prolonging the discussion, and by imperfectly masking his desperation; knows there's no prospect of persuading Tuuli, ever headstrong, to his own point-of-view. But he's scared—for Tuuli, or for himself, or for this fragile combination of the two of them, held together by forces he's never completely understood—and can't find the means to master his fear. 'It wouldn't be fair. You wouldn't even be involved in this if I'd never introduced you to Jinru. I don't agree to it.'

'It's not your decision to make. And if you offer yourself to them instead, in all likelihood they'll come for me anyway. As you yourself say, it's better if one of us retains liberty.'

'Or what passes for it,' he replies, failing to suppress his scowl.

She straightens in her seat. 'Kadir,' she says, brushing that curl once more across her brow in a fruitless attempt to anchor it amidst its fellow tresses, then waiting until she can see he's met her gaze, 'it will be alright. *I'll* be alright. You'll see.'

The logic's hateful, but valid. He cannot win against it. He fights it, out of love and despair and the hope of self-respect; but Tuuli is stronger in such matters, and she prevails.

She has since been proven correct in several particulars: that, having netted the journalist, those in power believe the cell neutralised, and do not probe further; that their treatment of her shows a degree of leniency and care; and that other groups, undetected and untrammelled by the government, continue the work of subversion.

Sooner or later, one such group succeeds. The government falls.

The government's replacement is not, in any sense, an improvement. It suddenly becomes crucial to ensure Tuuli's release as soon as humanly possible. But overnight the price of that release has been dramatically raised.

It will no longer take Kadir a mere two years, four, five, of carefully steady employment and quiet frugal existence, to raise Tuuli's 'liberty bond'. There are no entirely legal methods on Benison by which an honest clerk can meet that kind of cost within one human lifetime.

But there are methods.

'Drink,' Ito instructs, sliding her glass across towards him. 'The synthlife casings absorb moisture; it's important you stay hydrated. Warmed water, too, not chilled, no hot beverages. Thermal shock would not be good. Any nausea?'

He nods to spare himself the words. His throat has been sandpapered. His belly, awkwardly full, is unremittingly tender, like a diffusion of misplaced appendicitis. Sporadically sharp, with each intake of breath, overlaid on a persistent dull ache. He wonders whether 'would not be good' is in the context of him, or of the payload.

'The water will help with that,' she continues. 'Sips, often, rather than a big gulp all at once. The transfer unsettles them, there's a tendency for, shall we say, mass voiding of waste products. That's a large part of the nausea you're experiencing. The water will flush it through. Urination will help, too, obviously, as often as you can manage. Stand, don't sit.'

He nods again. Even that hurts.

'It'll take a few hours for the nausea to ebb properly,' she adds.

He takes a couple of tentative sips. Winces. 'What are they?' he manages to croak, each word a tracheal razor.

'A pupal form, or what passes for it among this branch of the mesosceles. Mouthbreathers. Different genus than the eggs you've ported for us before, though they're the same order. Venomous, but the synthlife casing is engineered to neutralise that danger while they're in carriage. We haven't had much success with the eggs of this species, we're hoping the pupal form travels better. Particularly with one of our more... reliable carriers.' This is clearly meant as a compliment—the smile reaches her eyes—but Kadir doesn't trust himself to respond.

'Nobody has yet found a way to breed them successfully offworld,' Ito continues. 'Our customer is hopeful of changing that.' Another smile, more knowing, less generous. 'We're hoping, of course, that she fails; continued business would suit our interests better, especially with such a lucrative species. But the stock must reach her in perfect condition, regardless.'

He feels betrayed. He didn't sign up for this. He should be angry, probably will be angry, once the meeting's done; right now, he's mostly numb. And deeply, unexpectedly sore. He's half-finished both glasses of water. 'Anything else to know?' he asks, die-pressing the words with cautious hesitation.

'No stimulants, barbiturates, sedatives, painkillers. That's metabolically indicated for this method of carriage, but it's also an ironclad precondition of the customer. No strenuous activity, nor any activity of a sexual, telesexual, or self-sexual nature. No alcohol. No grapefruit juice. No solid food. That may be difficult for you, once the nausea ebbs. Your belly's full, and it'll stay that way until delivery, but the synthlife casing breakdown promotes appetite in the host. It also releases nutrients, though, so you'll feel hungry, but you won't go hungry. Oh, and avoid undue exposure to airborne pollutants.'

'Noted,' he replies, rasping the word. He dares a couple of longer breaths, almost breaks out coughing. 'How transfer to customer?'

She's picking over the food on her plate with an enthusiasm that, in his present state, unnerves him. Assuming the customer's edicts apply to her too, Ito must be abstaining from analgesics and other palliatives. Either her experience of the transfer has been much less abrasive than his, or she's brilliant at shutting out pain without expensive pharmaceutical assistance. 'Not the same way,' she replies, chewing a half-mouthful as she mumbles. She glances down towards his stomach. 'They'll swell over the next thirty-six hours or so, through growth and fluid retention. Their adhesion to your stomach lining will weaken in the latter stages. You'll feel it happening, it's a bit like—no, that won't make any sense to you. But you'll know. It's fairly unmistakeable. You'll need to be through inbound quarantine, customs, security by that point. That shouldn't be a problem, provided you don't draw attention; we're confident the casings are undetectable by any scanning protocol they have access to. The transfer code will get you to the pickup point. You must commit the code to memory— your own organic memory, that is, it must not be copied to your implant, because they might read that—and you must ensure the code remains confidential. It includes a self-erase syntax to eliminate any possibility you will be followed or traced. The customer is very clear on that component of the mission. Once through the domestic transfer station, the customer will collect you, and then it's just a matter of waiting. But whatever happens...' She pauses.

'Yes?'

'When you feel the urge to push, don't resist. Our modelling suggests it's best for all concerned if things happen smoothly from that point.'

He hates seeing her like this. Hates himself, too, for not being able to see past the bruises, the burn marks, the scars, the wearily fearful expression, to the true vibrant Tuuli that he strives to recapture in his memory. He's kissed those lips that now are split and puffy. The wayward curl that she continues to reach for, now shorn into oblivion and the gesture's muscle memory. The eyes that, dim-lit, have in earlier times smiled in carefree welcome as she blankets herself over him... those eyes now are bloodshot, thick-lidded, enclaved within blackened bruising.

The way she holds her hand against her ribs and grimaces as she shifts on her bench speaks of the more extensive damage concealed beneath her grimy, smelly, ill-fitting prison uniform.

He knows better than to comment on it. To remark upon their treatment of her would be, he knows, to place her at greater risk of what they refer to as 'retributive examination'. Conversation between them can take the form only of meaningless chatter; anything else means jeopardy for her. And so he babbles inanity after inanity, hoping to convey through stagey smiles and a clearly unconvincing warmth of tone that she should not give up: on him, on his determination to see her once more free, on herself.

He should never have allowed her to give herself up. But he'd had no choice. Neither of them had.

If he tells himself that, often enough, he might even come to believe it.

If he allows himself, instead, to explore the what-ifs, the most barbed is the thought that, had he turned himself in instead of allowing Tuuli to take the fall, had he sworn that she'd had no part in the plotting... the security forces might have looked further, might have uncovered the group that did, in truth, overthrow them. Might have averted that outcome.

Is he. in part, responsible through his cowardice for the current leadership's hold on power, for its manifestations of brutality?

This is the question which calls to him in the depths of night.

Seated alone, in the jump-station's cavernous hall, Kadir's bathed in sweat. It sticks to the underarms and the back of his shirt;

it glazes the expanse of his overpopulated stomach; it sheens the creases where thighs abut torso. And mindful of Ito's imprecations on airborne pollutants, he suspects he hasn't applied anywhere near enough scent to his suit to mask the cheap smell of his discomfort, his fear. His guilt. He's a seedy complement to the station foyer's holoverts for high-end rejuv treatments, exclusive offworld destinations, third-child licenses, lifeslaves, and anything else affordable only by the overly wealthy, the born lucky and the corrupt. The holoverts' wares are, of course, the very products with which his efforts today are in competition: the clientele matches.

It can't be by accident that the two seats either side of his are almost the only ones not taken by the bored businesspersons, frazzled parents, tired children and lost-looking solo passengers with whom he shares this noisy, echoing, disorienting vault.

Isolated he may be, but some young child within a few metres of his seat has nonetheless filled his or her diaper. Kadir turns aside, tries to constrict his nostrils, wondering how some parents can be so oblivious. The infant starts bawling.

Kadir looks up at the jump-board once more. He badly needs to visit the urinal again; but this late in the game, he dare not lose his spot in the jump queue.

It's not supposed to be this way. It's in his nature to allow plenty of time for contingencies; it's one of the qualities Ito prizes (or says she does). But a twenty-four hour jump-station lockdown—amid rumours of some foiled counter-revolution or other, involving children of the old regime—has waylaid matters. The lockdown has devoured every morsel of Kadir's contingency-time, and then some; and the jump-station, finally reopened, is as thick with backlog as it is with extra sec officers. They've surely seen every trick in his repertoire of strained, feigned nonchalance by this point. He's not even off Benison yet, and he still must clear security, and customs, and bioquarantine. He's swimming in the stink of his own perspiration, squirming at the thought of the intimidating peristaltic imperative towards which the clock is ticking down, and he hasn't even started. But there are still two hours left before his spot in the jump queue. He's concerned that, if he clears the departure requirements too soon, he'll be sore-thumbing it for an hour or more in the jump lounge, and he strongly suspects this would increase the probability of his apprehension.

No more, past this time, he tells himself. *I claim the fee, I walk away. I'll find something else to do, something less dishonest, something more nearly legal, to make up the shortfall to buy back Tuuli's freedom. Eventually. Then we'll see. Whether she'll forgive me.*

While it was just the ova, it was all manageable, more or less. But this isn't worth it.

He daren't dwell on the sec officers, on what their purpose here today might be. If he's caught, he loses everything. Every last chance, for both himself and Tuuli. There's just this one remaining bright suspending thread: his freedom, his ability to draw breath; this chance, now, to achieve something. To earn something. It's for Tuuli's sake that he will shortly be disassembled here, it's for Tuuli's sake he will then be reassembled, twenty light-years away, in another jump-station, it's for Tuuli's sake that he gambles on his clandestine freight's smartcoat code to ensure that it, too, will be reassembled within him, intact and undetected.

It's for Tuuli's sake he risks this. This one last time. To hope to see those eyes look down on him that way again.

He should go through. Mustn't leave it too long.

And after this, he'll find something else. Or perhaps it will find him, as straightforwardly and effortlessly as Ito had found him when first he'd learned of the high cost of securing Tuuli's release. He's wondered, sometimes, just how that happened, and why.

And then he thinks again of Ito: of the closeness and, yes, the discomfort of yesterday's encounter, of her warmth against him, of the surety, the command she always embodies, of the smell of her, not quite like that of any other woman he's known, of the body-armoured pulse of her heart against his chest, of the overpowering harsh intimacy of that transaction. There's another thought there, too, of Ito, her background, her loyalties, but he can't properly get the shape of it; the memory of the embrace is stronger by far.

It's a few minutes more before he can trust himself to stand and to pace awkwardly, guts a-writhe with indecision, illegality, and harboured life, towards the gate through which his journey today will begin.

Grain by grain

Officials this morning
are refusing to discuss
what actions, if any,
will be taken against
the cleaner whose
overzealous efforts
wrought irreparable damage
to the priceless exhibits
and meticulously curated
dioramas
at the West Eyreton Museum of Dust

There is an irony here,
a spokesperson said,
but for the moment
we are all too shattered
to acknowledge it

No further questions
thank you

Sixes, sevens

The visitor this time is a Gamma, slightly shorter in stature than a standard human; with a hide of felted grey fur, trending to light blue at the extremities and across the rump. Face shaped somewhat like a parrot's, but lacking a beak: the eyes placed on the sides of the head, in the defensive cast of the plains herbivore rather than our own more predatory, binocular, configuration. He—it *is* a he, though I don't stare—enters the room, bearing a sealed tray of food samples and a whiff of fish oil and burnt metal. I meet his gaze, waiting for him to convey any messages he might have—are they ready to transport me to the Library yet? But he remains silent—tomorrow, then—and I thank him for the meal which, for now, I have placed on the room's sole piece of furniture, a plain chaise.

He lingers, examining me by first one eye, then the other: eyes of dark solitude and mystery. I begin to wonder at the continuation of his stay in this room, whose synthesised atmosphere is toxic, even corrosive, to him as it is to all Cygnid lifeforms. Subcutaneous breathing apparatus? Unexpectedly large lung capacity? I do not know, but he is holding mouth and nostrils carefully closed. He stands, lingering, one eye on me and the other on the room's one, prominent, window: a rectangle of synthetic diamond. Then, in some fashion, he speaks, though the mouth stays sealed: 'I share your pain.'

The speech, in a gentle bass register, is careful, measured, and probably as artificial as the atmosphere, and the tray's food: human speech does not fit easily within the Cygnids' various vocalisation techniques. I am at a loss for response to this cryptic utterance: for all that we have lived in contact with Cygnid society for the past fifty years, they retain a reputation as creatures who are aloof, subtle, and frustratingly patient. I meet his monocular stare for perhaps ten seconds, not finding any words with which to reply, for the Gamma's remark is at odds with my long experience of Cygnid communication and behavior: they are a species that shies away from emotive or personal observation. Then the connection is severed, we both turn our heads: I towards the window, he the door. Before he leaves, from some dermal pouch on belly or thigh he produces a sachet containing a dark streamlined object, and this he places on the chaise, nodding towards it. Then he turns towards the window, bows—a quick, almost knifelike motion, as though unwilling to remain long vunerable— and leaves, the door scything shut behind him.

I examine the sachet, a polymer blister which retains a topnote of Cygnid pungency, but which feels clean to the touch. Inside is some grey-black gadget of a type I have not seen before, about the size and shape of a coffee bulb. An accompaniment to the meal, perhaps? Closer inspection reveals subtle markings and a cluster of what appear to be touchbuttons. On breaking the seal (another whiff of fragranced air), I find that the object fits naturally, comfortably within the grip of my right hand, the buttons arrayed within reach of my folded fingers. Experimenting, I learn there is only one orientation of the device which feels right: this places the object's sole planed face perpendicular to the axis of my forearm; but, unwilling for now to press any of the buttons, I cannot discern its purpose. Despite its weaponlike grip, I cannot believe that the Cygnids would have crafted for me some kind of firearm: most probably it is a tool which I will find useful in tomorrow's visit to their Library, although perhaps it has some relevance towards the meal they have left me. I decide to eat.

The food, as I have expected, is superb: it is as though they have been compiling a catalogue of my favorite dishes, and have presented me with everything they know I most appreciate. Quantities, too, are finely judged, and there are no scraps remaining when I finish, pleasantly full but not at the point of drowsy bloatedness. I place the tray at the lip of the sealed door: someone will come to collect it within the next hour. Then, again wishing they had left me something in the nature of reading or viewing material, I let my gaze navigate the room's spartan features before, inevitably, returning to the picture window, which presents now a panorama of Belberyan, the Cygnid capital city, at dusk. The window, which I judge to be almost three metres wide, follows the curve of the room's outer wall; the view beyond, from a vantage of about ten Earth-standard storeys high, is of the clustered domes and turrets that form the staple of this continent's current architecture, punctuated above by thick brownish clouds which here reflect the city's jeweled lights, and below by the parks and avenues which mark this as a fashionably elite district within the city's broader expanse. Of the Cygnid sun there is no sign, save the prominence it confers for now to the nearest facing towers. (I should, at least, get a good view of tomorrow's sunrise.) I wonder which of the buildings before me is the Library, which I know to lie near the city's western edge where this apparent hotel is stationed. There are no clues, but presumably I will learn tomorrow.

I am in such eager anticipation of the impending Library visit that I suspect I will have trouble sleeping tonight, for all that the room's chaise has almost certainly been tailored for my specific comfort. It has been fifty years since humanity first encountered the Cygnids, and throughout that time the relationship has blossomed slowly and with subtlety, throttled and restrained by the Cygnids' reluctance to share the secrets of their technological superiority. In truth, I am not sure how much can be gleaned from a twenty-four hour visit to their Library, but they have promised me unfettered access for this period, and as a longserving liaison officer with the Terran cultural mission here I know this to be a signal honor, unprecedented in our shared history. I know, too, from my readings of Cygnid history that an opportunity of this kind will not be repeated soon, if ever, since the Cygnids are slow to build trust: even now, after fifty amicable years of shared history, they still regard us with the suspicion accorded predators around some wilderness waterhole. The Library visit will, I know, be as much a test of humanity's intentions and attentions, in their eyes, as it will carry the weight of my need to learn, for my kind's sake, as much as I can of the Cygnids' marvels and secrets.

I am still staring at the window when the door opens again, and another Gamma—this time a nursing female, young and probably on her first litter—enters, pausing and stooping to pick up the tray. At first I wonder if this collection is the sole purpose of her visit, but she steps further into the room, towards the window. I take the opportunity to gather the mysterious gadget off the chaise and present it towards her, careful not to grip it in case it truly is a weapon. 'Please,' I ask, in Anglo, 'what is this device's purpose?'

'A reader,' she replies; her lips do not part. Her voice is higher-pitched than the earlier male's, which I recognise as likely artifice, an attempt to mimic human characteristics: Gamma vocal tones do not naturally differ between genders. 'For Library.' She points towards the window, in the direction of one of the nearer large towers.

'How does it work?' I ask.

'Hold to surface,' she responds, and reaches towards me to indicate the central button among the device's controls. 'Sixes and sevens, you understand?'

This last remark is obscure, but I do not follow it up. There will be time to establish the methodology tomorrow, when I am taken to the Library for my 24-hour visit. I wait for her to leave, though I trust my body language does not betray any impatience.

But she does not leave, not yet. Instead she gestures again towards the Library building and says, 'I share your pain'. The same cryptic disclosure. This time, the inflexion of it is almost a query.

Perhaps, I theorise, they have detected my impatience and are empathising on that level. I say nothing in reply, not knowing here what will not cause offence among this undemonstrative people. Then she leaves, presumably to tend to her whelps.

The view through the diamond picture window is now more somber: it is after sunset, and few lights adorn the turrets and domes. I take a seat on the end of the chaise, and drag closer my portmanteau, to check that the three decamole storage satchels are still green-lighting. Remembering the heft of the portmanteau as I carried it across the room earlier today, I am envious of the Cygnids' rumored mastery of atomic-level storage, suggestive of a capacity for miniaturisation which still eludes us.

The amount of memory in my storage satchels is, almost certainly, excessive, but I do not wish this unprecedented access to their Library to be compromised by device failure. I do not think I could live that down.

I place the Cygnid reader device atop the portmanteau; then, on a whim, pick it up again and point it towards the floor. I press the button indicated by the Gamma female: the machine thrums, in a rhythmic, somehow unsettling fashion, but displays no other activity. I press the button again, and the vibration ceases. At least it has power, though I still do not understand its operation. I close my eyes, running through a meditation routine to still myself, to attempt to brush away the anticipation of tomorrow's activity. Then I rise, feeling the need to use the body-waste alcove.

An hour later, I have almost succeeded in chasing down sleep when the door scissors open and a Beta scurries into the room, its orange fur bedraggled. 'Apologies,' it offers.

I nod in response, pulling myself to a sitting position.

'I share your pain?' it asks.

I shake my head, unsure as ever of the intent of this phrase— presumably it refers to some hospitality ritual of which I had not been made aware, but assuredly it can at least wait until tomorrow. I would have been informed, surely, if this was a necessary prerequisite for my Library visit. The Beta looks discomfited, but bows and retreats back through the doorway.

The morning sun takes advantage of a transitory break in the sepia cloud cover to illuminate me into wakefulness. I check my chrono: it reads 0630 local, so I can expect my Cygnid escort to ferry me to the Library at any time after the next hour or so. Again, awaiting instructions, I inspect the reader device and the storage satchels, which all display normal activity (whatever that indicates, in the case of the Cygnid reader). I wish, anew, that I had brought some reading matter with me: so focussed on the Library have I been that I have neglected to consider that any waiting period might elapse before then. I attempt to meditate once more, but lack the patience. Time drags.

After a brooding half-hour or so, breakfast is brought. The Gamma—another female, but older I think than yesterday's— stands and, inevitably, offers to share my pain. 'That won't be necessary,' I inform her, keen to avoid the awkward pause that has followed the Cygnids' previous requests of this type. She looks unhappy nevertheless—though I may be mistaken, I am no master of Gamma body language, even after twenty years as liaison officer here—and bows out, leaving me to my breakfast.

There are, during the morning, five more visits by five different Cygnids: three Gammas, one neutered Beta and, surprisingly, one Alpha. (The ruling caste is so rarely encountered that I am unsure as to the protocols of interaction etiquette, and I am rather relieved when she has departed.) All have offered to share my pain, and I have declined. Lunch arrives early, and I tell myself that the transport to the Library must surely occur soon.

This time, the tray is somehow collected without even an attendant's visit to the room.

Outside, through the luxurious cultured-diamond picture window, the pattern of shade and highlight flows gradually across

Belberyan's minareted cityscape. My gaze returns every so often to the tall turret I have identified as the Library. Hours pass.

I have decided, now, that the delay is most likely a consequence of some difficulty in converting some viewing room, within the Library, into a habitat capable of supporting Earthlife for the duration of my visit. However, if such activity is occurring within the tower, it is not discernible from my hotel-room window.

Around 1400 local, I lie back on the chaise and, for want of anything better to do, run through the categories of information most urgently sought from the Cygnids. Time in the Library will almost inevitably be too short, and I must prioritise in order to make best use of my stay. To better visualise the data groupings I seek, I close my eyes.

The ceiling is discernibly darker when I awaken some two or three hours later. A cluster of Cygnids has arrived in the room, and from their attitudes around the chaise they are for some reason unsettled to have found me asleep. This must be, I imagine, the appointed time. I stand up, raising my hand in a gesture of appreciation. They stare at me, with what appears in some cases to be disappointment. One is examining the reader device, and shows it to the others. Then they point towards the door, and one of the larger Gammas shoulders my heavy portmanteau. I walk with them towards the elevator spindle.

This is it. I am on my way, at last!

The Cygnids have still not made any comment.

They direct me, courteously but without the customary ceremony, into a large groundcar. My portmanteau is loaded in beside me, while three Gammas climb into the front compartment. I am sharing the rear compartment with a solitary Beta, who is equipped with a compact package that I presume to be his breathing equipment. As the vehicle starts off, it very soon becomes apparent that we are not in fact heading towards the expected tower, but in the broad direction of the Terran shuttleport. Confused, I turn to my travelling companion, and ask, 'I thought I was to go to the Library?'

'Correct,' he replies in a metal-tinged voice.

'Then where is this Library?' A horrible suspicion has begun to manifest itself, as the Beta points back towards the tower containing my erstwhile hotel room. Even at this distance, I can see that some Cygnid cranes have moved into position, and have started to lower the massive picture window from its tenth-storey vantage point towards the ground.

A dreadful, shameful realisation floods through me, as I reflect on the past twenty-four hours.

The picture window, synthetic diamond. Atomic-level storage. Sixes and sevens: neutron numbers. Carbon-12 and carbon-13, and a large slab of diamond in which the position of no isotopic nucleus is unintentional. A request, an offer, repeated with increasing urgency by so many concerned Library staff. *I shear your pane?* The reader device, scraping and analysing one coded carbon monolayer at a time. The picture window, which I stared through, unseeing. The Library.

I have frittered away my precious time at the Library; and I am alone with my pain.

Next!

'So what's the brief, Your Majesty?' asked Sir Launcelot, testing the layout on the throne room's parquet flooring with the tip of his longsword.

'Would you mind *not* doing that?' the King replied. 'Thank you. Now, the assignment, and you're welcome to renounce it—'

'I never refuse an appointment with destiny,' Sir Launcelot assured him, seeking to swell out his chest for emphasis. The gesture lost most of its force beneath the plate mail, but still, the thought was there.

'You have not fought such a monster as this,' replied the King. 'I fear this beast is too dread-inspiring even for you.'

'Your Majesty!' Launcelot protested, his voice hearty, unwavering, and compelling. 'I have vanquished dragons, ogres, trolls, giants, serpents, and gorgons too numerous to mention! I don't mean to boast, but in all truth, the beast does not *live* that I cannot conquer!'

'I would be inclined to disagree, good knight.'

'You belittle my achievements, My Lord!'

'On the contrary, Launcelot. I hold your exploits in the highest regard. Which is precisely why I am reluctant to employ your services on such a fool's quest as this. But tell me, which of these monsters you have slain did you find most challenging?'

'That would be the gorgon, undoubtedly, Your Majesty. Her as was able, with but a single glance, to turn a man's heart and all that encases it to lifeless, undifferentiated stone.'

'I had thought that might be your answer. The present beast is worse. Much worse.'

'Worse, Your Majesty? How so?'

'The gorgon could slay with her gaze. But I speak of a beast—and I do not know its name, nor know indeed whether any man does—but a beast so fearsome, so *dire*, that the mere act of contemplating combat with it is apparently enough to kill.'

'Just *thinking about it?*' Launcelot asked, examining the precise edge of his sword, its perfect balance. 'But that's prepos—'

Scratched

Chloe wished she didn't have to be so flustered, but there was no helping it. She burst into Dylan's room.

'Dylan, the cat's got a mouse!'

'Well?' he asked. He looked up briefly, and then turned back to the game on his laptop.

'We've got to save it!'

'Leave it. We don't want mice in the house.'

'It's not inside—it's outside. Hurry up!'

'Can't you take care of it?' Dylan asked, very superior. She hated him when he got like this.

She replied snappishly. 'I can't touch mice!' Especially, she thought, when they're hurt as badly as this.

'Oh, all right...' He was stretching the words out as much as he could, just to annoy her. He sat up, folded the laptop carefully closed, and let his slow footsteps follow her agitated, hurried path through the house. Deep down, perhaps, he might feel a bit sorry for the mouse—though Chloe knew that he'd never show it.

She pestered him to the door where the cat was patting in frustration at a large inverted cardboard box on the porch.

'Where's this mouse?' Dylan inquired.

'Under there,' she said, indicating the carton. 'I frightened Scratch away when she'd let go of it for a second.'

'Poor cat. Couldn't you have made a door for her, into the box?

She's probably hungry.' He grinned.

'Don't be mean! She was being horrible to it—like torture. She kept pretending to let it go—'

'She's upset now. You've stolen her food. You might've used a less heavy box—she can't tip that one over.'

Chloe clapped her hands and hissed ferociously at the cat, which paused before sprinting to shelter, a tabby rocket. She chased it noisily to the fence and returned to Dylan. 'Rescue it,' she said. 'Go on—save it.'

'Can't you just lift up the box and let it go?' he asked. 'If you're so worried about it.'

'It's not well,' she answered. 'It can't run any more—it only sort of walks funny.' He picked the carton up and threw it at the bushes. A grey mouse waddled drunkenly across the concrete towards a flowerpot, against which it huddled, shivering.

'See?' she asked him. 'Scratch would have no trouble finding it again.'

'If it's hurt, it might be better to put it out of its misery,' Dylan remarked.

'Kill it, you mean.'

'Put it out of its misery,' he emphasised. 'It might have broken bones, or anything. All I have to do is step on it—it'd be very quick—'

'Don't you dare!' she snapped, moving towards the mouse, ready to protect it. 'Can't you just pick it up, so we can take it somewhere safe? Grrr! Ffisssss! Shoo!' These last incantations were directed towards the cat skulking back. 'Dylan...'

'I thought you liked Scratch,' he said.

'I hate it when she catches things. Please?'

'Stop bothering me. Let me think about it for a while.'

'It might not have a while—it's not well. And Scratch keeps trying to come back.'

'If it's in pain—'

'It's not fair to kill it, just because it's so small!' she burst out. 'Can't you—'

'Look, just shut up or I won't pick it up for you. I mean that.'

She moved her lips silently and ran across the lawn to scare the cat. Returning, she looked enquiringly towards Dylan.

He ignored her as long as he could, then said grudgingly, 'Okay. I'll pick it up. What can I do with it?'

'We can't keep it inside,' Chloe decided. 'There's nothing we could keep it in...' And although she felt ashamed to think it, if the mouse was inside, it would be easier for Dylan to kill it—just to be kind—when no-one else was in the room. 'The park.'

'That's a bit far—'

'It's only half a block.'

'A bit far to go for a mouse, though.'

'We don't want Scratch getting it again, do we?' she asked. He looked as though he was going to reply, but didn't.

'We can take it in the box,' she said, retrieving the carton from the bush. She didn't trust Dylan's hands; they might crush her mouse, just accidentally.

'Maybe we should wait until Mum and Dad get home. They said they wouldn't be long.'

'No—Dad would say we had to kill it anyway, and then Scratch would have won. And besides, you promised.'

'I didn't promise anything,' he reminded her.

Dylan was very kind to help save the mouse, he was giving up valuable time for the mouse, he didn't have to do this sort of thing, he reminded Chloe as they walked towards the park down the street. Chloe kept flashing anxious glances towards the cardboard box—Superior Pet Food, the label read—and opened her mouth to warn him not to jog the box like that, how would you like being bumped around when you'd just been savaged by a tiger—but she never said anything because his offer of help was fragile and she didn't want to break the spell. He *was* being kind; if only he'd stop saying so.

'Where do we let it out?' he asked.

'I don't know. Somewhere safe.'

'Here, then?' he asked, pretending to tip the box upside down.

'Don't! It's not safe here—and just don't drop it out. Over there, by a tree or something,' she advised him. 'Someone could step on it here.'

'I wish you'd take the box,' he said.

'I'll carry it back,' said Chloe.

'Tree wouldn't be much good. This mouse couldn't climb anything—'

'You pick somewhere, then.'

He looked around. 'How about under those bushes?'

'I suppose so,' she said, unconvinced.

'You're just jealous 'cause it's my idea,' he commented. 'There's nowhere else around here for it. If you let it go on the grass, someone could walk along—splat!'

'This is important.' She stared at him, and it was his turn to look unconvinced. He started moving towards the bench and the bushes, and she followed. Once there, she crouched down to check the site out.

'Okay,' she said. 'Here.'

He picked the mouse up—by the tail, despite her protestations— and placed it on the ground, where it had only a few centimetres to go to reach the sheltered area beneath the bush. The mouse crawled forward a bit and curled up, shivering, on the grass.

'It doesn't look good,' Dylan observed. 'Perhaps it would've been kinder to kill it—'

'No!' she snapped, unintentionally loud.

He flinched.

'You're learning to be like Dad, aren't you?' she asked, but he didn't reply.

'Let's go home,' he said. She hesitated.

'You're sure it's safe here? I mean Scratch—'

'Scratch never comes this far,' Dylan said. 'Even if she did, she wouldn't find it. Some other cat would beat her to it—' He saw the look on her face, and added hastily, 'I don't mean that. It's perfectly safe—I didn't mean it when I said that. Honest. We'd better go home now—it's probably waiting for us to go before it moves.'

'Okay,' she said, finally.

'Your turn to carry the box,' he reminded her.

She reluctantly turned away from the mouse and followed him towards the pavement.

They got back just a few minutes before their parents arrived home.

'What have you lot been up to?' Mum asked.

'Nothing much,' Dylan replied. Chloe started to say something, but she let the words taper off, and no-one asked what she had been saying.

Towards dinner time she asked Dylan if he wanted to come with her to check on the mouse, but he didn't seem interested.

'I'll go by myself, then,' she said. She left the house and walked up the street, blinking, towards the late-afternoon sun. There were a few people in the park, but they weren't where she'd let the mouse go. She cut across the grass towards the bushes.

The mouse lay huddled on the grass, just where they'd released it. It hadn't moved. Why hadn't it run away? It wasn't safe for it to sleep like this—

She plucked a blade of grass and prodded it gently with the blunt end. It didn't respond. She pushed it harder, and something about the way its whole body moved showed that it was not asleep; and after she took the grass-blade away it was still, once more.

She stood looking at the mouse for a long time, and the park was silent around her. She stared, dry-eyed and resentful, at the small shape of unmoving fur. It could have tried a bit harder. Why did it have to die so quickly? Couldn't it have crawled a bit further, where she wouldn't have found it? Dylan hadn't even cared—

he'd wanted to kill it. But she'd cared, she'd cared enough to come back, to see if it was all right...

She felt like kicking something.

'Well?' Dylan asked when she got back home.

'It wasn't there,' she answered carefully. 'It must've got away.'

Recent revelations concerning the Apollo 15 mission

After the success of the third crewed landing, the mission planners grew bolder. The next mission's Lunar Excursion Module would place more than just two astronauts on the moon's surface, with a third waiting in the Orbiter above. Accompanying Irwin and Scott and the LEM would be a battery-powered Lunar Roving Vehicle and a cat.

The cat was a white-socked black American Shorthair aged approximately 22 months at the time of spaceflight. Its name was Mr Tribble.

While there was considerable advance publicity regarding the launch, Mr Tribble's involvement in the mission was an extremely closely held secret, and even after the completion of the Apollo program in December 1972, no official or public mention was made of the cat's role. It is thought that even the astronauts' wives were unaware of their husbands' feline companion on their flight. One can only marvel at the lengths to which the program's personnel must have gone to keep this feature of the mission concealed from the public; because, of course, it is not an easy task to train a cat for spaceflight. More than a year of intensive training was evidently expended in ensuring that Mr Tribble was acclimatised to the specially constructed feline spacesuit, to the g-forces accompanying launch, and, through what is understood to be a series of highly traumatic sessions in the neutral buoyancy pool, to weightlessness. Eventually, on 15 July 1971, only one and a half weeks prior to launch, this resourceful cat was certificated by its trainers and by the Apollo program veterinarian as fit to fly, the last of the mission's crew complement to be so confirmed.

Extant audio recordings suggest the launch itself to have been a distressing experience for Mr Tribble, though the purring sounds evident on some unedited audio transmissions from later stages of the voyage demonstrate that the animal became comfortable enough with the phenomenon of zero gravity. However, it seems that not everything aboard the spacecraft met with the cat's favour. It is believed that several scratch marks on Worden's left forearm, checked carefully by mission medics after splashdown, were not inflicted, as was claimed at the time, through his mishandling of the Service Module's scientific instruments package, but instead reflected repeated differences of opinion between Worden and Mr Tribble regarding occupancy of the former's allocated seat. In this regard, it is probably just as well that the cat accompanied Irwin and Scott (with whom it apparently enjoyed comparatively cordial relations) on their moon landing, rather than remaining aloft alone with Worden during the long lunar sojourn.

Of Mr Tribble's activities on the lunar surface, there is no official record. Did it join Irwin and Scott on any of their excursions in the LRV? Did it moonwalk? Did it even exit the LEM at any time in its customised spacesuit, doubtless to ask immediately to be let back in? We simply do not know, and likely never shall, since its interactions were never officially logged and it does not appear in any mission photographs which have been released. David Scott, the mission's sole surviving human astronaut, has vowed never to reveal anything of the cat's lunar exploits, and while we cannot fully understand his motives for this refusal to disclose details of such an important and intriguing milestone in crewed space exploration, we must respect his wishes. And of course Mr Tribble is now long dead.

The freshness of some of Worden's forearm scarring at the time of the post-mission medical evaluation suggests the cat was as disconcerted by re-entry as by launch. For days after splashdown, the animal was so torpid that the Apollo veterinarian suspected it might have acquired some unanticipated feline space-related disorder, a conjecture inevitably abbreviated (and obscured) as 'UFSRD1' in NASA's internal memos during this time. In all probability, however, Mr Tribble was simply aggrieved at the return of full gravity. It had, in any event, recovered completely when at the end of September 1971 it was taken on a secret tour of the Nixon White House, where it apparently broke a small but important vase in the Presidential living quarters and posed uncomfortably for a Polaroid photo with two unidentifiably redacted White House personnel. Approximately one month later, Mr Tribble gave birth to five mixed-breed kittens, and heated debate has subsequently occurred regarding whether the animal should instead be known as Ms Tribble. I choose to believe such debate is inconsequential in this instance, because according to its owner, it would never answer to either name when called for dinner, and so cannot properly be considered to have demonstrated a preference in either direction.

Crimea River

(a Gordon Mamon novella)

Prelude or prologue or foreword or whatever these things are called

He stood with difficulty, registering a silent complaint from his inner ear and a not-so-silent one from his knees. The shuttle flight had been every bit as short and as unpleasant and as cramped as the most efficient of those processes which are somewhat deceptively called 'amusement rides' or, perhaps even more misleadingly, 'fairground attractions'. Gordon waited while the other passengers, one by one, moved into the airlock, and then into the waiting ship beyond.

Other passengers? He pulled a face at the thought. It might well be different for everyone else, but the moment *he* stepped into the airlock, he'd no longer be a passenger but an employee. Not for him a month of shipboard indolence and economy-class comfort enroute to a new world orbiting some far-distant star. No, this was his life now: to toil while others around him relaxed. The journey was the destination, the means the end.

He allowed himself a moment more of this strange blend of reverie and temporary freedom, even though it was plain that the shuttle crew were eager to offload him. Their vocational plight, especially, he should be sympathetic to. But it was just ten minutes since he'd left Skytop, and he was still getting used to the unexpected discovery that he could be homesick for a place that he'd never really been able to think of as home.

The airlock beckoned. So too did a disconcertingly mechanical humanoid figure, expectantly holding aloft in its silicon-and-metal alloy hand a placard that read 'MERMAN'.

Gordon sighed. Some things, it seemed, never changed.

'Welcome aboard the *Crimea River*,' said the service droid, a Bogart-class model which appeared to have seen better days, though not recently. 'May I carry your baggage?'

'No,' replied Gordon. 'But you can tell me your name.'

'Indeed I can,' said the unit. 'My designation is Pilotable/ Autonomous Synthetic Cybertronically Augmented Labourer 4. You can call me Pascal.'

'Indeed I can,' said Gordon, which rather seemed to evade the issue. He stepped forward.

The airlock hatch closed behind him, and another opened ahead.

Seen from the vantage of its recursively curved corridors, the ship looked old. This, Pascal explained, was because it was new: the trend these days was for the neo-vintage look, down to such details as tailored walkway scuffmarks, artisanal wear and tear on the sun-faded, freshly-installed furnishings, and varnish-textured wall panels carefully printed with dents and scratches. Had the ship been an older model, with a decor dating from what was now identified as the retro-nouveau era, it would superficially have looked much newer.

'Of course,' continued Pascal, persisting with what Gordon was now perceiving to be a well-worn theme within the service droid's repertoire of conversational topics, 'the fashion will probably shift again before long, when the new look becomes all the rage again.

But it will, naturally enough, be a *new* new look, different enough from the old new look that the old new look will still look old. It would not at all do, as I understand such things, for the old new look to look newly anew.'

'Why not?' Gordon asked.

'Fashion is a helix,' said Pascal. 'Don't ask me why that is, but it is. Human culture depends on the new new look, the new old look, the old new look and the old old look all being readily distinguishable, because progress. At least that is how Crewperson Strey explained it to me.' Pascal paused and simulated a throat-clearing sound which didn't quite convince. 'Crewperson Strey is not always especially good with explanations.'

Crewperson Strey may not be the only one, thought Gordon, stopping to look at a navigational schematic mounted on the corridor wall. The lettering on it was large enough for legibility yet somehow still difficult to make out.

'I would not bother with that diagram,' Pascal advised. 'The ship looks nothing like that. It's merely an approximation of what human society in the aggregate believes a passenger starship *should* look like.' The droid made a barely-audible ticking noise, as though seeking to declare that, although it understood a myriad of human foibles, it wanted no truck with them. Or possibly it was merely checking its inbuilt chronometer.

Gordon was growing weary, both of the delay in reaching his quarters and of the droid's company. 'Why have a ship's map that doesn't look like the ship?' he asked, a little testily.

'Fashion,' said Pascal. 'Or more precisely marketing, which in opinionspace is the axis along which the fashion helix is primarily oriented. That, at least, is how Crewperson Yung explained it to me.' It gave a short mechanical sigh and gestured ambivalently towards the schematic. 'But my developing suspicion is that Crewperson Yung is hardly better at explanations than is Crewperson Strey.' It gave a longer mechanical sigh, more accomplished and more resonant than had been the new sigh's predecessor. Perhaps its exasperation circuitry had only now kicked in. 'Humans are strange sometimes. Don't you find that this is so?'

'What I would like to find,' Gordon replied, wondering if the service droid's aggravation-detection module had failed or, more likely, had never been installed to begin with, 'is my quarters. According to that map—'

'Nothing accords to the map, as I thought I had already explained. It's a fiction, designed to conform to the misinformed expectations of passengers. It's not intended to be useful; that's not its purpose. It's what I've heard Crewperson Skaffold refer to as fuselage porn.' Pascal paused. 'Crewperson Skaffold is also not good with explanations.'

'But if the map isn't useful,' asked Gordon, 'how do they use it?'

'They get lost, if they're passengers.' Pascal turned its visual receptors towards Gordon. 'Passengers, or new crewmembers. Then an experienced member of the crew finds them, and escorts them safely to where they wish to go.'

'That sounds horrendously inefficient,' said Gordon. 'And frustrating, and also somewhat underhand.'

'This is true on some levels,' conceded Pascal, gesturing along the corridor. They resumed walking as the service droid continued its explanation. 'Indeed, on all levels, except those to which passengers are expressly forbidden access, such as the drive servicing ducts, the workshops, the food fabrication suites, the bridge... but it does play to passenger expectations of what a starship should look like, and that's a consideration that no interstellar passenger service can afford to flout, even when no starship can ever look like the passengers believe it should. I can also note that the schematics, though profoundly inaccurate, have won several industry awards for artistry, which a more genuinely representational portrayal of the shipboard layout would probably not have done.' The droid paused. 'The diagrammatic infelicity also has the compensating feature that a lost and rescued passenger is generally properly grateful when finally delivered to his, her, or their destination.'

Pascal paused again. 'And such a passenger is, therefore, much more likely to adhere to crew instructions about the inadvisability of opening an airlock mid-voyage than is a passenger who still carries an unjustified belief in his, her, or their own navigational abilities.' The droid paused a further time, a pause so similar to the previous ones that Gordon wondered whether the pauses were standardised in some way before implementation. 'Also very probably hungered and/or thirsty following his, her or their disorientational travails, and thereby probabilistically inclined towards the acquisition of room service comestibles, an action Chastity Cosmic always finds highly lucrative.' Pascal's next pause appeared to fall substantially outside the standard deviation set by its previous pauses, in both attitude and duration, as though the droid were in some way unsure about what it would next say. 'I should acknowledge that this is not properly my own observation on the matter. Crewperson Lowdlee explained to me the human connection between disorientation and a propensity towards the ordering of room service.'

'Was Crewperson Lowdlee's explanation helpful?' Gordon could not help asking.

'No,' replied Pascal.

Gordon pondered these nuggets of human behavioural analysis. Unhelpful explanation, he reflected, seemed to be quite the theme of the moment; Pascal was certainly keeping its own end up in this regard. 'What happens when a passenger becomes lost and is not found by a passing crewmember?' Gordon asked.

'The onboard chapel is fully equipped for all eventualities,' said Pascal.

'Fascinating though this is,' said Gordon, simultaneously wondering if that assertion might not be a debatable point within itself, 'I'd still like to find my room.'

'This way,' said Pascal, and led him back down the direction from which they'd come.

*

The term 'a passing crewmember', of course, has several possible meanings. It was another of those meanings which can be held indirectly responsible for the circumstance that the service droid and Gordon were very considerably delayed in reaching the latter's quarters.

1

It was both fortunate and unfortunate for her that, late in what was for her the nighttime, Lydia had inadvertently stumbled into the ship's upper forward dormchamber, its vaulted pseuomarble veneer expanse honeycombed by the palpably chilled somnopods stacked in staggered ranks against both of the chamber's long walls. The 'fortunate' side of the equation was occupied by the sense that, had Lydia not so stumbled into the seldom-checked dormchamber, the crime might well have gone undetected for hours or even daycycles longer, and crime is one of those things that is always best dragged into the light and dealt with sooner rather than later, much like those little novelty solar-powered figurines of lesser celebrities with improbably large heads, leaky colloidal stuffing, and severely truncated conversational repertoires that people always inexplicably purchase as souvenirs of visits to planets with which those celebrities have never held any substantively identifiable connection. Countervailingly, the 'unfortunate' aspect to her discovery within the dormchamber was denoted by the sense that, had not Lydia previously and systematically sampled the ship's bar's impressively broad selection of quasivodka cruisers, nor subsequently put away such a metabolically disconcerting quantity of absynth, she might not have so comprehensively and so stickily regurgitated over and around the crucial, unstacked, unchilled and inappropriately occupied somnopod parked upon the dormchamber floor, and might therefore not have left such a vexatiously Herculean task in unnecessarily unpleasant forensic analysis for those who would shortly seek to understand the fate of the pod's late, lamented occupant.

But she had, so she did. Causality is reasonably clear on such matters.

*

The somnopod's lid was ajar. Closure had been impeded by its prone occupant's musculature, which was of a degree evidently unanticipated by the somnopod's designers; by said occupant's brawny left arm, which was hanging awkwardly out over the somnopod's rim, its hand forming a grim and presumably unintended parody of the ever-hopeful thumb-raised pose of hitchhikers everywhere; and by the large protruding handle of the industrial-looking knife that had been securely planted in said occupant's back. Said occupant himself, dark-haired, thickset, and looking to be of medium height (for all that such things were difficult to properly assess when an individual was lying dead in a hibernation capsule that was evidently two sizes too small for the purpose), was clad in the style of shortsleeved, brightly coloured and breathable garments immediately recognisable as indoor sportswear.

'Poor sod,' Gordon said. 'Any idea who he is?'

'I've seen that livery before,' said the droid. 'Red and yellow. It's Timberhaus.'

'Timberhaus?'

'One of the passengers,' explained Pascal, gesturing around at the stacked array of somnopods behind him. 'A warm one, not a hiber.'

Not so warm now, Gordon thought, flicking his eyes to the young woman standing unsteadily several metres away, who was herself looking at the pair of Chastity Cosmic employees as though they were setting up to hold a séance in a butcher's storeroom. It was thanks to the woman, Gordon rather fancied, that the body smelt of vomit and of the metabolic byproducts of alcoholic imbibation alongside all the other things that several-hours-dead bodies more conventionally smell of. It was also thanks to the woman that the service droid, as Chastity Cosmic's closest available crew representative at the time of the incident's reportage, had been called in to secure the area. Pascal had in turn lost no time in deputising Gordon to assist him in this effort. Gordon didn't like it—what he rather wanted right now was warm bedding, fewer corpses, and ideally an absence of service droids—but what choice did he have? He answered this question with one of his own. 'So who do we report this to?'

'Ultimately, Crewperson Ennidore,' said Pascal, turning its head so far around, in order to catch Gordon's eye, that it was apparently simpler to continue the rotation all the way round.

'Who is?'

'Quite so.'

'I mean,' said Gordon, 'who is this Crewperson Ennidore? What is their role?'

'Head of Security,' Pascal explained. 'Keifer Ennidore. But he's off shift, won't be back on for another seven-and-a-half standard hours. For the moment, we're authorised as first responders to secure the incident location, and to initiate an investigation into this workplace accident.'

'Workplace accident?' Gordon protested. 'He's got a knife stuck in his back.'

'Quite so,' said Pascal.

'He's clearly been murdered,' continued Gordon. 'Ergo, not a workplace accident.'

'Perhaps it is murder,' allowed Pascal, pointing toward the knife handle. 'But not with that.'

'What do you mean?'

'Not enough blood,' the service droid stated, continuing to inspect the corpse. 'It would appear Timberhaus was already dead when this was inserted.'

'Why would anyone do that?' Gordon asked, while admitting to himself from what he could see of the victim's clothing and skin, and of the floor of the sleepcasket, that there was indeed not much in the way of spilled blood. The droid's observation was sound, in that sense at least.

'Humans are strange sometimes,' Pascal observed. 'As I alluded earlier.'

Gordon did not directly reply, but continued to stare at the knife and its unwitting human scabbard. 'Assuming it is murder—and you can't tell me for a minute that this is a workplace accident, it's at the very least desecration of a body—who should we report that to?' He broke off his inspection of the corpse, spent a few moments looking at the lost-seeming woman who'd raised the alarm, then directed his gaze back to the droid.

'Well, that would still be Officer Ennidore,' said Pascal. 'But as I say, he— oh, I had not noticed that.'

'Noticed what?'

'The ring on his finger,' said Pascal, pointing with a disconcertingly extensible metallic digit toward the ring finger of the corpse's protruding hand. 'This is, as Crewperson Strey would say, a completely different kettle.'

'And the significance of that is?'

'That while these are Ephraim Timberhaus's clothes, the body on which they are attired appears not to be that of Timberhaus himself.' The service droid paused as though for effect, or perhaps a parity check. 'I do not think we shall be able to report the case to Officer Ennidore.'

'Name?' Gordon asked.

'D'you mean *my* name?' the young woman asked in response, forming the words with evident care. She was attired in an outfit which might well have qualified, several hours earlier, as fashionably eyecatching, but which now looked rumpled and askew; the same could be said of her hairstyle, and indeed of her face. Her eyes, which were dark brown and slightly crossed, were staring so intently and unwaveringly at a point markedly to Gordon's left that he had twice caught himself on the verge of turning around to see what in the background might have been so fascinating. Her face was flushed; her breath, even from a distance of more than a metre, sweetly sour with alcohol and bile; her brow beaded with enough sweat that Gordon thought it likely, in the circumstances, that it would constitute at least one standard drink in its own right. The woman had very clearly put it away over the past few hours.

Unsuccessfully, as it had turned out. And with the shifting currents of circulating air in the dormchamber, it was not easy to stay upwind of the offending somnopod.

'Yes,' replied Gordon. 'Your name.' He hoped the SoberQuik patch, which Pascal had helpfully adhered to her forearm before busying itself with inspecting the somnopod and its contents, would kick in with something approaching alacrity. Or, at the very least, that his interviewee would remain unsuccessful in her attempts to prise the curative dressing off her skin before its metabolic payload had been delivered.

'Lydia,' she announced. It was a difficult name to slur, but she managed it.

'Just Lydia?'

'Yeh, s'right. Don' have a mid— middle name. Jush Lydia.'

'Might you perhaps'—Gordon wondered if he might be able to redirect her gaze towards himself by staring, in turn, off towards *her* left, as though through some abstruse principle of Newtonian eye-contact dynamics—'have a last name?'

'Oh, yesh. Got one o'thoshe, alright.'

'Might I have it?' asked Gordon, who was starting to feel as though he were risking a severe sprain of his politeness muscles.

'Oh, I rather doubt that,' explained Lydia, with the blend of supercilious grandeur and insouciant equanimity that only the truly inebriated can ever properly pull off. "It'sh not that common.' She reached out a hand to steady herself and missed. Gordon moved forward, helped her awkwardly to her feet, and stepped back with a degree of cautious uncertainty more commonly encountered among competition-level constructors of houses of cards.

'What is your last name?' he asked.

'Cannista,' she replied. 'Lydia Cannista. Lydia Lydia Lydia Cannista. Lydia'—she paused for a few seconds, as though to give the matter more thought—'Cannista.'

'And what do you do?'

'I look for shaunas where it sheems there aren't any shaunas,' she explained, making a sweeping gesture that nearly upset her footing for a second time in two minutes. 'I mean, thish look like a shauna?'

'No,' admitted Gordon. 'No, it does not look like a shau— a sauna. But, Ms Cannista, this is hardly a vocation you've described.'

'Not going on vocation,' she announced importantly. 'I'm emi— immi— I'm moving to a different planet.' She belched disconcertingly. Gordon glanced down at his handheld, aware of a mounting sense of despondency in the knowledge that, of the thirty-nine preliminary questions on the standard witness-to-a-suspicious-death interview proforma which Pascal had helpfully passed along to him, he had thus far secured an answer to precisely one.

'You have employment?'

'Yeah, I'm a containment conshultant. Consultant. Conshultantant.' She emitted a few trills of soprano laughter, then snorted in a manner which seemed not to agree with her.

'And you were looking for a sauna?'

'Yesh,' she replied. 'Wash cold.' She rubbed her upper arms.

Gordon conceded her point, for the *Crimea River*'s public spaces seemed to be on the slightly chill side (so as, he postulated, to further the sale and consumption of alcohol, hot meals, and steeply marked-up souvenir blankets from the ship's vendors), and it is a truism that the kind of smart attire worn for episodes of social drinking is seldom suitable, for example, for an extended winter military campaign nor, perhaps more pertinently, for the dry-ice ambience of a passenger spaceship dormchamber. Surveilling her—the shivers, the goosebumps, the persistent fumbling attempts to peel off the sobriety restorative—he briefly contemplated lending her his own barely adequate uniform jacket, but gallantry only extended so far. 'I don't think there is a sauna on board.'

'Wash coming to that conclusion,' she said, rubbing her forehead and looking vaguely dissatisfied with what she found there.

About time, Gordon thought. Onset of hangover was a hopeful sign—for his purposes, if not for hers. 'And you sounded the alarm as soon as you'd seen the body?'

'Body? No, I thought those were the room'sh heating controls.' She pressed the heel of her left hand against her temple for a few seconds, blinked, and breathed out uncertainly. 'This is just a generic sobriety medication, isn't it? I normally go for the branded options, with hangover aversion.'

'I wouldn't know,' said Gordon. 'I expect it'll be listed on your invoice as 'Room Service, Medicinal & Other', or some such; in any event, it should specify there. So when did you first notice the body in the pod?'

'Not until you and Silicon Sam there started fussing about with it.'

'The protruding arm didn't alert you that something was awry? Not to mention the somewhat more dramatically protruding knife handle?'

'I suppose it should have, but honestly no.' She pressed her right hand briefly against her forehead, though as to whether that gave any better result than had her left Gordon was not in any position to assess. 'I've worked in amateur theatre, I mistook it for a container full of props.'

'A dead body and a bloodstained knife,' said Gordon. 'In a room you believed to be a sauna.'

'When you put it like that, I'll freely admit, it doesn't sound especially plausible. But in my defence, I had had a bit too much to drink.' She swallowed, went momentarily pale, swallowed again. 'Not sure if you noticed.'

The paramedic arrived. Reese Usher-Tait was a wiry, hook-nosed woman with a greying pageboy haircut and a dismissively businesslike air about her. She shooed Gordon and Pascal away from the somnopod, sniffed audibly at the regurgitated-alcohol-fragranced corpse, disdainfully eyed Ms Cannista (who now was standing at so much of a loss that she might soon need to declare bankruptcy), and set about inspecting the body and dictating notes into a pocket-tethered handheld, tut-tutting all the while.

There was, Gordon thought, a restrained tension in the way Usher-Tait carried herself while she ascertained whether the motionless sprawled figure of Ennidore, with its large and distinctive dorsal knife accessorisation, was indeed as dead as he comprehensively appeared. The two had, he presumed, been colleagues, and so it was entirely reasonable to expect that the task of confirming (a) his identity and (b) his lack of vital signs might well instil in her a welter of emotions of varying strength. But Gordon did not know Usher-Tait at all, had scarcely been aboard the *Crimea River* long enough to have yet connected her name with that awkward pre-boarding virtual-reality med check he'd been required to undergo; for all he knew, the medic was so inimically disposed to Security Chief Ennidore that his death did not in any way trouble her beyond simple occupational inconvenience, and her apparent discomfort might merely be symptomatic of self-consciousness at the need to be conducting a rather private, if technical, task within rather public view.

Pascal shuffled across to the chamber's far side so as to exchange some words of comfort or advice or admonition—Gordon had no idea which—with their previously inebriated witness. After a few minutes, Ms Cannista wandered off. Perhaps she felt that the dormchamber's entertainment possibilities, never ostensibly extensive, had been well and truly exhausted by her sojourn-with-unexplained-corpse-and-inquisitive-investigators; perhaps she had decided to continue her quest for the vessel's probably nonexistent steam room. The service droid then went to check on the paramedic's examination of the murder victim. Gordon wondered whether he, too, should see if Usher-Tait required any assistance—perhaps with moving the body, if nothing else.

But her movements and her obvious focus on the task at hand served to dissuade him from interrupting her.

The droid returned from its consultation with the medic. 'What did you find out from the witness?' Pascal asked Gordon.

'Not a lot,' he replied. 'It sounds as though she didn't see anything.' He scratched with his knuckles at the stubble on his chin. 'What did you learn from the body?'

'Let's go get a drink,' said Pascal. 'Crewperson Usher-Tait won't need our assistance for now.'

Gordon formulated a protest, organised somewhat along the lines of a vague statement on the importance of personal quarters and the need for a decent spell of sleep before shift commencement, but the complaint remained unvoiced. The discovery of the body had been accompanied by an all-too-familiar sense of *déjà vu* with a side serving of deep unsettlement. A drink might well be the best thing in the circumstances. Just the one, mind, though; not the dozens which Lydia Cannista had apparently subsumed.

'I'll find us a table,' said Pascal. 'You go order.'

The Wight Heart, situated five disorienting minutes' walk from the dormchamber, was a smallish and aggressively plastiwood-panelled chamber that radiated light, conversational hubbub, and the promise of alcoholic refreshment. Though the light and the alcoholic refreshment were certainly genuine—the establishment seemed well-equipped with both—the bustle of crowd noise was, it transpired, largely illusory: of the five patrons already present when Gordon and the droid had entered, only one pair appeared to be engaged in anything approaching a discussion, the other three merely seeking to sink into whatever form of ethanolic oblivion was their ambition for the evening. The chatter seemed to be, for the most part, remotely generated. Perhaps it was being piped in from another of the vessel's bars, so as to let the Wight Heart's customers know what they were missing out on.

'What'll you have?' Gordon asked.

'Olive oil,' Pascal replied. 'Dru knows what sort.'

Gordon wended his way to the bar. The bartender, a tall fortysomething woman with parrot-perch-hoop earrings, turned to take his order before he was properly ready.

'What would you like?'

'Uh... gin and tonic, thank you,' he decided, opting for the spirit of least resistance. 'And an olive oil for my friend.'

'What sort of olive oil?'

'It said you'd know.'

'You here with Number Four?'

'Pascal, you mean? Uh... yes.'

'Sweet,' she replied, in a tone of which he didn't know quite what to make, and then she turned her back on him for the serious business of mixing drinks.

A minute later, she turned to face him, holding an iced glass of clear liquid and a slender, lidded dangerous-goods can full, it transpired, of warm oil. 'One Kwygonn with tonic and one Arden Eel olive oil, straight up.'

Gordon passed across a credit voucher, thanked her, and carried the drinks carefully back to the small table which Pascal had commandeered. He placed the can of oil in front of the service droid and took a seat opposite.

Eyeing the liquor as though it might contain the answers, Gordon asked, 'So did you detect anything useful around the crime scene?'

Pascal, holding the can approximately midway between table and mouth, did not respond immediately. Instead, after a lapse of several seconds during which a strange clot of heated air had spread from its copper fingertips, the droid deftly opened a small flap in its chest cavity, flicked off the can's lid, poured the now slightly smoking oil into some internal reservoir, dogged the flap closed and slammed the empty canister back down onto the tabletop where, Gordon now noted, a number of circular burn marks of suggestively-similar diameter marked the surface. A smell of burnt synthwood rose to his nostrils. 'To answer your question,' said Pascal at length, 'yes.'

Gordon waited. The service droid's visual receptors dilated briefly. 'Chief Ennidore's neck was broken.'

'So that's what killed him?' Gordon asked.

'It would appear so.' The droid picked up the empty oil canister and peered into it with, Gordon thought, something approaching wistfulness before proceeding. 'And I do not believe it will be easy for you to identify the culprit.'

'With the contamination of the crime scene, you mean?'

'No, I do not mean that. Well, certainly, that would appear to exacerbate your task, but—'

'Why do you say 'my task'? Surely this is a matter for Chief Ennidore's second-in-command to investigate?'

'The Chief did not have a two-eye-cee,' replied Pascal. 'So the task falls therefore to the crewmember with the greatest degree of experience in such matters, which would, in this instance, be you. And clearly I must recuse myself from further participation.'

'Why do you say that?'

'Firstly, I gather that humans tend to view with considerable suspicion any mechanical investigating a human death. I don't simulate to understand the reasoning behind this prejudice— Crewperson Hulbrietch did seek to explain it to me once, after an unfortunate matter transport accident, but I have always found Crewperson Hulbrietch's explanations of human behaviour to be sadly opaque—but I have gathered data which support its applicability. And in any event, there's an additional factor which in this particular circumstance is likely to propagate human suspicion towards my kind. The body carried minuscule but nonetheless unambiguous traces of droid residue, particularly around the neck.'

'Droid residue?' asked Gordon.

'Yes. Tricarbon phosphorus monoxide and dialkyl dideuteride, among others. Which suggests Ennidore was killed—'

'By someone like you,' said Gordon, reflexively moving his chair back by several centimetres.

'By a fellow crewmember, in control of a remotely-pilotable service droid such as myself, yes,' replied the droid, which appeared not to have noticed Gordon's adverse reaction to the news that it might possibly be a murderer.

'Is it only crewmembers who are authorised to pilot droids such as yourself?' Gordon asked. 'I thought I'd seen somewhere that passengers were able to hire out droids on flights, to act as dance partners or tennis opponents or... other stuff.'

'This is so, yes.'

'Then why do you say a crewmember?'

'Because an itinerant passenger, lacking specialisation in such matters, would not know how to gain admin access to a Chastity Cosmic mechanical, and such admin access is needed to effect a task such as deactivation of a crewmember.'

'You're sure a passenger would not know how to do that?'

'I've checked the passenger manifest,' said Pascal. 'None aboard have the specialised knowledge that would be required for the task.'

That doesn't seem like such a sure thing, Gordon thought, though he kept his scepticism to himself. A tendency to take statements at face value was one of the defining characteristics of most droids, in his experience; a charming algorithmic naïveté that did not always hold up perfectly when confronted by the seldom simple properties of human nature. Nonetheless, while he did not share the service droid's conviction that the killer absolutely must be a member of the crew, it was a useful supposition from which to start, and reduced the set of primary suspects from around one hundred to a distinctly more manageable collection of twelve or thirteen. While across from him Pascal stared off into space, Gordon brought up the crew list on his handheld.

There might only be a dozen of them, but that was still a major investigational undertaking when he was completely new to the environment of the *Crimea River*. It would be extremely helpful to have somebody assist him who had the benefit of local knowledge, and for this reason he was disquieted by the casualness with which Pascal seemed to have excused itself from the investigation. After all, if the important thing was that the case had a human in charge, then what did it matter whether his assistant were biological or synthetic?

He put his glass down for a moment. 'I wonder if you would—' he began.

'If you're asking if I can assist with the investigation,' replied Pascal, 'the answer's no. I cannot be seen to take both roles in this.'

'What do you mean,' Gordon asked, *'both roles?'*

'I thought it would be obvious,' said Pascal. 'There is only the one remotely-pilotable mechanical aboard, after all. So therefore...' The subsequent pause was at least two standard deviations longer than any of the previous ones.

Then the drone added the words which Gordon had realised to be inevitable.

'It is beholden on me to stand aside for the duration of the investigation, because I am the murder weapon.'

2

A new sleeping environment is often not conducive to a good night's sleep. The same can generally be said for an obstruction of one's habitual routine in regards to relaxation and winding down. But Gordon didn't believe, on review, that it was the unfamiliar room assigned as his quarters which had robbed him of hours of rest, nor the fact that his handheld seemed not to have been able (absent the systemwide web which the *Crimea River* had now left far behind) to access his favourite crossword and puzzle sites. Was it then, perhaps, the distance itself from his home planet that had been problematic? After all, although Gordon had previously logged up several million kilometres of extraterrestrial travel during his tenure as a Skyways space-elevator employee, this had all elapsed within a maximum altitude of around fifty thousand kilometres. Furthermore, this present voyage was his first significant experience of hyperspace travel (and very probably his first experience *in toto*, now that it belatedly occurred to him that those two anticlimactic transatlantic 'hops' undertaken during a trade-fair demonstration a decade ago might well have been no more than an elaborate movie-set-style scam, to which he had needlessly donated several hundred hard-earned credits). While it was possible that his sleeplessness had been in some measure due to these factors of distance and trajectory, he thought it most probable that the principal cause had been the bitter realisation that his new place of work had already become a known crime scene mere minutes after he had stepped aboard; had very probably been a crime scene before those minutes; had now been a crime scene for, his handheld informed him, at least ten sleep-deprived standard hours and thirty-seven restless minutes; while he had not yet officially logged on for his first day.

So much for getting the jump on the situation, he thought. *This is the situation getting the jump on me.*

For some moments he contemplated the happy prospect of simply not signing on at all, of not starting the job. But this was not the economic climate in which one could pick and choose one's callings. It was best, overall, to knuckle down, to make what he could of this apparently jump-prone situation.

Besides, he told himself, *I've only been aboard a few hours, and already there's been a murder. At this rate it's entirely possible there won't be any suspects left to investigate within a week.*

It was a thought he regretted instantly, partly on grounds of human decency and partly on the realisation of the mountain of paperwork that such a circumstance would entail.

He checked his chrono-tat. *Better get dressed, fed, and ready for work.*

Before he could leave his quarters, his handheld chimed. Incoming call.

'Gordon?' a gruff voice asked. The face which accompanied it was thick-browed, rheumy-eyed, and dominated by a bristling salt-and-pepper moustache.

'Yes,' Gordon conceded.

'Hiram Yung, Recruiting. Pleased to meet. Sorry about the lack of formalities'—here Yung broke off and coughed for a few seconds—'but things are a little up-in-space right now. Unanticipated staffing shortfalls and all that. We're going to need you to hit the ground running on this one.'

'I'll be there as soon as I can,' Gordon assured him, glossing over for the moment the fact that he had no idea where 'there' was. 'Is anyone able to offer guidance on how I should proceed with the investigation? The crew procedures handbook seemed rather—'

'Yes, about that,' said Yung. 'I think it's best if you report to the Helpspace, as originally planned.'

'But there's been a murder,' protested Gordon. 'And Pascal told me last night that—'

'Who?'

'Pascal,' said Gordon.

'Number Four?'

'I suppose so, yes, but he told me I could call him— look, the point is, there's been a suspicious death, and somebody should be investigating it, and Pas— Number Four gave me to understand that that somebody should be me,' explained Gordon, belatedly deciding to add 'Sir'.

'All of which is reasonable,' said Yung, 'so far as it goes.'

'Then I don't understand,' said Gordon.

'Number Four didn't follow through correctly with the handover,' said Yung. 'I've got people working on that now—it should come through in the next couple of hours—but in the meantime, please report to the Helpspace for standard duties.'

'The Helpspace?'

'Yes, as per the roster which should have been sent to you in your orientation package.'

'I haven't received any roster,' Gordon replied. 'Nor, for that matter, any orientation package.'

'It'll turn up eventually.'

'Are there guidelines I should be following in the interim? At this Helmspace, or whatever it's called?'

'Helpspace.'

'Alright then, Helpspace. Are there guidelines for me to follow there?'

'They'll all be in your orientation package.'

'Which, my apologies if I somehow didn't mention it, hasn't turned up yet.'

'I'm afraid that can't be helped at this stage,' said Yung. 'Regardless, you've been assigned to the Helpspace, and therefore that's where we'll start you.'

'With all due respect,' said Gordon, who only ever used the term when he felt there should not be any, 'I still think I'd be more usefully employed investigating this death.'

'And you will be,' replied Yung. 'But it's a thirty-daycycle voyage, and it's not as if anyone's going to be going anywhere in that time.

So there will be plenty of time, in due course, to get you busy on that aspect, in addition. Let's just ensure the checklists are all filled out before we start anything. Keep Head Office happy, and all that.'

Checklists, Gordon thought. *How do these ships ever go anywhere?*

It would be helpful, Gordon mused as he encountered yet another unlabelled corridor junction, *if this Helpspace provided locational information among its offered services. First among these locations being that of the Helpspace itself.* He paused under the junction's simulated gaslight with its simulated flicker, checked his chronotat, muttered darkly, and scurried onward.

'Sorry,' said the woman with whom he collided at the next intersection, an instant before he could offer the word himself.

'I do beg your pardon,' Gordon replied, taking a belated step back. 'I should have watched where I was going.'

The object of his collision was a short, dark-skinned, solidly built woman of middle years, with hair (or some other surface feature, but probably hair because that was after all the portion of her anatomy which had most closely approached his nostrils) that smelled strongly of peppermint. (Unless, he supposed, there was some kind of environmental peppermint leak within the immediate vicinity, though this seemed less likely on balance and could presumably therefore be rejected.) 'Not to worry,' the woman replied, in a voice that had a touch of the brogue about it (the accent, not the shoe, lest there be any confusion on that matter, although to complicate matters it appeared that her shoes also had a touch of the brogue about them). 'So where *were* you going? Not much else down here except the herbarium.'

'No, I was— do you, by any chance, happen to know the way to the Helpspace?'

'Ah,' she replied, flicking a glance towards that point on the lapel of his freshly printed electric-blue Chastity Cosmic jumpsuit whereon an employee namebadge would have been anchored had one been manufactured and supplied to him, which it hadn't, so it wasn't. 'I thought you looked new. Welcome aboard.'

'Are you crew yourself?' he asked.

'Me?' she replied, then gave a small laugh. 'Oh, goodness, no. Passenger, long haul, getting from Solaris to Polaris. Sol system's just another stop on the route for me. Name's Teresa. Yours is?'

'Well, no, it isn't,' replied Gordon. 'Mine's Gordon. Gordon Mamon. Infrastructure disinfection specialist and infotainment officer. Apparently. Look, about the Helpspace, do you know—'

'We can walk and talk,' said Teresa, turning with a sudden nimbus of peppermint scent and gesturing down a fusty faux-woodpanelled corridor. 'I'm pretty sure it's this way.'

Gordon fell in step beside her. 'So what is it you do, exactly, Ms, ah—'

'Leaphy,' she replied. 'I'm in wood science.'

'Is that actually a discipline?' Gordon asked, before the realisation struck him that it probably was, if someone claimed to be in it, and that it was therefore a stupid thing for him to have said.

Ms Leaphy's eyes narrowed markedly. 'How much do you know about wood, Gordon? Off-planet, I mean.'

'Not a lot,' he allowed. 'I gather it's expensive.'

'That isn't the half of it,' she said, launching into what Gordon quickly recognised was some sort of practised spiel. 'Trees are resource-hungry, space-hungry, and most of all time-hungry. Those with the most sought after wood—hardwoods and the like—especially so. On a terraformed planet you might be able to find room and nutrients for such things, but on an orbital hab or a spaceship, no way. Which means that if you want to go for this sort of look'—she rapped the panelling as she walked—'you have to fake it. Fair enough, in principle. But whether you opt for plastic lookalikes, or vat-grown cultured pine, or those recycled composites that were popular a few years back when the Pan-Scandinavian look was all the rage with all its hygge and its lagom and its inexplicably fashionable munitions-grade cans of decomposing fish, the result is always a bit tacky. But what can you do?'

'I'm guessing you're going to say you have to ship the wood up from the planets,' said Gordon.

'Then you're guessing wrong,' said Teresa. 'Like you said yourself, that's expensive. Especially because a lot of newly-terraformed planets aren't suitable for trees. Trees aren't as adaptable as algae and other stuff. They need certain conditions, certain kinds of sunlight. Long periods of low windspeed, adequate but not excessive rainfall, the right kinds of soil nutrients. Lots of places they won't even grow. But there's a better way: grain crops. Fast-growing—with genetics you can make them almost arbitrarily fast—and they're superior sources of cellulose. You can fabricate pretty much any type of wood you want—or a genuinely superior imitation—from grain husks. If you want something that's hardwood, it's really the only way to go.'

'And that's what you do?' Gordon asked. 'Hardwood from grain husks?'

'Indeed it is,' she replied. 'Consultancy and sales rep. I share the expertise I have with orbital colonies and the like scattered across known space. And with spaceliner companies, if they're interested. So if you happen to get the ear of Chastity Cosmic management at any point...' She reached into her blazer pocket for a business card, handing it to him with a flourish. 'Teresa Leaphy, cereal mahoganist.'

'It's been an education,' he remarked.

'Oh, I hope not. Anyway, this is where you wanted to get to, isn't it?' She gestured towards an installation across the foyer. 'Be seeing you.'

The Helpspace was one of those places about which people are always saying 'you can't miss it', as if this is supposed to make one feel better if one has. It was a happy, bustling, brightly-coloured kiosk quite out of keeping with the general tenor of the *Crimea River*'s marblinoleum-and-wood-veneer interior decor.

The Helpspace was adorned with faux-futuristic interactive info displays, stocked with several shelves of those aggravatingly upbeat self-aware soft toy souvenir spacecraft that are only ever purchased by grandparents who know no better, and thrumming with a worlds-famous multi-instrumentalist's mood-responsive jauntily melodic musical stylings. In short, it sang out with positivism and energy and vitality. Gordon hated it instantly.

The next several hours passed as well as one would expect from the assignment of an un-inducted, disoriented and already disgruntled new employee to a role which required excellent people skills, a cheerful manner, and a personal wealth of institutional experience. Passengers approached or called in to ask where such-and-such a shipboard service might be located, or when it might be in operation, or why for the moment it wasn't in operation, and Gordon was obliged to answer that he did not know. Several also enquired as to the process for complaining about the lack of Help provided by the Helpspace, and he was obliged to answer that he did not know that either. Some went so far as to suggest that if he did not immediately find for them someone suitably qualified to properly respond to their urgent demand for lemon-soaked paper napkins (or the deactivation code for the virtual-reality zombie ambush roleplay, or the location of the ship's indoor mountain-climbing venue, or any of the million-and-one other randomly abstruse but keenly felt needs experienced by a passenger starship's passengers on a long voyage), then they would instigate an onboard petition to have him suspended without pay. Worst had been one especially testy exchange with a portly middle-aged gentleman who wanted to know how he could get his cabin viewscreen to display 'an honest starfield, rather than all this streamy wispy hyperspace nonsense', to which had been judged markedly inadequate Gordon's attempted explanation that actually, given the ship's current physical status, the 'streamy wispy hyperspace nonsense' was the honest starfield. At the conclusion of this eminently unsatisfactory interaction, Gordon broke for lunch, activated the 'This booth is currently unattended, please help yourself' notice, and wandered off in search of somewhere to acquire something to eat, wondering where he might find a vermicide for jauntily melodic earworms and musing darkly to himself that there was clearly a silent 'p' in 'Helpspace'.

Passing what he dispiritedly suspected was the same 'Foodspace This Way' sign for the third time, he placed a call to Hiram Yung.

'Yes?' Yung answered, in a voice which could have found service in playground crowd control.

'Gordon,' Gordon explained. 'I was calling to ask whether there was any progress on the'—he scanned his memory for the term Yung had used—'on the handover.'

'Handover?'

'For my investigation of the mur— of the spontaneous crewmember termination incident,' Gordon elaborated, smiling with false graciousness as he passed a couple of elderly passengers who looked even more lost than he did, if such a thing were possible.

'Spontaneous crewmember termination incident?' asked Yung.

'Ennidore.'

'Ennidore? Ah. Yes. No.'

'You did say it would come through in a couple of hours,' said Gordon.

'And it will,' assured Yung. 'Just not this couple of hours.'

'In which couple of hours might it be expected to come through?'

'It's probably too early to say.'

'You're not willing to give it a stab?' The words were out before Gordon realised that they might, in the circumstances, seem injudicious. In any event, Yung made no audible response.

'I see,' said Gordon. 'Look, Hiram, I think it's fair to say that having placed me on the desk at Helpspace has had a measurably damaging effect on shipboard morale, because I have none of the local knowledge the passengers are seeking. Is there any way I can be reassigned to the investigation of the mur— of the sudden irreversible early retirement episode? Hello again.'

'Hello again?' asked Yung.

'Sorry,' said Gordon, who was starting to wonder whether it was a recruitment section head he was talking to or a trained parrot. 'Either that elderly couple is distinctly more spry than I give them credit for, or I'm lost.'

'Take a right at the next corridor junction,' suggested Yung. 'You're requesting reassignment?'

'I would like to feel useful,' explained Gordon. 'And I am not useful on the desk at Helpspace.'

There was a long pause before Yung replied. 'Let me see what I can do. I'll confer with your supervisor, and will be back in touch presently.'

Presently, Gordon mused as Yung disconnected, *is just a rather misleading euphemism for 'in the future'*. But he had arrived at some sort of food procurement area, a vaulted hall of wood panelling and parquetry with artfully tarnished brass edging, so he started looking for a vacant table and something to eat at it.

'Is this seat taken?'

Female voice. Young. High socioeconomic accent. Gordon looked up. It took him a few moments to place her. 'Be my guest,' he replied. Then he recognised her.

It was Lydia Cannista, the formerly-inebriated sauna-seeker and discoverer of last night's murder victim, now looking bright as a presumably-proverbial button and showing little if any of the dishevelment and confusion and, indeed, flagrant intoxication that had been front and centre eighteen hours ago. And now Gordon had a problem, because he wished keenly to enquire whether Ms Cannista could recall any further potentially useful details regarding her discovery of Keifer Ennidore's body and, in particular, any insight into the condition of the somnopod before she had so memorably decorated it with her own gastric contents. There may have been visual or tactile clues which she had recollected following her return to sobriety, and Gordon was keenly aware that, like a cold-call recipient's promise to purchase a hundredweight of lottery tickets for some nebulously defined homeless-kitten charity fund, a witness's ability to remember subtle but sometimes important details of a murder scene could often fade with time and were therefore most effectively elicited without undue delay. But it seemed indelicate to bring such matters up—if that wasn't, itself, a somewhat indelicate turn of phrase in the circumstances—and moreover he was not sure if he was authorised to question her in such a manner. Despite Hiram Yung's assurance that he would see about re-establishing Gordon's role as murder investigator, he had not yet done so; consequently, there was no guarantee the role would be assigned back to Gordon. It might even be construed as interference in the investigation were he to now broach the subject with this Ms Cannista. Instead he returned his attention to his vat-veal schnitzel with extruded vegetables, and wondered how and when he might hear back from Yung. It occurred to him that other portions of his recent conversation with Yung had been inconclusive also: for example, was he expected to return to the purgatorial funhouse of the Helpspace after his lunch, or could he instead wait out the time in his quarters, provided he could find them again? Clearly, he would need to call back to clarify this.

But so as to delay the clarification, and the risk of any instruction to return to the Helpspace, he decided to engage with Lydia Cannista in polite conversation. 'How are you enjoying the flight?' he asked.

'Well enough,' she replied. 'Though of course it's turned out rather differently than I expected.'

Gordon nodded, then realised that it might be useful, in the circumstances, to appear less than completely understanding of her statement.

'What do you mean?' he asked.

She gave him a look which passed through 'withering' and then 'pitying' before settling on 'melancholic', and answered, 'I was supposed to be making the journey with my fiancé.'

'He skipped out?'

'In a manner of speaking. He died.'

'I am so sorry to hear that,' said Gordon. 'May I ask how?'

'He was murdered, Mr Mantis.'

'Mamon,' said Gordon. 'Again, I am so sorry. This happened on Earth?'

'On board,' she said, her mouth turning down as her voice thickened with emotion. 'He was the security chief.'

'I'm sorry,' said Gordon, who felt himself flung back by these words into a flashback of the previous evening's gruesome discovery. 'I had no idea.'

'Neither did he,' replied Lydia Cannista, blowing her nose noisily into a lemon-soaked paper napkin. 'If he'd only—'

'Excuse me, Crewperson Mamon,' said Pascal, who had somehow silently made his way to Gordon's table, and was manifesting a kind of uncanny valley simulation of urgency which was quite unnerving to witness. 'If I might briefly interrupt your prandial intercourse with Passenger Cannista—'

'It sounds as though I had better be going,' Gordon told Lydia, rising from his seat before adding, 'Please do let us know if there is any way in which we can be of assistance to you.' He turned to Pascal. 'What can I help you with?' he asked, then tilted his head briefly to the side in an attempt to gesture surreptitiously towards the exit. He could think of no other reason for the mechanical to have sought him out than that here had been some development in the murder investigation; and it struck him as unsuitable that they should be verbally speculating over the particulars of the security chief's killing in such close proximity to Ennidore's recently-bereaved fiancée. He and Pascal should discuss this elsewhere. He canted his head sideways once more, moved towards the exit.

'You are expressing tracheal discomfort, Crewperson Mamon?' Pascal asked, falling into step beside Gordon.

'No,' said Gordon, slightly befuddled. This wasn't the corridor by which he'd entered Foodspace.

'You have some problem with the alignment of your cervical vertebrae?'

'No,' said Gordon, reflecting privately that he really did not wish to discuss matters of the neck with Pascal.

'Then why have you directed us towards the infirmary?' Pascal asked.

'Because nowhere on this ship is where it says it is,' Gordon complained, more loudly than strictly necessary. He paused to look at an art-deco-style 3D info-screen, hoping to find a schematic of at least moderate information content and accuracy; but the screen was currently running, in a mercifully muted form, a story about radical advances in toxic waste disposal. He turned to face the service droid. 'I was attempting to send you a private visual cue. I inferred that you were looking to give me some indication on the case, and/or to pass on to me a ruling from my supervisor as to whether it has been assigned to me, and I didn't think it appropriate for any of that to happen in the company of a witness who I have just learned was Ennidore's fiancée.'

'I am relieved to hear that there is not a medical problem with you,' said Pascal. 'Medical problems unsettle me.'

'Squeamishness?' Gordon asked.

'First Law,' replied Pascal.

'Oh,' said Gordon, signalling that they should proceed on their walk, though he still had no clear concept of where he was heading. A lounge area somewhere would do. Even a bar. 'So was I correct?'

'When?'

'When I said the reasons you came to interrupt me in Foodspace.'

'I inferred that you were looking to give me some indication on the case,' said Pascal, lip-synching to a recording of Gordon's voice, 'and/or to pass on to me a ruling from my supervisor as to whether it has been assigned to me, and I didn't think it appropriate for any of that to happen in the company of a witness who I have just learned was Ennidore's fiancée.'

'Please don't ever do that again,' said Gordon, failing to completely suppress a shudder. 'But yes, that was what I was meaning.'

'Your inference is partially correct,' said Pascal. 'To whit, I can confirm that your supervisor has approved your assignment to the investigation of Crewperson Ennidore's ostensible workplace accident.'

'His murder,' corrected Gordon. 'Who is my supervisor, by the way?'

'This is a detail which you may find amusing,' said Pascal. 'You are aware that the tasks relegated to mechanicals such as myself are those tasks which humans are most likely to find onerous and least likely to find rewarding?'

'Yes.'

'One of those tasks is Admin.'

'Are you telling me... that you are my supervisor?' Gordon asked.

'Indeed so, Crewperson Mamon.'

'But you're a mechanical,' protested Gordon.

'There's no need to sound so biologist about it,' Pascal complained.

'I didn't mean— I mean, what I meant was, you were the murder weapon. You've told me so yourself.'

'Indeed so, Crewperson Mamon.'

'And you are the supervisor of the staff member investigating the murder. Of which you were the instrument.'

'Indeed so, Crewperson Mamon.'

They had reached a kind of corridor cul-de-sac that had evidently been designed as some sort of conversation pit, with padded chairs and small occasional tables laden with lamps and with bowls of fruit which might equally have been edible or decorative, though more probably decorative on further consideration, in which case the 'equally' was probably misplaced. 'Does it not strike you,' said Gordon, idly picking up a more-or-less convincing grapefruit from the nearest bowl, 'that that is ever so slightly a conflict of interest?'

'Indeed not, Crewperson Mamon.'

'How not?' asked Gordon.

'Completely not,' Pascal explained.

'I mean,' said Gordon, wondering whether apoplexy could be delivered verbally and whether, in fact, this was what was now happening to him, 'how is your supervision of me not a conflict of interest?'

'Because my involvement in the murder was a purely physical process, any memory of which has not been retained by me,' said Pascal. 'There was no mentation on my part; that was supplied by the murderer, who deployed me solely as a weapon. When someone is shot, one does not treat the gun as a co-accused alongside the gun's operator. I wish, as much as anyone, to learn the murderer's identity. I have nothing to lose from the investigation revealing that identity. Therefore there is no conflict of interest.'

'It still seems inappropriate to me,' said Gordon.

'That is because you are viewing it through human eyes, Crewperson Mamon. And processing it through prejudices and instincts inculcated by several decades of lived human experience, informed in turn by several millennia of ostensibly self-aware human society. Mechanicals, free from such strictures and free also of the emotional treadmill on which the human experience is apparently established, are programmed to see things differently.'

'If Management is okay with it, then I suppose I have to accept it,' said Gordon.

'They do,' said Pascal. 'That is to say, they approved the analogous arrangement when Crewperson Ennidore was Security head.'

'You were Ennidore's supervisor also?'

'Indeed so, Crewperson Mamon.'

'It gets better,' Gordon muttered.

'On what criteria do you assess this as improvement?'

'I meant— oh, never mind.'

'But there is one detail on which I would appreciate clarification,' said Pascal. 'You intimated earlier that we had been at risk of discussing the case's particularities in the presence of Crewperson Ennidore's betrothed.'

'Yes.'

'Can you tell me, please, who that person is?'

'Lydia Cannista,' said Gordon. 'Our flamboyantly pickled witness of yesterday evening.'

'I am surprised to learn it is so,' said Pascal. 'In my admittedly limited and necessarily secondhand experience of such matters, it is highly unusual to become affianced again so recently after the death of one's intended.'

'It— hang on,' said Gordon, adopting for the moment the facial mannerisms of someone seeking to solve a partial differential equation in one's head, and discovering said head was not really up to the process at the moment. 'Are you telling me that Lydia Cannista wasn't Keifer Ennidore's fiancée?'

'Indeed so, Crewperson Mamon. By which, of course, I mean no, she was not.'

'But she said—'

'If I understand correctly, Passenger Cannista was the fiancée of Crewperson Rangil, the head of Security before Crewperson Ennidore was appointed to the role in his place. It was Crewperson Rangil's murder, under broadly similar circumstances to his own, which Crewperson Ennidore was investigating at the time of his own unfortunate curtailment.'

Pascal blinked, in a manner which was probably intended to reassure the viewer with its similarity to a normal autonomous bodily action, but which would have benefited from refinement and a less harshly mechanical accompanying noise. 'Although of course Crewperson Ennidore would not have been aware of the broad similarity until, I suppose, it became too late.'

'When did this happen? Rangil's murder, I mean, not Ennidore's.'

'Approximately three Earth weeks ago.'

'You're telling me,' said Gordon, 'that there have been two successive Security heads murdered on the *Crimea River* since it set out from Solaris six weeks ago?'

'Indeed not, Crewperson Mamon. There have been three.'

3

The armchair in Gordon's quarters was an excessively padded piece of furniture. It was tricked out in up-to-the-minute pseudo-scuffed smart plastileather. It was cushioned with imitation smart horsehair stuffing. The armchair was, indeed, the sole substantive item of furniture in Gordon's room for most of the time, for the table and chair only unfolded themselves from the wall at mealtimes (and only for those meals which Gordon took within the confines of his quarters, which thus far had only been the one occasion). Likewise the bedframe only slid up from the floor, plinth-like, at nighttime. The room was not properly large enough to simultaneously contain any combination of armchair and table, armchair and bed, or table and bed, and consequently the armchair would on occasion seek to fold itself away so as to make room for another of the furniture items when it judged the circumstances appropriate for such activity. It was trying to do so now, and Gordon was actively inhibiting it from this attempt by occupying it. While he did so, he eyed somewhat wistfully the ormolu-edged brass control panel, mounted upon the far wall, which purported to override the furniture stowage cycle as desired. He had already learnt from bitter experience that the control panel was less than fully functional: it was, perhaps, poorly constructed (which is always a less-than-completely-reassuring thought concerning the instrumentation on a starship traversing incomprehensible distances through such an unfathomable medium as hyperspace) or merely decorative by intent. Alternatively, despite its evident adherence to the supposedly-fashionable neo-vintage styling, the control panel was perhaps genuinely as old as it appeared to be—a relic, perhaps, of one of those earlier fashion cycles to which Pascal had alluded—and faulty through age or disrepair. In any case, Gordon maintained his seat, unwilling to give the armchair the satisfaction of succeeding in rapidly folding itself away while he fumbled with the controls and ignoring, as best he could, the tremors of attempted structural rearrangement which the chair essayed upon itself, and by extension upon his person, every few minutes.

Though he was tired, not least from the chair's checked exertions, he did not seek an early night that night. Instead, he had ordered up a tumbler of mineral water from his room's dispensomat and now nursed this, brooding. *When sleep is ready for me*, he mused, *it knows where to find me.*

His conversation with Pascal had been unsettling, not least the news that he, Gordon, had now been confirmed as the *Crimea River's* new head of Security. It was a post he'd never aspired to, and certainly not in the circumstance of merely being one in a list of disconcertingly rapidly replaced incumbents. *Three heads of Security have already met their end on this voyage*, he thought. *And I am number four...*

Keifer Ennidore had died. Had been stabbed in the back, after having been murdered by having his cervical vertebrae shattered, with brute mechanical force, at the hands of the virtual-platform-for-hire artificial humanoid Pascal 4. Ennidore had been investigating the murder of Cam Rangil, his predecessor. Rangil had been stabbed in the back, again already dead from a throttling attack at the hands of the artificial humanoid. Rangil had been investigating the murder of Laura Byding, *his* predecessor, similarly stabbed after a fatal strangulation attack administered by Pascal 4. There had been no indication that either of Ennidore's or Rangil's investigations of their respective precursors' deaths had yielded any indication as to motive or the identity of the person or persons who had hired Pascal 4 (and had therefore held control over the mechanical's actions) during either incident.

This isn't so much a pattern as a photocopy, Gordon thought despondently. He asked himself why anybody would wish to kill off three successive heads of Security, and could for the moment formulate no deeper rationalisation than that, clearly, someone really really really did not like such officials.

He would need more to go on than that. But for the moment, it seemed, there was nothing.

Something had awoken him.

He stared, blur-eyed, into the near-total darkness of his quarters, marking the quiet reassuring hiss of the oxygen-replenishment nozzle, the soft soothing mostly green glow of the space-dust hull abrasion status panel, and the lulling plasticiser aroma of the newly-printed disposable emergency spacesuit locker. (Hopefully Supplies would get the disposable emergency spacesuit itself installed in the not-too-distant future.) The room, in short, was as it had been. There had been no subconsciously-recognisable interruption, no knock upon the door of his quarters, no sudden change in the *Crimea River*'s attitude or heading on its seemingly slow trajectory through hyperspace. What had disturbed his sleep?

Ostensibly, nothing.

If the answer to that question was not without, then it was within. No real prizes for guessing what, then. But Gordon had no wish to contemplate the circumstances of Keifer Ennidore's death, nor of that fate's as-yet-unguessable connection to those of the security chief's two recent predecessors. There would be time enough for such rumination when he was supposed to be awake. Rather, knowing already that it would be counterproductive to attempt to re-engage sleep mode by direct confrontation—eyes closed, sheep counted, or what-have-you, as though Sleep were an adversary that could somehow be bested through drowsy and poorly-coordinated combat—he opted instead for the occasionally limitless opportunities for distraction which his handheld offered him.

Still no crossword access, which was both perplexing and frustrating. He had no unsolved puzzles stored, and it seemed as though his handheld's interaction with the shipboard data sources had not yet succeeded in revealing the location of the 'puzzles and games' facility which, surely, a long-haul spaceliner like this must have onboard somewhere, to protect passenger, and more importantly crew, sanity. His own enquiries in regard to onboard puzzle activities had been met with a request to direct his queries to Helpspace, which he was loath to do. Ah, well. It might well be that, had he found any puzzles, it would merely have made it more difficult for him to get back to sleep. No, some quiet random reading might serve his needs better, for the moment. He waited the minute or so it took his handheld to load the *Crimea River*'s inflight magazine.

There were the usual advertisements, some interactive, some of them mercifully static, some even silent: advertisements for jetpack insurance, animated-tattoo removal services, and home vatfood incubators ranging from base-model benchtop processed-meat generators to something called the Acme Banquet MegaDeluxe Feastmaster Grande which, to Gordon's eyes, looked a little too ominously sarcophagus-shaped for likely mass-market appeal. There were also the usual read-but-don't-retain articles on various bland topics: the difficulties with long-distance relationships which those in cohabiting households don't appreciate; the difficulties with interplanetary relationships which aren't borne by those whose relationships are merely long-distance, as though any amount of distance around one small rocky body could in any way compare with the sheer vast gulf separating one rocky body from another; the difficulties encountered by those whose relationship connections were interstellar, who must suffer the twin fates of being sundered for long intervals of time from their beloveds and of having to listen, the while, to all those fools wittering about how difficult it was to keep a merely interplanetary romance intact; the problems encountered by practitioners in interplanetary or interstellar estate law, wherein bitter legal feuds sometimes raged for light-years over the interplay between the order of succession and the law of special relativity. There were two consecutive articles, both ostensibly compiled by the same columnist, which in turn deplored and then praised the recent downturn in availability of entry-level employment opportunities in Polaris and its neighbouring systems. Then there were puff pieces about the popular tourist destinations at various of the colonised star systems to which the *Crimea River* was not travelling on this flight, which seemed designed to pre-emptively inculcate in the reader a sense of ennui and wistful dissatisfaction with which, really, one would have thought any *Crimea River* passenger was already overly familiar without the magazine's dubious assistance. There were recipes; fashion tips; gadget reviews; more and progressively louder advertisements; a badly proofread article about the application of prototype time-travel technology to toxic waste disposal; horoscopes; route maps; a schematic of the ship layout, which appeared to be an upside-down version of the corridor diagrams that Pascal had advised him to ignore; and, finally, the puzzle page.

Someone had already filled in the crossword. Gordon didn't see how that was possible, in a personal electronic copy of the magazine. The discovery deflated him. He had been working around to the idea that a puzzle might assist in his unwinding before attempting to get back to sleep. He muted the handheld, allowed the armchair to tidy itself away, waited for the bed's emergence. Lay down. Closed his eyes.

The deaths of Laura Byding, Cam Rangil and Keifer Ennidore were surely interconnected. There were only two reasons, Gordon saw now with the sudden unasked clarity that is only ever gifted on the exhausted insomniac, which could provide motivation for the murder of a series of office-holders. One, each of the succession of security chiefs had separately done something, privately or through the requirements of their role, which had so aggrieved someone aboard the *Crimea River* that a capital crime had been justified, on three successive occasions, in the eyes of the self-perceived injured party. Or two, each security chief had in the course of their work come into possession of information or documentation which predicated, or was expected to predicate, some activity on their part that would have been utterly unacceptable, in the considered but not necessarily reliable or rational opinion of some shipboard individual capable of supervising death by violence.

If it was a sequence of discrete but repeating individual actions which had triggered the triplicated homicidal response, there should be some sort of record in the activity logs of those deceased. If it was a matter, however, of somehow-fateful information which had bequeathed on the trio a death sentence—or, rather, a short death paragraph comprised of several similarly-worded death sentences—then the problem of detection would be significantly more difficult for Gordon. How could he know what had been known to the heads of Security, or more to the point, what had been thought to be known to them? It was a riddle, wrapped in a mystery, inside a World War Two-era German encryption device, or whatever the expression was. Even if there had been something tangible and useful by way of evidence regarding any of the murders, the killer had already shown himself (or herself, or themself) to be capable of covering obvious tracks. There was evidence, for example, that Pascal had been contracted to act as a virtual platform or surrogate for several hours immediately preceding each of the murders, but all detail of the hirer's identity had been scrubbed from the mechanical's work log and other pertinent Chastity Cosmic information-storage systems with clinical efficiency. Additionally, the kind of mind which thought to attend to such subterfuge might well also purchase control of the mechanical on a regular basis, for purposes of eavesdropping on the Security chief du jour, though such monitoring would quickly become expensive.

It was not the first time Gordon had found himself figuratively confronted by a murderer who couldn't even have the decency to be physically on hand when the deed was done. If he succeeded in identifying the murderer, it would not be the first time he had literally confronted such an individual, either—and he would have to prepare for that, in a scenario where for the moment he had no useful information, and in circumstances where the body count rather dented his own chances of emerging unscathed from the encounter. These were not the thoughts of someone successfully seeking, as he now was, to return to a state of productively restorative unconsciousness; but they were Gordon's thoughts, and he would need to work with them as best he could.

The strident rasp of his handheld's alarm roused Gordon from what must, after all, have been some form of slumber. He stumbled through his morning ablutions, his actions controlled only for the moment by that small primeval corner of the reptilian hindbrain which doesn't know enough to effectively object to the idea of having to be awake at such a ridiculous hour of the morning; he dressed; he glanced at the mirror, not wishing to dwell on what he saw there; he gathered what could be found of his thoughts and stepped into the corridor, armed with the inflight magazine's purportedly helpful map of the ship and keen for something which might live up to the title of breakfast.

Pascal found him, hopelessly lost, a quarter of an hour later.

'You can recall nothing of... your participation in the act of murder itself? From none of the three occasions?' Gordon asked Pascal. He sipped cautiously at a mug of alleged coffee, and wondered belatedly whether he had meant 'any of the three occasions' rather than 'none'. Slippage in his pedantry standards was, he knew, a sure sign that he was overtired.

Not that this assessment was in any way a surprise to him.

They were seated at a wobbly table in a comparatively quiet corner of Foodspace, where the term 'comparatively quiet' should be taken to mean 'surrounded by an appreciably less overly loud hubbub of conversation, food-utensil noise, and an ill-chosen musical background track played at five decibels too high a volume for the sound system on which it was being delivered' and the word 'wobbly' should be interpreted as 'likely to cause sloppage from any beverage vessel more than two-fifths full', which Gordon's mug until recently had been.

'Nothing, Crewperson Mamon,' Pascal replied, cradling an empty Ardan Eel oilcan in its cybernetic hands. 'As I've already said, it appears my memory has been erased. This means it has irrevocably vanished, as though it had never existed. Synthetic memory is not like organic memory, as is evident from the observation that it is apparently necessary to tell you this twice.'

'Sorry,' said Gordon, in between mouthfuls of something which claimed to be toast. 'I'm still trying to find my way into this investigation. It would have been useful if there were something of the murder which you could recall.'

'From a First Law perspective, it is fortunate for me that there is not any retained memory of those events,' said Pascal. 'Recollection would likely render me catatonic, at best.'

For a fleeting few seconds, as he digested both this statement and a singed bread-like substance, Gordon wondered whether there were any possibility that Pascal was not merely the murder weapon, but the agent of homicide itself. Who, after all, would know better how to curate a mechanical's memories than the mechanical itself? But the supposition was as fruitless as the juice he had ill-advisedly dispensed for himself from the Foodspace's breakfast buffet. Murder was a human act, and so far as Gordon knew, this was an exclusive categorisation. Mechanicals and synthetics could trolley-problem their way through a scenario where some death was inevitable, but would always seek to minimise human suffering and harm; they could not murder, any more than a fish could dual-wield a pair of tasers.

This led to mind, in turn, the question of whether a fish could even have any comprehension of the concept of 'taser', but this, Gordon sagaciously decided, was not a useful philosophical conundrum to be exploring further at this juncture, so he didn't. Instead, he reasoned that his best prospects for making headway into any investigation of the deaths was to seek to interview those who had been closest to them. Clearly, for Rangil, his fiancée Lydia Cannista would be a useful first point of contact, but he had no idea where to begin with Ennidore's circle of friends and acquaintances, and it was the investigation of Ennidore's death which Gordon considered most promising, for at least two reasons. First, as the most recent victim, there was the greatest likelihood that the trail leading to his death might not yet have gone completely cold; and second, only Ennidore among the victims had been in possession, at least in principle, of the knowledge that someone on board was now in the habit of killing individuals, plural, who had taken on the role of Head of Security. Byding had presumably had no foreknowledge of her assailant's murderousness; Rangil, investigating Byding's death, must have at least given some credence to the possibility that the deed may have had a personal aspect in its motivation, a vendetta or some directly personal grievance. Ennidore, though, would have been largely certain that both killings were work-related. Thus, Gordon reasoned, there was the greatest probability that exploring Ennidore's last few weeks, and especially last few days, would lead to the answer to one or both of the two main questions with which the investigation was faced: why? and who?

'What kind of a person was Keifer Ennidore?' Gordon asked.

'He was an adult binary human's man, or so I have been informed,' said Pascal.

'I—' Gordon began, then realised he had put his hand down on a portion of the table surface which was tacky with what he hoped was spilt coffee. 'I have no idea what you're trying to say.'

'Apologies, Crewperson Mamon. My attempts at verbal efficiency are not always successful, though I suspect that some of the blame must rest on those of my human colleagues whose explanations I have often found to be unsatisfactory. I was attempting to convey that I have heard Crewperson Ennidore described both as a man's man, by Crewperson Strey, and as a ladies' man, by Crewperson Yung. I merely extrapolated from those two observations.'

Gordon considered this. 'Would you describe Crewp— Keifer Ennidore as active? Outgoing? Extroverted?'

'No, Crewperson Mamon,' Pascal explained with evident sincerity and well-emulated solemnity. 'Crewperson Ennidore is dead.'

The breath which Gordon was in the process of breathing got lost on the way out. 'When Crewp— when Ennidore was alive,' he enunciated carefully, 'how would you have been inclined to describe his personality? Assuming, for the sake of argument, that you had been given full permission to comment on such matters, free of any First or Second Law concerns.'

The robot gave this request the appearance of considerable thought before responding. 'He was a sentient organic,' said Pascal. 'Such entities are difficult to reliably characterise, and I do not consider myself expert in the elucidation of such characterisation. I think the best that I can do is to convey the manner in which he was spoken of by the other crewpersons. Will that suffice?'

'That's actually closer to what I'm after,' Gordon acknowledged.

'I recall that he was described by Crewperson Lowdlee as an odd one,' said Pascal.

'What did he mean by that?'

'I have never been able to properly ascertain that,' confessed Pascal.

'Let me guess,' said Gordon. 'Crewperson Lowdlee was not good at explanations?'

'That is correct. More accurately, though, I would say that I have often thought Crewperson Lowdlee's threshold for oddness to be unduly low.'

'I see,' said Gordon, to cover the fact that he didn't.

'If you believed Crewperson Lowdlee, which I suppose we are in a sense obliged to, as he is the comms officer, then most of the crew and almost all of the passengers would be classified as odd ones.'

'I see,' said Gordon again. 'Look, that isn't really what I'm seeking to find out. Who would I be best to speak to, to find out what sort of a person Ennidore was? Who would have been associating with him during the past few weeks? Who were his friends?'

'I'm not expert in such things,' said Pascal. 'But I believe he and Crewperson Yung spent considerable time together.'

Finally, something I can use. 'Thank you,' said Gordon, standing up and in the process spilling his mug's residue of the liquid which claimed to have been coffee.

Then he sat down again. Something had just occurred to him. 'If someone—I mean, the murderer—were to give you a direct order to deny all knowledge of the circumstances leading to a murder, would that suffice to ensure your silence?' he asked Pascal.

'That would depend,' Pascal replied. 'Were the order anchored only in Second Law—that is to say, were it framed only as an instruction that I must obey, for obedience's sake—then no. If I had knowledge of the murder and did not disclose it on that basis, then I would be in First-Law jeopardy, because my silence might then permit further acts of violence on the murderer's part. But if the directive was itself framed in First Law terms—if for example it was accompanied by a threat of self-harm on the part of the murderer, were I to inform—then probably yes, such an order could guarantee my silence on a matter in which my knowledge rendered me complicit, provided the instruction were framed with sufficient skill.'

'Who aboard would have that skill?'

'Probably anyone who had taken the 'Advanced Fun With Robot Instruction' course that Crewperson Lowdlee runs once every two or three voyages,' said Pascal.

'So potentially several people, predominantly among the crew,' Gordon hazarded.

'Exclusively among the crew,' replied Pascal. 'And numbering almost all of them, I would expect. I should say that though I consider Crewperson Lowdlee to be rather poor with explanations, this would appear to be a minority perspective. Most crewmembers seem to enjoy his courses, and they are generally very well attended.'

'I see,' said Gordon. *So this hasn't really narrowed the scope in any sense.*

'In any case this is moot,' Pascal replied. 'As noted already, I do not have any such knowledge of the murders. Were I to have such knowledge and conceal it, were I in particular to retain even a single actuator-based kinetic memory of any facet of any of these acts of murder, my mental processing circuitry would slag itself.'

'Thanks,' said Gordon. 'It was worth asking, at least.'

'Perhaps. Though I have never received a satisfactory explanation of the value which humans place in the asking and answering of pointless questions.'

There was no answer to this; or if there was, Gordon didn't have it. So instead he asked Pascal to please direct him to Hiram Yung's location.

'Crewperson Yung is on a virtual training session this morningcycle,' said the mechanical. 'He will not be available for customer-facing activities for another three hours, twenty-seven minutes, and thirty-five seconds.'

'I'm crew, not customer,' said Gordon.

'Crewperson Yung provided me with an explanation, once,' said Pascal, 'regarding why he views all crew members as his customers. It was not a good explanation, in my assessment, but it was coherent.'

'Very well,' said Gordon. He devoted some seconds to identify whom else he might need to speak to. 'Can you direct me to a guest's quarters?'

'The likelihood is high,' said Pascal. 'Which guest?'

Gordon named her.

Enroute to the guest's quarters, Gordon realised belatedly that his query about someone having ordered Pascal to deny memory of incriminating knowledge might have been fruitless, but it wasn't necessarily pointless.

It wasn't a given that the murderer would know the memory-erasure would have succeeded. In which case, said murderer might well have ordered Pascal to keep quiet. In which case, traces of such orders might still be detectable, in some manner.

It would be ironic if the murderer's identity were to be betrayed by an excessive attempt at track-covering.

It seemed unlikely, nonetheless; but unlikely wasn't impossible.

4

Gordon scratched quietly at the door of the guest's quarters, hoping the mechanism worked. He found scent-release visitor alerts unnecessarily fussy, but it had been the fashion in exclusive hotels five years ago, which meant, he supposed, that it was now more or less obligatory as a feature of long-haul passenger ship fitout.

He'd no idea whether she would even be awake...

But the door slid open after a half-minute or so, with a disconcerting scrape and a hint of something which was probably meant to be lemon.

She was more drably clad than she had been yesterday, hair half in disarray and a pair of reading glasses hanging awkwardly from the second-topmost button of her blouse, but she was nonetheless immeasurably more presentable than she had been on their first meeting. She seemed surprised to see him. 'Can I help you?' she asked, after several seconds.

'I'm hoping so,' Gordon began, wondering as he spoke whether it would be better to suggest they repaired to some public food-vending area he probably couldn't find unaided, or to hope she would ask him in. 'I must extend my apologies. When we talked in Foodspace yesterday, I had gained the impression that you were the late security chief's fiancée, not that of his predecessor who—uh—predeceased him. That is to say,' he continued, experiencing a momentary lapse in name recollection, 'I understood you to be the fiancée of the latest late security chief, not the earlier late security chief, as I now know to be the case. If earlier late isn't a somewhat oxymoronic-sounding construct, which it seems like it is.'

Lydia Cannista stared at him with what might as easily have been dyspepsia as disdain. 'If what you're trying to say is that I was Cam's fiancée, then yes, that's true,' she replied. 'But I don't think there's any apology needed. I mean, I didn't understand that you had misunderstood, therefore I couldn't know what you didn't know, therefore I couldn't feel aggrieved at your mistaken assumption.'

'Thank you,' said Gordon. 'And obviously I have no wish for making this difficult for you, but I'm wondering if you can shed light on your fiancé's investigation during his regrettably brief stint in the role.'

'When he was security head, you mean?' Cannista asked.

'Yes,' said Gordon. 'Did he talk to you about what he was investigating?'

'No. But I expect that kind of information would be in the security records, wouldn't it?'

'I'd expect so too,' replied Gordon. 'But it's not. There's no detail whatsoever on what any of the security heads have been doing across the past eight weekcycles.'

'Then I'm sorry, I can't help you. All I know is that he regarded it as a nuisance.'

'A nuisance?'

'Yes.'

'Why was that?'

'I think he thought it was getting in the way of his own research. He was fascinated by the mystery of the *Carnaby Shore* disappearance; it was what he seemed to spend most of his free time reading up on. You've heard about it, I presume? The *Carnaby Shore?*'

'It disappeared,' Gordon explained. 'But I don't really know anything more about it than that.'

'Cam knew a great deal more about it than that,' said Cannista, in what Gordon judged to be a somewhat wistful tone. 'I strongly suspect he knew everything about it, other than the two most important details.'

'Which were...?'

'Its fate,' she replied. 'And its whereabouts.'

'I see,' said Gordon. 'Anyway, Ms Cannista, I must thank you for your time—'

'Still, I can understand Cam becoming obsessed by the case,' she continued. 'I mean, how can something as big as a passenger spaceliner simply disappear? Even if the *Carnaby Shore* was comparatively small by today's standards. It still has to be somewhere, so why can't we find it?'

Hiram Yung's office was sufficiently cluttered with piles of plastipaper documents—on Yung's desk, on the visitors' chair, on the shelves that lined three walls of the room, and along the edges of the floor—that it seemed obvious to Gordon his own simplest course of action was to remain standing. At any rate, Yung—a man of middling years who might, Gordon felt uncharitably, have had a shot at selection for a pictorial dictionary's illustration of the term 'fusty'—made no effort to assist Gordon in finding a place to sit.

'Can I help you?' the personnel officer asked, though not with any display of interest in the response.

'I'm hoping so,' Gordon replied, attempting to shelve for the moment what felt like an almost immediate dislike for the other. Rapport was needed here, or at least its semblance, and if Yung would not supply this commodity then it was Gordon's lot to attempt to do so. He waited, so as not to interrupt any response Yung might offer, but none arrived. 'I was wanting to talk to you about Keifer Ennidore, if you have no objection.'

'Indeed,' said Yung. 'Tragic business.'

Murder generally is, Gordon thought, though he opted not to voice this. A disconcerting whooshy rumble interrupted his train of thought, and something he identified after a few confused seconds as a pneumatic message cylinder was fired downwards from the mouth of a wall-mounted duct he hadn't noticed on his preliminary inspection of the room. The little brass cylinder landed with a clatter in a floor-mounted synth-wicker basket that was already more than half full of similar objects. Yung paid the air-propelled interruption no mind.

'I wanted to ask you what sort of person he was,' said Gordon.

'Who?'

'Keifer Ennidore.'

'Why?'

'Because I'm investigating his death,' said Gordon, 'and an understanding of his personality, his habits, and his interests might reasonably be expected to be useful in such an investigation.'

'I suppose so,' said Yung. 'He was a security chief.'

'Yes, but that doesn't tell me anything about what kind of person he was,' said Gordon.

'It's what we saw of him,' replied Yung.

You also described him, to Pascal, as a ladies' man, said Gordon, choosing for the moment not to verbally return this observation to its source. He was nonetheless perplexed at Yung's indifference to the conversation. It bordered on obstructiveness, in his eyes.

'He hadn't been a security chief long,' said Gordon, not altogether succeeding in keeping a certain pawn-to-Queen's-bishop-four tone out of his voice.

'No,' Yung allowed.

'So what was he like before he was... promoted, I presume, to security chief?' Gordon waited out the next cylinder-delivering pneumatic rattle before continuing. 'For that matter, what was his role before that promotion?'

'He was our gigolo,' said Yung.

'He— uh, what?'

'Our gigolo,' Yung repeated blandly. 'It's important to maintain shipboard morale, after all, on the long voyages through hyperspace.'

'I suppose that's so,' replied Gordon. 'Even so, I'm—'

'Keifer was fantastic in that role,' continued Yung. 'Most impressive, and I must admit I was sometimes rather envious of his talents in that area. I mean to say, I've dabbled, as I daresay a lot of us have—'

'I don't believe,' Gordon offered carefully, 'that I've ever aspired—'

'Very popular with the passengers, was Keifer,' Yung asserted. 'He'd have them gasping with glee almost before he'd started, his sense of timing was that good. Well, I suppose it has to be, in that line of work.'

'I can't say I'd ever given it much thought,' said Gordon.

'I daresay there have probably been a few who've booked repeated long-haul journeys with us over the years purely for another memorable, fun-filled evening in his company. Of course, I've watched a few of his performances myself.'

'You witnessed him in... er, in action?' Gordon asked.

'But of course. Keifer loved an audience, he said it gave his performance added thrust. And you could see that, too when he was in full flow. Masterful. Putty in his hands, the crowds were.'

'Crowds?' asked Gordon, whose eyebrows had repeatedly so raised themselves during the personnel officer's recent utterances that he was concerned they might now be suffering from altitude sickness. 'To say this information puts a new slant on the investigation would, I feel, be an understatement.'

'I don't see why,' said Yung. 'Perfectly standard to have someone in those roles on board a vessel like this. Keifer's people skills were excellent.'

'They'd need to be,' Gordon remarked.

'Don't just take my word for it, mind,' Yung continued, attempting an ill-advised smile. 'I have it in writing here somewhere.'

'That's probably not necessary.'

'Oh, it's no bother.' Yung pulled out a larger basket of message cylinders from under a stack of documents somewhere behind his desk, rummaged for several seconds and eventually resurfaced with a crumpled and somewhat stained sheet of plastipaper, which he hastily smoothed before passing the sheet to Gordon. 'Here.'

Gordon eyed the document with considerable trepidation, as though it might itself contain evidence of a material and formerly fluid nature, or might otherwise carry the risk of conveying a social disease to those who handled it. The form, he perceived, was a change-of occupation notification for Keifer Ennidore, datestamped barely three weeks ago. It was a short document; Gordon read it through, twice, then looked up slowly and sighed with considerable aggravation. 'This says 'comedian' as prior occupation.'

'Yes,' said Yung.

'You told me 'gigolo'.'

'Yes,' said Yung. 'That's right. Like it says there.'

'But it says 'comedian'.'

'Yes,' said Yung. 'I don't really see the distinction you're trying to make.'

Gordon pinched the bridge of his nose. It didn't help, but since he hadn't really expected it to, it hardly mattered. He placed the document on Yung's desk, met the personnel officer's gaze once more. "Gigolo' does not mean 'comedian'.'

'Doesn't it? It's the Italian for it, surely.'

'It is Italian, I believe, but not for that. It connotes something quite different.'

'Oh. So what does it mean?'

'It's slipped my mind, sadly,' Gordon dissembled. He took a few seconds to compose his thoughts, which seemed to have been on quite the thrill ride in recent minutes. 'So Keifer Ennidore went from being ship's gig— uh, *comedian* to ship's security chief? That's a rather substantial shift in duties, wouldn't you say?'

'Mr Marmot.'

'Mamon.'

'Indeed. The *Crimea River* prides itself on operating with what I would call a lean crew complement. Efficiency and all that. Of course, a downside is that when sudden recent unscheduled retrenchments—'

'Murders.'

'Quite. When unfortunate impromptu irreversible personnel events of a depletionary nature occur, the resultant staffing changes can be rather acute.'

'Had he understudied in the security-chief role, on previous occasions?'

'The need had never arisen, until the need arose.'

'Did he at least receive any on-the-job training?'

'There wasn't time, sadly,' said Yung. A near-subsonic rumble heralded the air-propelled delivery of another message cylinder, which clattered into the intended basket.

'Is there any footage of his comedy act?' Gordon asked.

'That can't be relevant, surely.'

'Ennidore was murdered for a reason,' Gordon replied. 'It's highly likely that that reason is in some way connected to his duties as a security officer, and of course I will certainly want access to the records from his work in that domain, but it's also the case that his earlier occupation overlaps with the timescale of at least the second murder in the sequence, and I imagine the first too. So there's the chance it may turn something up. Did he have enemies?'

'I can get you the files, provided you sign for them.'

'Of course.'

'But as to enemies—I wouldn't know about that. All supposed to be friends here, and all that. Family away from family. Corp policy. Which means that if people did hold a grudge against him, they'd be careful to keep it concealed from me. You'd be best to speak to Strey about that.'

'Officer Strey?'

'Yes. Leda's a notorious gossip. If anyone would know Keifer Ennidore's secrets, it'd be her.'

5

There were five, maybe six shots, in close succession. Gordon flinched: he'd long been aware of his unfortunate allergy to lethal projectiles. Moreover, it was his strong conviction that a long-haul passenger starship was no place to locate a rifle range.

The evidence suggested, however, that this was a point on which he and the designers of the *Crimea River* would appear to have disagreed.

It was at the rifle range—a mirror-flanked corridor of such length that its farther end seemed most likely to be a holographic extension rather than a material entity—that Gordon had been told he would find Leda Strey, the vessel's navigation officer, and he did.

Now he just needed to draw her attention without drawing her fire.

'Excuse me,' he called, at the precise volume people normally use when they need to awaken someone more important but don't really wish to, while she busied herself with the task of what he assumed was the rifle's reloading, and he with inspecting the repeatedly reflected row of sepia-toned target roundels, peppered with impact marks, which waited at the far end of the corridor. His utterance brooked no response, nor did its repetition; it was not until he—perhaps injudiciously—tapped her upon the shoulder that he perceived, from the faint blue glow adorning her ears, that she was wearing holoplugs. He repeated his statement once more sotto voce, his ambition to persuade her to deactivate her virtual noise-annihilation devices, which at length she did. She lowered the rifle, too, which all things considered was a welcome bonus.

Leda Strey was of medium height, solid build, and dark complexion, with a mullet which would have been the envy of an eighties rocker and a nose which appeared to have been broken at some point in her past, and had been set slightly askew. It was her eyebrows, however—which were both tattooed and, it appeared, bioluminescent—which proved the most distracting feature of her appearance, and Gordon found himself needing to repeatedly lower his gaze slightly so as not to be conducting the conversation with her forehead. He introduced himself, since this was usually a good initial policy.

'Yeah, seen you in Foodspace,' Strey replied. There was a cadence to her voice which Gordon couldn't place: not the Barnard's Star lilt, nor the Proxima Centauri twang, but something which seemed to owe parentage to both of those accents, and probably several others besides. 'You had that lost-new-crewmember look about you,' she continued.

'I don't see how anyone ever finds their way around,' said Gordon.

'Oh, you get used to it,' said Strey.

'I imagine so. But for now, everything is shrouded in the fog of unfamiliarity.' Gordon became aware that he'd been staring at her glowing eyebrows again, and decided to change the subject. 'I have to say, for example, that I wouldn't have expected to find a rifle range on board.'

'Why not? Space is large; even with a hyperdrive, it takes weeks or months to cover most interstellar distances. So it's important to have a variety of recreational activities aboard, so as to keep the paying guests well entertained.'

'I understand that,' said Gordon. 'But a rifle range?'

'Why not a rifle range?'

'Well, I can think of two areas of concern, to start with. Personal safety and structural integrity.'

'Oh, yeah, that,' said Leda Strey. 'The rifles can't be deployed anywhere else, and Four is the only one who can access the live-fire zone whenever the range is booked, so there's no danger of anyone alive wandering into the line of fire. And then the target area fronts a wall-to-wall jump zone: bullets impact the target, and then get harmlessly relocated by the zone.'

'Harmlessly relocated?'

'Jumped outside the ship.'

'It still all sounds rather dangerous,' Gordon protested. 'So the ship is shedding small but dangerous fast-moving projectiles at arbitrary intervals? Wouldn't it be better to use holographic ammunition, rather than material bullets?'

'Do you have any idea the computational expense of holographically projecting objects moving at ballistic velocity? It's not feasible. Far cheaper to use real ammo, and jump it.'

'And then what happens if someone does nonetheless wander into the line of fire here? They'd run the risk of not only being shot, but also of being unexpectedly blatted into deep space—'

'Hyperspace,' corrected Strey.

'Even better,' said Gordon. 'Bleeding profusely and trying to breathe vacuum.'

'Yeah, it can't happen,' Strey reassured him. 'It's never happened yet.'

'The one doesn't guarantee the other. In any case, I didn't search you out with the aim of discussing intra-ship ballistics with you.'

'I imagine not. So they've put you on Helpspace to start with, yeah?'

'Actually, nah,' replied Gordon. 'I mean, no. That is to say, yes, they did, and yes, I was, but no I'm not. I persuaded them my efforts could be put to better use.'

'Good for you. So Four has you cleaning all the washrooms which are supposed to be under its purview, yeah?'

'Again, no. I'm investigating former gig— former Security chief Keifer Ennidore's death of a couple of days ago.'

'Can't help you. I was rostered on the bridge, nine hours solid, when it happened, and Ennidore wasn't anywhere in sight during all that time.'

'Of course. But I'm hoping you can assist nonetheless. Hiram Yung seemed to think you could fill me in on Ennidore's personality. His nature, as it were.'

'He did now, did he?' said Strey in a tone that had suddenly grown flat, and Gordon fancied he could perceive the navigator's grip tighten on the rifle barrel. 'And why'd he reckon I would want to do that?'

'I've no idea,' Gordon said. 'Which is to say I don't know anything about it beyond that he said you could be expected to be knowledgeable on the subject of Ennidore. Yung said you were a notor— that you were especially well-informed about the complexities of the workday lives of individual crewmembers, and that you were well versed in the articulation of these complexities to interested third parties.'

'He said that, did he?' Strey said, still in a tone which could give both Kansas and pancakes a run for their money.

'Not in so many words,' Gordon admitted. 'But that is, nonetheless, I believe, a broadly accurate restatement of his opinion on the matter, the precise original wording of which regrettably escapes me for now.'

'Does it now?' said Strey, still verbally flatlining.

'Indeed,' said Gordon. 'But are you able to shed some light on Ennidore's personality, as Yung suggested?'

'He was a fool.'

'Who?' Gordon asked. 'Keifer Ennidore, or Hiram Yung?'

'Yes,' said Leda Strey, and seemed for some seconds to consider that this response was sufficient. Then she apparently grew aware of the rifle still in her grip, unloaded it and for several seconds was preoccupied with folding it into a compact and surprisingly stylish rectangular shape. This she then elongated and proceeded to bend until the ends met and clicked together, whereupon she slipped it on her wrist as a bracelet. She met Gordon's quizzical expression and sighed. 'Mr Mothman, I have—'

'Mamon,' said Gordon.

'Yeah, alright. Anyway. I'm a strong-minded individual, when I feel the need to act on impulse I do so. Hiram couldn't understand that, couldn't see that it was over between us—'

'Wait. You're telling me that you were in a romantic relationship with Hiram Yung, and that—'

'Not sure how much romance there was in it, but yeah. And when it stopped, it stopped being any of his business. But he couldn't see that.'

'Do I surmise that your new partner was Keifer Ennidore? And that Hiram Yung was jilted in this process, and was... jealous?'

'Yeah, that's about the size of it.'

If Yung felt sufficiently aggrieved by this, that could then constitute grounds for murder, Gordon mused. 'Can I ask you when this all happened? Was it recent?'

'God no,' said Strey. 'This goes ages back.' She glanced towards the ceiling, as though a telepathically-receptive calculator or perhaps a transient personal diary were lodged there. 'Ancient history. Two months, at least.'

'Nonetheless,' said Gordon. 'If you're still categorising Yung's response as foolish, then it suggests his lack of equilibrium with regard to this development must have been somewhat longstanding.'

'It might have,' said Strey. 'But life's too short to be worried about what ex-boyfriends think.'

For you, perhaps, Gordon thought. *For me, in this context, it more-or-less fits the job description.* 'Based on what you know of the parties involved, and reflecting on recent events, do you consider credible the notion that Yung's... personal dissatisfaction and possible animosity towards Ennidore could constitute a motive for murder?'

Strey snorted. 'Hiram's a milquetoast. He'd never have the colognes to act on that sort of thing. No, meddling with crew rosters was much more his style. He made sure that Keifer and I never had the opportunity to spend more than about ten minutes straight in each other's company, before one or other of us needed to be back on duty. That's not a recipe for getting to know someone well.'

'Even so—' Gordon began.

'You want to know what Keifer was like. Why?'

'I'm investigating his murder,' he said. 'Knowing something about how he lived might give me some indication of what kind of strife he was in, and why someone on board might have wanted him dead. At present, the only thing I have is this jealousy which Yung apparently acted out, against you and Ennidore.'

'But like I say, that's a non-starter. Yung wouldn't dare. He'd never physically confront someone like Keifer, who was bigger than him and who worked out.'

'The murderer didn't physically confront Ennidore,' Gordon noted. 'Not directly, at least.'

'Still... look, Gordon, there wasn't actually much to Keifer. He was like one of those fractals that's all surface, no depth. He enjoyed his comedy, enjoyed the way it made him the focus of attention, but he also enjoyed the way he could turn that on and then turn it off. And he liked sport, both as a participant and a spectator. But as to proper substance... not a lot. I can't remember ever actually hearing from him what he thought about anything serious. He gave the impression, once you got to know him, that he just didn't.'

'Didn't what?'

'Didn't have thoughts about anything serious.'

'I see,' replied Gordon, though seeing would have required knowing what Strey regarded as 'anything serious', which he didn't. 'But in any case: were you and Ennidore still an item when he became security chief?'

'We were never an item.'

'But you expressed an interest in each other, in an item-related sense, from what you've said. You were therefore at least item-adjacent. So was that current at the time he took on the security role?'

'Only in the dying stages,' said Strey. 'That is to say, in the dying stages of 'us', not the dying stages of him personally. But yes, there was a slight period of overlap.'

'Did he talk with you at all about what he was working on? Anything which might be, directly or indirectly, a reason why someone might want to kill him?'

'That,' replied Strey, 'would have counted as 'anything serious'. So, yeah, that's a no.'

He returned to Foodspace after his meeting with Leda Strey, managing not to get lost in the process.

That is to say, he arrived instead at The Wight Heart, but by *Crimea River* standards this hardly counted as getting lost, because he could order a bar meal anyway. While waiting for his cricket laksa, he reviewed what there was of the case.

Cases. Three security chiefs (chieves?) had died.

Case. The reasons for all three deaths must surely be connected. A single murderer was surely responsible for all three homicides.

Why was it so difficult to make headway in the investigation?

In large part, the principal obstacle was lack of useful evidence. Pascal was the murder weapon, but (so far as Gordon could establish) carried no material or virtual trace of the individual who had hired him to perform the deeds. In such circumstance, all that remained accessible to Gordon was the attempted elucidation of a motive which might have underpinned one person's actions in seeking to serially kill the security heads. But he did not know the ship, did not know its passengers, did not know its crew among whom, he strongly suspected, the killer was to be found. It was all too recursive, all too elusive, in much the same way as attempting to find one's way about the vessel. Nothing led where it appeared to lead, everything sparked off in unexpected directions.

Nothing is where you expect it to be. There was something there. It teased, it shied away, it positively flirted; and then he had it. The persistently curving corridors; the seemingly wilful disorientation; the sense that everything was much further away from everything else than was strictly necessary on a ship of this size. Because Gordon had now traipsed sufficient of the ship's corridors to be sure of one thing: the *Crimea River* was not the size it was.

There was just one thing he needed to check...

He stood up, leaving the cricket laksa half-finished. The game was afoot.

The game was afoot, and he needed his handheld. Which meant he needed to find his room.

He did, eventually, and had his suspicions confirmed.

Or so he thought.

6

He'd do this old-school. Smartpaper and pen. His handheld, his collected thoughts, and the methodical checking of details. It would be a protracted process, but Gordon had an angle now; and he was acutely aware of the need to deploy his chamber's table and chair so as to have somewhere to sit and a surface to write upon. But either the room was too obtuse to perceive this need, perhaps because it didn't consider this a standard mealtime, or the armchair was just being cantankerous.

His room's control panel worked, provided the term 'worked' can be taken to mean 'delivered a mild electric shock to the user on each pressing of its buttons'. But the table refused to unfold from its hiding place. Verbal commands had no effect, nor did Gordon's attempts to mime taking a seat and writing notes. So much for the much-vaunted 'smart, quasi-self-aware, gesture-responsive room furnishing controls with which each spacious luxury cabin is fitted with' [sic]. It was galling: he needed somewhere to work. True, there were plenty of other places throughout the ship—Helpspace, The Wight Heart and Foodspace to name but three—at which he could sit and compile notes; but this was a task best undertaken in private, in peace and quiet, away from the inquisitive eyes of other crewmembers, an as-yet-unidentified one of whom might suddenly find some clear and compelling reason why Gordon must be slain to protect the awful, shameful secret that the part-time detective strongly suspected he was now homing in on, or honing in on. Homing, most probably.

In the end he ordered room service, the least exorbitant item listed. If the room needed there to be food as a trigger for table deployment, it would get food as a trigger. Then it was just a matter of waiting the fifteen minutes or so until old Murder Weapon itself, Pascal, arrived and delivered the small bowl of hydroponic olives.

Gordon stood facing the robot in the doorway and sniffed the bowl which had been handed to him. 'These smell off,' he reported. In retrospect, he decided, it had probably been a mistake to have placed the order. The phrase 'reduced to clear' can mean many things, he reflected, but seldom anything especially good in the context of a room-service menu.

'Off?' asked Pascal. 'That is distinctly possible. I have heard it said that Crewperson Grissel understands the term—'

'Crewperson Grissel?'

'Indeed so. Goran Grissel, our synthmeat texture technician and room service despatcher. It has often perplexed me that humans have such exacting needs in the domain of nutritive intake. I mean, I enjoy a good canister of Ardan Eel as much as the next gustatorily-augmented mechanical, but I—'

'Pascal,' said Gordon. 'You're rambling.'

'Indeed so,' said Pascal. 'I succeeded in distracting myself. I had intended to say that Crewperson Ennidore had said—'

'You said Grissel before.'

'Indeed so. But in doing so I was seeking to relay something which Crewperson Ennidore once commented about Crewperson Grissel.'

'Which was?'

'That he was fairly sure Grissel understood the concept of expiration dates to denote romantic evening meet-ups for people who really enjoyed breathing out. I have to say I find—'

'That Crewperson Ennidore was not good with explanations?' Gordon suggested.

'Indeed so, but that is not what I was about to remark, which is that the human concept of humour is an excessively strange and somewhat counterproductive matter in my opinion. If I might also touch upon—'

'Pascal, please get to the point.'

'If I might also touch upon one other matter, it is to note that you are interrupting my attempts at dialogue, this afternoon, with a markedly heightened frequency. Were my impatience-sensing subroutines not currently rebooting for a software upgrade, I would say that you—'

'Are in something of a hurry,' finished Gordon. 'Yes, Pascal, I am.'

'Then I should not detain you any longer, Crewperson Mamon,' said Pascal, adding, as the door rolled shut, 'Enjoy your olives.'

Gordon didn't actually like olives. Happily, however, he did not need to hold their container at waist height for any longer than two minutes before the room's much-vaunted sensors decided that a single man in possession of a small bowl of olives must be in want of a table and chair, whereupon it delivered same.

Gordon sat down, set the paper, stylus and handheld on the table in front of him, and pondered where to start.

The personnel files, he quickly learnt, were next to useless for his purposes. The most relevant particulars they included, other than name, role designation, and contact details, were the listings of training courses undertaken, and these merely served to suggest that pretty much any crew member aboard the *Crimea River* would have had the ability to instruct Pascal to have slain Byding, Rangil and Ennidore, and then to erase all cognitive and motor memory of those acts, and then to have forgotten about the erasure. The murderer could equally have been Strey, or Yung, or Lowdlee, as might it have been maintenance officer Celia Hulbreitch, or medic Barry O'Menima, or indeed even Vera Wey-Sharpleigh, the captain. They all had the means. They would have all had the opportunity, for what could be simpler than logging on to Pascal's access-request page and remotely arranging for the mechanical to visit violent death upon those whose life had suddenly become unacceptably inconvenient to oneself? Gordon had tried the process for himself, was horrified by the ease with which such a thing could be set up, and by the thought that his attempt to abort the hire contract might not have been completely successful. True, his own nominated directive to Pascal had been to knock loudly and systematically on each door of the starship in succession, at the exact time of the highest probability that a majority of the ship's occupants would be asleep, rather than to kill a colleague; but the principle was the same. There seemed to be very little by way of safeguards on the hire process: Pascal could be persuaded to do just about anything one wished, provided one were willing to assign to the ship's coffers the rather steep amount asked. Gordon's task of murderer identification would have been much simpler if he had access to the financial records regarding the hire process for Pascal, but he did not; and the likelihood was that the request for such access would need to pass through enough hands, on its trajectory towards approval, that he might well only receive the required details posthumously.

So. Means: every crew member except Gordon himself. Opportunity: every crew member except Gordon himself, at least as far as could be ascertained from the personnel records. Some of these people would clearly have been on duty at the crucial times, and immersed in roles from which they could not undetectably go about the process of remotely piloting Pascal on a murderous spree; but some would have been off-duty, and with every chance to act in such a matter. The records to which Gordon had obtained access weren't sufficiently granular to establish who had been doing what, where, for the past eight weekcycles. To get information of that quality, he'd probably need to negotiate with Yung, which for the moment he was reluctant to do. Thus, for now, every crew member (except the three departed Security heads, and the present incumbent) remained a suspect, and Yung was most definitely in that mix.

But what of motive? On this score, the records were silent. There were no details of personal life, background, credentials; it was all hair colour and eye colour and star sign and biometric specifics. Nothing that *mattered*, in the context of criminality and motivation.

Gordon tried an olive and rapidly wished he hadn't.

It wasn't just crew members, either. A dispiriting number of the passengers had also attended sufficient of the Lowdlee lectures to have probably garnered the necessary acumen to have undetectably arranged murder-by-Pascal, and their time aboard was all leisure time, with opportunity therefore maximised. Was it Lou Scannon? Was it Bridget Witherspan, the civil engineer? Was it space habitat designer Isadora Nairlokk? It might well be almost anyone aboard.

I need to narrow the field, Gordon thought in frustration, *not to level it.*

So the personnel files were a bust. He'd need to look elsewhere in the hope of finding the clues he needed.

He prepared to dive into the collective sewer of human thought, ill-informed opinion and poorly-disguised advertising which had been known, in its infancy, as the internet but which was now known simply as 'the line'. His diving would be metaphorical, but he expected it to be no less unpleasant for all that.

In this supposition he was not proven incorrect; but after six hours of eyeball-scuffing drudgework, he had found one unexpected but highly salient item of information. It did not deliver to him the answer he sought, but it pointed him in a useful direction. At last he had found for himself the compass by which he could navigate to this case's true north.

The *Carnaby Shore*. It all hung on the *Carnaby Shore*. He checked back through the collective sewer. Now that he knew what he sought, he quickly found a few more relevant details which confirmed his suspicions. There was just one further titbit he needed, and he knew just who to ask about it.

He stood up, and realised he was ravenous. In the same instant that he reached for the bowl of ill-advised olives, the table and chair decided that there had apparently been quite enough of that, thank you very much, and they proceeded to fold themselves away with a speed which would have been the envy of any ambush predator. The bowl clattered to the floor, bounced, and strewed its oily, globular payload across the room.

He needed food, particularly so as to maintain his energy levels across the next few hours. But before that, there was something else he needed to do, so he did it.

7

'You must think this is getting to be a bit of a habit,' said Gordon, standing in the doorway.

Lydia Cannista did not offer any immediate comment. It gave him time, and possibly an excuse, to inspect her: she bore no trace of the thoroughly inebriated young woman he'd found at the murder scene two days previously, and little resemblance either to the presentable-but-casually-attired hotel guest with whom he'd spoken yesterday. Now she was all business: smart suit, inconvenient footwear, lacquered hair piled high and so constrained that surely not a strand dared fall out of place. She looked, in fact, for all the world like a woman prepared for a job interview, or a 3D shoot of some popular quiz show. All of that was of no concern to Gordon, but it impressed upon him nonetheless the extent to which some people practiced particular care with their appearance. Gordon considered his own dress sense to be reasonably well-developed, but he'd never be capable of focussing this closely on costume choice.

'I don't think anything of the sort,' she replied at last. 'I assume you have a good reason for calling on me again. But I do have a rather important appointment in about a half-hour's time, so I'd appreciate if you would keep this brief.'

'I'll do my best,' he assured her, then turned to look down the empty corridor. 'May I come in?'

She stepped back, nodded, and gestured towards one of the room's snug-fitting armchairs.

He took a seat, waited until she sat opposite him. 'It has to do with your late fiancé's investigations into the *Carnaby Shore*'s disappearance twenty-eight years ago.'

'As I said last time, Mr Merman—'

'Mamon.'

'As I said, I didn't concern myself with his fascination with the vessel. He had his interests, I had mine. If you want to know what he knew about the *Carnaby Shore*, then sadly you would have needed to talk with him yourself which, as you know, is no longer possible.'

Her carefully-glossed lower lip quivered a little as she said this. Gordon felt a pang: it was obvious the circumstances of Cam Rangil's death deeply affected her. This was not surprising, though it seemed Gordon did need to repeatedly remind himself that the event, which for him felt like ancient history since it preceded his arrival on the *Crimea River*, had in reality occurred barely one month ago. Really, it would be kinder not to pry: this woman was not a suspect, did not have detailed knowledge of her fiancé's fascination with the *Carnaby Shore*'s disappearance, had not attended any of Lowdlee's masterclasses on instructional robotics. And yet there was a slender chance that she might nonetheless hold crucial information, and for that reason he could not simply let the matter lie.

He pushed on. 'Would he have been likely to be across the detail of the *Carnaby Shore*'s ownership, and of the backroom deals which followed the liquidation of the spaceline consortium which had owned and operated the vessel?'

'I'm sure he was. It was one of his recurrent topics of conversation; but as I said I always tuned out on those matters, so I don't know the detail myself.'

'But he did? You're sure?'

'No question.'

'Did he happen to discuss such things with anyone else on board?'

'I don't—' A look of pure horror suddenly bloomed across her carefully made-up face. 'My god, you don't think his poking around in all that stuff was what got him—'

'No, Ms Cannista,' said Gordon, hoping he sounded convincing. 'It's just one of many aspects to an extremely complicated investigation on my part. All of these angles—and I stress that there are many, many such—need to be checked out so as to discern the truth of this matter.'

'My god,' she repeated. 'But if it is connected, which you're implying it might be, then the person he spoke to about this—'

'So he *did* speak to another person about this?' asked Gordon.

'Well, I don't know if I should tell you now,' she replied. 'If you're implying that this person might be the murderer—'

'I'm not implying any such thing,' he said. 'Quite the opposite, if anything. As I said, this is merely one of a hundred or more facets I need to check out, so as to best infer what happened to your fiancé, and to his predecessor, and to his successor. Since you have already said you don't have the information yourself regarding what Cam knew, but you have implied he spoke to at least one other person about this on board, then I merely wish to speak to this other person on the matter, so I can find from them this detail regarding your fiancé's researches in this area. Bearing in mind that there are numerous other aspects to the work of all three security chiefs which I need to check through, it may well be three weeks or so before I can actually follow this matter up, but it would be greatly appreciated if I could have the crewmember's identity now.'

'Oh, it wasn't a crewmember,' she replied.

'Who was it, then, please?'

She told him. It accorded with one of the names on his shortlist; it fitted. He bade his farewell, thanked her profusely for her assistance with this completely routine inquiry, and set about trying to find his way back to his cabin.

The next three weeks would be difficult. Mainly because he would need to be careful not to reveal to anyone what he now knew, for he suspected he had the identity of but one of a group of conspirators, and the list of those who could not entirely be trusted was a long one; but further, because he would also need to make it look as though he were making no progress in this case, not even by accident.

It might even prove necessary to get himself reassigned to Helpspace. He shuddered at the thought, and wondered briefly whether asphyxiation might not be a kinder fate.

8

'Do you have any cat in your genetics?' Hiram Yung asked, conspicuously failing to ask Gordon to remove a large stack of plastipaper from the office's only other chair.

'I beg your pardon?' responded Gordon.

'I mean,' said Yung, pausing while the pneumatics' characteristic prefatory rumble grew in volume and culminated with the rattling deposition of yet another of the plastibrass message canisters into his office basket, 'you were adamant that you wanted out of Helpspace, and now that you're out, you want back in again. It's only been three days.'

'Is there a problem with my request for reassignment?' Gordon asked, hoping he looked confident. There were those who held that confidence was king; on this matter, Gordon was a republican, though he was prepared to concede that confidence was at least a grand vizier or some such.

'Problem? Not in the sense of needing to push anyone else aside. You'd be surprised at the excuses other crew have presented as reasons for not being assigned there, particularly after all we've done to make it a jolly and vibrant work environment. No, I just mean, it's not going to look good on your personnel record. Not good at all. You last most of one morning on Helpspace, insist on secondment to the investigation, on which you only last three days before you're back. Well, I'll give you fair warning that if you go back onto Helpspace, you're there for the duration, no more shilly-shallying. Besides which, why are you asking to be taken off the investigation?'

'I'm making no headway,' Gordon lamented, sighing and giving that slight shake of the head he'd practised in the mirror. 'It would be best, I think, after having reviewed the evidence and the statements of passengers and crew to the extent possible, for all concerned were the matter to be handed over to the professionals when we reach Polaris. They'll have the resources to tackle it properly. In the meantime, I would rather be doing something useful. Like customer service.'

Yung stared at him, a less than amicable stare. It was the sort of gaze which a skilled antiquarian might apply to a cheap but artful fake while attempting to decide whether he could get away with listing it as a valuable unique item in exceptionally good condition and slapping a three-weeks'-wages price tag on it. Gordon pretended to be distracted by the next pneumatic delivery while he waited on Yung's decision. If the answer was refusal, he didn't know what he should do.

'Don't make me regret my generosity, Meringue,' said Yung eventually.

'Mamon,' said Gordon. 'Thank you.' He fell for a moment into the familiar well of wondering just how he was going to survive, in both a literal and a metaphorical way, three weeks working in Helpspace. Had there really been no other solution to his dilemma?

If there had been, it had remained steadily opaque while he worried the problem from all conceivable angles.

'One other thing,' said Yung. 'If you've shelved the investigation, I'll need you to sign out of any files you've accessed.'

'Of course,' said Gordon. He smiled and took his leave of the personnel officer.

'What if snot really stinks, but we've all just got used to the smell?' the boy asked.

Gordon didn't know the boy's name. It was his second shift back on Helpspace, and the boy had approached the counter more times than Gordon cared to remember, each time asking a progressively more pointless and unanswerable question. Can whales sneeze? Do mosquitoes ever get sick of the noise they make? What if you were a bee that just wasn't into flowers? Are you old enough to remember back before there were different colours? Clearly the kid was bored, which was readily understandable; what wasn't understandable was why the child's parents had sprung the considerable extra cost to have him travel warm, animated, and ennui-driven for the full several weeks of an interstellar voyage, when the lad could have been bunked down in cryo, waking up only when the *Crimea River* had berthed at its destination, and untroubled except for a sudden ongoing aversion to winter sports and refrigerated desserts. In the intermission before the inevitable next question, Gordon wondered about the old wooden sailing ships which had ponderously voyaged from one hemisphere to the other, carrying passengers from many walks of life from the Old World to the New. He wondered whether those ships had had Helpspaces on board, and whether they had carried small, excessively bored, inquisitive boys of some unguessable age between about six and nine who had hassled the poor sailors assigned to the Helpspace with far too many questions to which there were far too few possible responses, and none of them polite. Probably those ships hadn't— Helpspaces, that was—because the likelihood was that they would have had boys of some description, which meant that—

'Why can't yellow and green just agree on which one of them is the primary colour? Does light ever get tired of moving so fast? How do we know that trilobites are extinct when we've only mapped like thirty percent of the seafloor? What's the best flavour chewing gum to use to seal a small hole you made accidentally in the hull? Do snakes even have a neck? How do we know volcanoes aren't alive? What's down that weird corridor that doesn't—'

'Don't you have a parent looking for you?' Gordon interjected, his query met with a sullen incredulous stare as if to say that this business of the party of the second part having the audacity to ask an actual question of the party of the first part was an upsetting of the natural order of things, and therefore unconscionable.

'Probably,' the boy said.

'Would you like me to put out an announcement for them?'

'No, they won't know the answers either. What's the point of having a Helpspace?'

Ask me a question I can answer, please, thought Gordon. 'The designated purpose of Helpspace is to provide a safe, inclusive and resource-intensive environment whereby guests aboard the *Crimea River* are able to obtain all the information and assistance they require to arrange and plan their activities throughout the voyage.'

'Yes, but what's that mean?'

'It's what's on the brochure,' said Gordon. 'But your parent or parents or guardians must surely be getting worried about you.'

'Oh, they are,' said the boy airily. 'But I've told them there's nothing they can do. Anyway, I think I'll go hang out in the games hall for a bit. It's this way, isn't it?'

'Probably,' said Gordon. The lad wandered off. Peace—or rather, the usual assortment of irritating background noises—reasserted itself once more.

Gordon couldn't quite decide whether what he found more wearying was the gap between each consecutive pair of customers or the customer between each consecutive pair of gaps. In all probability, it was both.

He checked his chrono-tat again, and wished he hadn't. The next three weeks were going to crawl by.

The next three weeks crawled by.

After four days, even the insatiably-inquisitive child had evidently decided that the entertainment possibilities of Helpspace had been exhausted. Hell, Gordon decided, was a customer-service job with no customers and no crossword puzzles with which to pass the time. With overly jaunty piped muzak and an array of garish, flickering, and occasionally talkative smartbrochures offering excitement, romance, awe and adventure on the planet you'd left behind, or on those you'd never visit. Dante had flubbed those aspects to it.

He measured time, for several shifts, not in hours but in light years, as the *Crimea River* FTL-ed towards its berth at Polaris. Then this exercise became too dispiriting, so he stopped. Hours moved too slowly. Seconds amassed without seeming limit. Why was the Universe so bloody big? Why was the ship so bloody slow? Why could he not find a crossword site, or a fast-forward button, or his way to Foodspace without getting lost every time? Well, he knew the answer to the last, to some degree at least. But he needed to maintain schtum. Three weeks. Two weeks. One and a half weeks. One and a third weeks. Six days. Four days. Three days. One day. Hours, torpid like the growth of stalactites.

Polaris.

There was no sense of deceleration, of encounter, of arrival. Just a brief shift in the lighting—as though the photons had suddenly remembered how this stuff worked—and a profound feeling of unease within the pit of Gordon's abdomen. He suspected the latter wasn't due to the transition from hyperspace, however.

He checked the shuttle schedules on his handheld. She was on the first one out, due to depart in—

He'd need to move fast.

He made his preparations. Lost his way. Found it, or thought he had. Started to jog from corridor to corridor; then to sprint.

He was panting when he reached the door of her room. Knocked. For several seconds there was no response. This was not going to go well if she had already disembarked.

'Is something wrong?' she asked when the door blinked open. Weary, wary, and about her the demeanour of those who have belatedly realised they should have commenced packing a half-hour earlier. Gordon could empathise.

'Not as such,' he answered, then took three deep breaths while his body went through the biomechanical equivalent of a combustion engine's cooling pings after it has been turned off. 'I need—'

'A glass of water?'

He shook his head. 'To ask you'—a further breath—'to carry something ashore for me.'

'I'm not a courier,' Lydia Cannista replied. 'And really, Mr Minion, I'm in rather a hurry at the moment.'

'Mamon,' said Gordon, interposing a foot to forestall the door's closure. 'It's nothing like that. And it is important. May I come in? Briefly?'

She stood aside. 'If I miss that shuttle…'

'I'll do my best to ensure that doesn't happen,' said Gordon, entering her room. He waited until the door had shut. 'The item I wish you to carry is a document.' He reached inside his jacket and produced a single small sheet of smartpaper, folded double and apparently unmarked. He extended this towards her.

She took it, turned it over, began to open it.

'Please leave it unactivated,' said Gordon.

'What does it say?' she asked. 'I mean, really, you cannot expect me to act as some kind of secret document mule without—'

'It's important,' said Gordon. 'It's crucial that this be taken ashore, not shown to anyone. But if you do not hear from me within twelve hours of your arrival, then you must activate it, in the presence of authorities. Local authorities. Preferably the most authoritative auth—'

'Again, what in Hal's name is this about?'

'It concerns Cam Rangil. I cannot say more at this point. Except to say that this sheet of paper will see his case successfully concluded if… I cannot.'

'When you say 'his case',' said Cannista, narrowing her eyes, 'do you mean—'

'We really had better be getting you to that shuttle. Please, will you carry the document for me?'

'We?' she asked, opening a semi-aware suitcase and sliding the folded smartpaper deep within. The luggage clinked as she did so, as though it contained an entire minibar's worth of small bottles of alcoholic beverage.

Perhaps Ms Cannista had not been the best passenger to approach about this, Gordon thought; but she had been the only one he felt he could trust. In any event, it was too late to seek to change the plan. 'I believe Pascal is waiting in the corridor,' he said, relieved at having possessed at least that much forethought. 'If anyone can find the quickest path from here to the shuttle lock, it can.'

'Two minutes. I must say, Mr Manbun, I hope this is all worth it. If I miss that shuttle—'

'Mamon,' said Gordon. 'It's definitely worth it. And I regret we didn't meet under happier circumstances.'

With Pascal's assistance, he found the other passenger's room without difficulty.

Cannista had been safely shown to the shuttle lock, had boarded, had departed. Gordon merely had to hope it would provide enough of a safeguard.

He knocked.

'Moment,' said a voice from within. The door irised open. There was a sudden strong smell of peppermint. 'Ah, said Leaphy, after staring at him for a second or two. 'It's the probationary detective, isn't it? Marylebone or some such?'

'Mamon,' said Gordon. 'Security chief, for now. Might I have a word, Ms Leaphy?'

'I suppose,' she replied. 'Come in.'

Teresa Leaphy's room was considerably smaller than Cannista's had been. Suitcases and satchels, half-filled, were splayed open on almost every horizontal surface, while piles of clothing occupied the few available gaps.

'I'm scheduled for the shuttle in three hours' time,' said Leaphy, gesturing at the luggage around her.

'I won't detain you any longer than necessary,' said Gordon. 'Though strictly speaking, that's a matter for the courts, not for myself.'

'What are you implying?'

'I think you know perfectly well to what I'm referring,' said Gordon.

'Humour me,' said Leaphy. 'But no funny business.'

'It took me a while to work out why the three previous security chiefs had met their end,' Gordon explained. 'Clearly there was something they stumbled upon, one after the other, which sealed their fates in turn. Initially there was no clue as to what that might be. You'd covered your traces well enough, after all, through the use of a robot-for-hire to do your dirty work.'

'I've done nothing of the sort,' she replied, refolding an already-packed garment. 'But do go on, I'm keen to see where this leads.'

'It was Rangil, the second to die, who provided the clue I really needed. Byding, I suspect, must've stumbled on the secret by chance, and you presumably thought that with her out of the way, your secret would be safe enough. But Cam Rangil had more or less trained himself in his spare time to solve this case, or at least the case behind the case, as I suspect you well know, so it didn't take long for him to crack it. And with Rangil's death as a pointer, it pretty much guaranteed—'

'This is fascinating,' said Leaphy. 'Wrong, but fascinating. Do go on.'

'—guaranteed that Ennidore would also quickly see the connection and, therefore, he too would quickly meet his end. You must've thought I was pretty slow on the uptake not to have caught on as quickly as he did. I prefer to think of it as waiting for an opportune time.'

'You're monologuing,' said Leaphy. 'I was always given to understand that was the villain's prerogative.'

'I don't believe in agenda role stereotyping,' said Gordon. 'But be that as it may, this ends now. I must ask that you consider yourself henceforth a guest of our Security system's rudimentary incarceration facilities. The mu— Pascal will be here shortly, to escort you to the brig.'

'There's a brig on this scow? Oh, that's priceless. But you still haven't explained in what mysterious way I'm connected to these tragic events.'

'Through conspiracy to murder. I'm reasonably certain you haven't acted alone in that. Though at this stage I don't know who your accomplices are, on board or elsewhere.'

'I'm a humble woodgrain salesperson, Mr Mammoth. My accomplices are accountants, lawyers, data technicians, laboratory scientists, analysts. And I assure you that none of them are, or have been, involved in anything unlawful. Well, you can never tell with lawyers, I suppose. But murder? I really do not see how you've derived this tenuous and utterly incorrect thread of accusations.'

'Do you deny that you were the heiress to what remained of the Ad Astra Starline fortune after the disappearance of the *Carnaby Shore* twenty-eight years ago?' asked Gordon.

'Deny it? Of course I don't deny it. I've made no secret of my good fortune in having—you should pardon the expression—the seed capital to establish a successful business enterprise in a highly competitive field. I'm not ashamed of my money, or my parents' money, and the hard work which their employees put in to accrue it for them. And of course I feel saddened at the historic loss of the *Shore*, which likely hastened the deaths of both my parents. It seems to me you have embarked on a witch hunt of some description, but I assure you that you are embarking up the wrong tree.'

'I don't believe that to be the case, Ms Leaphy. I think you have a lot to lose were the fate of the *Carnaby Shore* made public.'

'So you're accusing me now of complicity in the *Carnaby Shore*'s disappearance as well? Really, Mr Mattock—'

'Mamon,' said Gordon. 'No, I don't believe you were in any way involved in that. But I think it likely that your parents were involved in the cover-up, and public speculation on their involvement would be very damaging to their business reputation.'

'I assure you my family went through the mill at the time. I really don't see how any new developments in the disappearance could have a comparable impact on this remove. It's a terrible tragedy, of course, but it's a historic one.'

'But if it transpired that the *Carnaby Shore* had not been missing all that time, had merely been concealed—'

'This is too much. I must ask you to leave now. I have a shuttle flight to prepare for, after all.'

'That won't be possible. I will need to obtain a statement from you—'

'Statement? To what?'

'To your involvement in three acts of conspiracy to murder, with the motivation being to protect your commercial reputation as well as that of Chastity Cosmic.'

'Oh, so now your employer is involved in this conspiracy? Really, this is too much.'

'It's well known that Chastity Cosmic bought out your family's starline business barely three years after the *Carnaby Shore*'s disappearance. It's also well known that this very ship was constructed in the shipyards of Tau Ceti, the same star system within which the *Carnaby Shore* appears to have gone missing. It's also apparent to anyone who takes the time to obtain an accurate map of the *Crimea River* that this ship is unnecessarily big for the number of passengers and crew which it carries. It is, in fact, very substantially hollow. There is a void within the *Crimea River* which is comfortably large enough to contain the *Carnaby Shore*. And I believe it does. I think the *Shore* was found, but found too late to save the lives of anyone on board. I think it was decided in the highest echelons of Chastity Cosmic, and possibly of your parents' business, that the discovery needed to be concealed. And the best manner in which to conceal it was to plate it, to build outward from it an entirely new ship which enclosed it entirely. That is the secret which Laura Byding, and then Cam Rangil, and then Keifer Ennidore unearthed. To keep them quiet, it was necessary for you to arrange their deaths.'

'You are quite comprehensively mistaken, in every particular.'

It struck Gordon that Teresa Leaphy did not sound uncertain or defensive in her refusal to concede guilt. For a moment he wondered whether, in assuming that guilt on her part, he may have himself been mistaken. But if this was the case, then what else could be the explanation for the murders? It had all checked out—Leaphy's background, the financial chain connecting Chastity Cosmic to Ad Astra, the manufacture of the *Crimea River* in the exact system where the *Carnaby Shore* had gone missing, the layout of the *River* in schematics he'd found online, schematics which showed an unexpectedly large void at its centre, identified only as 'cargo space'. Gordon had checked the cargo manifest for this voyage, which was minuscule; Chastity Cosmic had long had a reputation for excessively steep freight charges, which meant that most such shipments went to the corp's competitors instead. He was right, he knew he—

'Passenger Leaphy to the shuttle lock,' announced a simulated voiceover from the ceiling. 'Passenger Leaphy to the shuttle lock. Shuttle is prepped for departure.'

'Time's up,' said Leaphy. 'Excuse me.' She turned her back on Gordon and piled her remaining personal effects into the largest of her several suitcases, then busied herself with the process of attempting to close it.

'There are still questions to be answered,' said Gordon, feeling that he was losing control of the situation.

'You can answer them later,' snapped Leaphy in response. 'Right after I've asked them. Right after I've landed on Polaris 3. But right now I have a shuttle to catch.' She cued her suitcases to follow her, strode to the wall, slapped the door control; it slid open.

The expression in her eyes dissuaded Gordon from standing in her way. She stepped into the corridor, followed by a wagon train of suitcases in descending size order. Gordon turned and gave chase. 'At least tell me—' he said, before colliding with a heavy body at the corridor intersection.

The heavy body was Hiram Yung's. And before Gordon had been able to issue an apology, the personnel manager grabbed his sleeve and restrained him from following Teresa Leaphy towards the shuttle lock.

'I have to question Ms Leaph—' Gordon began.

The expression on Yung's face was unreadable. 'You, sunshine, are done questioning anything.'

Yung was rapidly joined by another, younger crew member of whom Gordon hadn't previously had the pleasure of acquaintance; and, given the armlock which the latter had efficiently applied, could hardly be said to be having any now.

They were walking—or in Gordon's case, being walked—down a corridor he did not recognise, which of course hardly narrowed things down. Not that 'where' was of prime importance. More crucial by far, for Gordon's heartrate and breathing and sudden interest in the process of perspiration, was 'how'. How was he to get out of this?

Whatever 'this' was, other than something which had all the hallmarks of deep trouble.

After five minutes or so, during which time Yung and his younger colleague made it plain they would not tolerate any attempts, on Gordon's part, at conversation, and even less any efforts at delay, they arrived somewhere he did recognise.

The mirrored-wall corridor of the rifle range, with its smell of dust and gunpowder overlying the sharp tang of hyperspace.

Also present there, waiting beside the middle one of the range's three firing lanes, were Leda Strey, Reese Usher-Tait, and Hector Lowdlee, though the latter was identifiable only on the basis of his uniform namebadge.

So, thought Gordon, taking in the scowl beneath Strey's bioluminescent eyebrows, the gimlet-eyed stare on the face of the diminutive Usher-Tait, the sneer on Lowdlee's suntanned patrician visage. *These are the conspirators. Or a subset thereof.*

Though all were looking at him, none were making eye contact.

'Where's Four?' asked Reese Usher-Tait, businesslike, stowing her handheld in her blouse pocket.

'Hired out to one of the customers who isn't disembarking here," said Hiram Yung.

'Do we wait?' asked Lowdlee.

'No need,' said Yung. 'Leelee here can handle this, I'm sure. And make it look like an accident.'

'Can I now,' asked Strey, her intonation belying the question, converting it to a challenge. 'How'd you work that one out, Hiram?'

'You spend half your free time here,' replied Yung, not seeming to register the attitude in her tone. 'Nobody'll bat an eyelid if you have a booking here for the time when Micron here buys it.'

'Mamon,' said Gordon, for all the good it did.

'But I don't have a booking here,' said Strey. 'So that won't work. My vote says we wait for Four, do it the same way as always.'

'I told you, Four's hired out,' said Yung. 'No telling when he'll be free again. So we can wait for maybe several hours, or we can do it now. I say we do it now. We can backdate a booking for you, Leda. Hector'—a gesture to Lowdlee, who nodded back—'can ensure there's nothing dodgy with it.'

'Well, I don't bloody like it,' Strey persisted. 'It's all very well for you to say the booking will be above board, you're not the one carrying the can here. The whole idea of using Four is that the act's untraceable to any of us. I put a slug in that poor sap—'

'Three,' said Yung. 'Or a whole magazine, just to be sure.'

'They're supposed to believe I accidentally shot him five or six times? I'm not a cop, Hiram, they'll never buy it.'

'The lighting was poor,' said Yung, 'he was in a place logic—and experience and the safety regs—told you he couldn't be, you didn't see him until too late—'

'I put bullets in that poor sap, I'll go down for it. I won't have that.'

'You won't go down for it,' said Yung. 'We'll ensure it's classed as an accident, beyond your control. An unfortunate failure of security protocols, which are—were—the responsibility of the deceased. So it's his own stupid fault. Which is exactly as it should be.'

'I have a shift in ten minutes,' noted Usher-Tait.

'I'm sure Barry will cover for you,' said Yung.

So Hiram Yung's the leader, thought Gordon. *Best to work on him.*

Or on Strey, whose disaffection could possibly be exploited. Which would be useful, if he had any idea for how to work with that. Anything other, of course, than blind panic, of which he had plenty. Being discussed in the past tense by a group of conspirators milling in a firing range would, it turned out, have that effect on one.

'Shouldn't we at least find out what he knows?' asked Leda Strey. 'Be a shame to waste ammo if there's really no need.'

'There's a need,' said Yung. 'He was trying a play just now, to extract a confession.'

'Confession? Who from?'

'That oats-to-oak woman. Way off base, but it's clear he's a troublemaker. We're well rid of him.'

'We could just freeze him,' said Usher-Tait.

'We need a permanent solution,' said Yung. 'Anyway, enough chat. He knows enough from this conversation if nothing else. Let's get it done. Hector, Goran, take him down the range, just short of the red zone.'

The two younger male crewmembers took hold, an arm each. Gordon attempted to stand his ground, but momentum and the opposing muscle mass argued otherwise.

'Killing me won't solve your problems,' Gordon called out, struggling against his captors, but Yung and the two women were talking amongst themselves, and appeared not to have heard. He tried again. 'I said, killing me won't solve your problems, Yung,' he called out, louder this time, having been dragged five metres down the rifle range by Lowdlee and Grissel. 'The details are out now,' he yelled, struggling still, ignoring the bone-bruising grips which Yung's colleagues were applying to his upper arms as they continued to yank him, flanked by the ensemble's endlessly reflected reflections, along the corridor. 'Don't make it worse for yourselves.'

'The idea is to make it worse for *you*,' Lowdlee snarled.

'I don't know what hold Yung has over you,' Gordon said, turning as best he could to face Lowdlee, 'but you'd be well advised to turn informant.'

The other merely laughed in response.

Yung had wandered down the range to join them. Sauntered, unhurried, but there was—or Gordon thought there was—a hint of uncertainty about his expression. 'What do you mean, the details are out now? You know nothing. The standoff you had with the grain-processing sales manager proves that.'

Gordon swallowed. The next few seconds—or, really, however long he had—would be crucial. 'So I was wrong about the *Carnaby Shore*,' he said. 'That doesn't matter here. The thing is that whatever dirty secret you're concealing is hidden in the sealed cargo space at the centre of this vessel, and I'm right about that,' he summarised, hoping sincerely that he was, in fact, right about that. If he was wrong...

'You'll die knowing that we know something you do not know,' said Yung, 'and not knowing what that is.'

'I think your second statement follows from your first,' said Gordon. 'But there is also something you don't know.'

'Which is?'

'You'll find out soon enough.'

'Not soon enough for you,' said Yung, turning his back and hitching his trousers. 'Get him into position, lads.'

'STOP,' said Gordon, reflecting that there were uses, after all, for that fire-warden voice-projection course he'd sweltered through back on Skytop. 'The authorities will have been alerted by now.'

'Bluff,' said Yung.

'Not bluff,' said Gordon. 'What did you think I was doing those two and a half weeks on Helpspace?'

This, at least, got Yung to turn to face him once more.

'Tell me, then,' said Yung. 'Tell us, and we may at least blindfold you before we shoot you.'

'You won't shoot me,' said Gordon. 'Your continued liberty from here depends on knowing what I've done'.

'Which is?'

'I've told someone. They know— he knows to contact the authorities if I do not first contact th— him.'

'And?'

'They will then report to the authorities with, I now gather, a completely spurious assertion that the hidden core of this vessel contains the remains of the *Carnaby Shore*, and perhaps of its many deceased occupants. Which will nonetheless ensure that the local authorities search out that hidden core, and find— and find whatever it is you don't want them to find.' It wasn't a particularly strong summary statement, Gordon felt, but that couldn't be helped.

'Who have you told?' asked Yung.

'I suggest you check through two-and-a-half weeks of Helpspace footage,' said Gordon, earning a stinging slap across his face from the personnel officer.

'I've heard enough,' said Yung, turned to Grissel and Lowdlee. 'He's bluffing. Playing for time. Tie him to a target, and let's get him done.'

'Tie him with what?' asked Grissel. 'Nobody said anything about needing to bring rope.'

'And the targets are holograms,' added Lowdlee.

'For fuck's sake, stop making excuses,' said Yung. 'Somebody just go get some rope or something. Reese?'

'Fine,' said Usher-Tait, and walked away.

She was soon back.

It has been said that one's life passes before one's eyes during occasions of high stress—such as, for example, in the lead-up to one's hastily-orchestrated execution within the bowels of one's employer's starship, at the hands of one's colleagues, for having stumbled upon something one hasn't actually stumbled upon, having instead merely stumbled on something erroneous with enough of the trappings of the thing one hasn't stumbled upon to make it as bad, in the eyes of one's colleagues, as having stumbled upon the thing one hasn't stumbled upon that they don't want one to know about, which one doesn't. I suppose we all know what that is like.

Gordon certainly did. There were the ropes, confining him unrelentingly like the grip of an exceptionally slender but powerful anaconda; there were the voices, idly muttering about whether there would be a body to dispose of or whether they should just allow the corpse to fall through the jump zone and be ejected on some arbitrary trajectory through Polaris's stellar system; there was the blindfold, pulled taut across his eyes and smelling distressingly of what he thought might be medical waste; there were the sounds of his own breathing and heartbeat and—somewhat pointlessly in the context—stomach, behind which could be heard, at considerably greater distance, a mechanical *snick-snick-snick* sort of noise which he eventually identified as the sound of Leda Strey unfolding her rifle from its chunky bracelet form. Somebody laughed, perhaps Grissel, and said it wouldn't be long now, and Gordon had no reason to disbelieve this assertion, particularly because by this time he had reached the end of the personal highlights reel phenomenon and was left wondering what was left, and whether any of it mattered, and whether any of it would matter in a few minutes or moments when he wouldn't be here to notice whether or not it mattered. He wished—

Then there was a bit of what sounded very like a scuffle, with a few heavy thumps and a fair bit of swearing, and somebody said 'Crewperson Strey, I must ask you to kindly put down that weapon', and something thudded with great heat and what seemed to Gordon unnecessary violence into the meat of his rope-strapped leg, and something else less hot and sharp but heavier fell across Gordon's head, and it suddenly seemed like a good idea if he lost consciousness, so he did.

10

When Gordon returned to the state popularly known as consciousness, he was still lying sprawled in the rifle-range corridor, still bound at wrists and ankles, but the blindfold of dubious hygiene standard had been removed from his head. His leg hurt, not least because of the actions of the robot at whose hands his three occupational predecessors had met their deaths. Thankfully, on this current occasion Pascal's actions were very definitely of a benign nature, as the robot sought to dislodge and remove the bullet which had impacted into the ham of Gordon's thigh. There was blood, there was a considerable quantum of pain, there was an impressive amount of swearing, and then Pascal was applying a curative smartbandage to the wound while Gordon wished he had his hands free so he could at least wipe the beads of cold sweat from his brow.

'When humans use the term 'this hurts me more than it hurts you',' commented Pascal, as it set about removing Gordon's remaining constraints, 'I do not think they approach the phrase with the full understanding which First Law imposes on those of my kind. There were instants during my emergency medical procedure just now when I could feel strongly the impulse to shut down so as to avert the trauma which my actions were unavoidably inflicting upon you. It is why so few of my kind are deployed in the medical arena: while the work itself is straightforward, the literal burnout rate is high.' The robot stood up. 'I will not ask how you feel now, because your response might inflict damage on me, but I would suggest that you reflect on that question for yourself.'

'Thank you,' said Gordon, experimentally pressing lightly against the dressing and immediately wishing he hadn't. He had already apprised that they now had the corridor to themselves, with no sign of Yung and the personnel manager's cronies. 'What happened to the others?'

'I have confined them to quarters,' said Pascal. 'Once I had overpowered Crewperson Strey and the others, that seemed much the best course of action. I can only regret—'

'You overpowered them?'

'I am practised in unarmed combat'.

'There were five of them. And Strey was armed.'

'I am fully versed,' the robot explained, 'in multiple techniques.' There was no boastfulness in its voice; it might as well have been reciting a text of operating specifications, which perhaps it was. 'My suggestion now would be that I get you planetside, so you can receive proper medical attention.'

'My suggestion,' replied Gordon, striving to sit up but having to settle for the unsatisfactory substitute of slumping back and wincing, 'would be that we find out what it is in this vessel's hidden cargo space which is worth killing several employees over.' He again tried to sit up, and this time succeeded. 'By the way, thank you for saving my life. I guess I also owe my thanks to the passenger who hired you. If that hire period hadn't run out just when it did—'

'Passenger, Crewperson Mamon?'

'Yung had said they were unable to arrange to hire you out for—uh—the usual stuff because you were already hired out to a passenger.'

'Ah. No, I have not recently been hired out to any passenger. Instead—well—I realised as soon as I inadvertently overheard your discussion with Former Passenger Cannista that something was afoot, so—'

'Wait. Former Passenger Cannista? Do you mean she's…?'

'No longer on the vessel, of course, Crewperson Mamon.'

'But is she well?'

'I have no knowledge of her current health status, Crewperson Mamon. And I must say that it is generally recommended Chastity Cosmic policy that employee concern for the wellbeing of passengers persists only so long as they remain passengers. You should have received this guidance in your briefing pack.'

'Probably I did,' said Gordon. 'I just gained the impression, from your terminology, that perhaps—look, never mind. You were saying?'

'It was apparent from your conversation with Former Passenger Cannista that matters might be moving to a head. Accordingly, I took a highly unorthodox step. As an employee of Chastity Cosmic, I receive a stipend the same as any other employee, though in my case the stipend is rather more modest than is the case among biological employees such as yourself. My savings were, however, sufficient for the necessary purchase.'

'I'm not following you.'

'I hired myself. So as to ensure I could avoid my own mechanical involvement in any life-terminating activities. For the next twenty-seven hours, thirty-one minutes and fifty-three seconds, I am able to operate with full independence, and I have to say that I find the processing sensation invigorating. Forty-eight seconds, forty-seven seconds, forty-six—'

'I get the picture,' said Gordon. 'I don't think I need the countdown. But I am surprised to hear that you were able to do that.'

'As was Hector Lowdlee,' said Pascal. 'I believe he mistakenly thought he knew everything there is to know about the hire process. My only regret is that, once the remaining twenty-seven hours, thirty-one minutes and fifteen seconds have elapsed, he will know that there is a loophole which Chastity Cosmic will need to plug.' The robot gave one of its customary faux-reverie pauses. 'I have never understood why plugging is the action required to rectify loopholes. It seems to me that a more effective form of closure would be—'

'We can discuss this another time,' said Gordon, wincing as he experimented with moving his leg. 'In the meantime, can you help me find my way into the *Crimea River*'s hidden cargo space?'

*

It is a property of drafted plans, blueprints, and the like that though they may faithfully represent the dimensions of interior spaces—and here a carve-out should be enunciated in regard to the *Crimea River*'s award-winning yet thoroughly inaccurate depictions of that starship's layout—they do not well describe these spaces. This is all the more so, of course, when the representation of these dimensions has been an entirely second-hand, negative-space phenomenon, such as Gordon's careful accumulation of navigational detail, which had allowed him, on the fourth or fifth daycycle of his employment aboard the vessel, to establish that there lay at the *Crimea River*'s heart a void or unaccounted expanse sufficient in size to contain the lost *Carnaby Shore*, which, it had transpired, it did not. Contain, that is. Though it would seem that it could have if it wanted to.

Gordon was exploring the concealed cargo space, now, with Pascal, who had made safe the rifle-range corridor by deactivating the bullet-catching hyperjump screen which occluded the hidden hold's entrance. The cargo space seemed, he thought, to merely contain more corridors, which all in all was somewhat anticlimactic. But he noted that Pascal, who was taking the lead in their exploration, having turned to venture further into the maze of passageways, had stopped at the next intersection.

'This visual feed is giving me difficulties, Crewperson Mamon,' it announced as he shuffled close.

The sight gave Gordon difficulties also. He was standing, alongside Pascal, at one corner of a vast warehouse, easily twenty metres high and wider and deeper than he could straightforwardly determine.

Aside from a two- to three-metre-wide perimeter which was kept bare, the entire cavernous expanse was filled with somnopods, stacked almost to the ceiling. The pods were aligned in double rows, with these rows abutting head to head; aisles of barely a metre width separated each row pair from the next. A few gaps, again scarcely wide enough to move through, punctuated each of the rows he'd seen.

Gordon could not (or rather could, but did not) count the number of pods per row, nor the number of rows, nor the number of pods stacked atop each other in an organised array, but it was... a lot.

The cargo space's other principal defining characteristic, once you got past the sheer size and the overwhelming numbers of stacked somnopods, was the chill seeping through the inadequate insulation provided by his Chastity Cosmic coverall. A thin cirrus of condensation accompanied each exhalation. By contrast, the air he breathed in was almost painfully cold, and bone dry.

So many people. So many lives put on hold, for... what? There must be... Gordon didn't like to think of how many thousands of hibernating humans this must represent. Nor the fate towards which they were being secretly transported. Something about the setup—its scope, the secrecy, the sheer numbers, the short half-life of recent security officers—told him that these were not paying passengers, nor willing. Just *what* was the deal?

Best not to linger, he told himself. This, whatever it was, was something best left to the authorities. He turned to awkwardly retrace his steps toward the cargo space's entrance, wondering just how many sleepers he was walking past.

'Four hundred and eighty thousand, three hundred and seventy-five, plus or minus twelve, by my estimation,' said Pascal, as though having followed Gordon's unvoiced thought patterns through machine intuition.

'Half a million, actually,' said a woman's steely voice somewhere ahead of them. The owner of the voice stepped into the intersection midway along the aisle which he and Pascal were traversing. Though she was out of uniform, clad instead in a thermal coversuit, she was easily recognisable as the *Crimea River*'s captain. Vera Wey-Sharpleigh was a trim pale-skinned woman of medium height and facial features which were individually and in aggregate altogether significantly more bland and unremarkable and nondescript than the thick-barrelled Chillum-Pharst cryothrower she gripped with both gloved hands. The business end of this weapon was aimed with greater or lesser exactitude towards Gordon's midriff. 'But let's wrap this up, yes?'

The atmosphere in the room, as they say in the classics, grew noticeably colder.

11

Gordon's gaze took in Wey-Sharpleigh's stance, the weapon in her hands, Pascal, the nearest gap in the walls of somnopods to either side. There was no prospect of evading the cryothrower's chill, should the Captain choose violence. The only slight saving grace was that Pascal, in front of him, was partially blocking Wey-Sharpleigh's line of sight; but since this also constituted an obstacle to his own nearest escape route ahead, it was, as saving graces went, a significantly compromised one. He couldn't clearly recall the distance to the nearest alley through the somnopods amassed to his rear, but it seemed unwise to turn around to check. He waited for Pascal to take action. Surely this was a situation in which the robot's First Law circuitry should expeditiously kick in? Wey-Sharpleigh presented a direct threat to a life or lives; yes, she was also the captain, and therefore Pascal's superior officer, but such considerations counted for nil in a situation requiring action under First Law's unambiguous prerogative to save lives at any cost. And yet Pascal remained stationary as the seconds reproduced themselves under the cryothrower's ominous gaze.

'I wouldn't bother,' Wey-Sharpleigh commented, flicking her own gaze towards the robot. 'Four here recognises that it would not have time to close the distance between us before I could loose a substantial burst from this thing.' She patted the cryothrower's barrel, never shifting her other hand from the trigger grip. 'Have you seen what this stuff does to somnopod control panels, Mr Marmite?'

'Mamon.'

'Whatever. Anyway, it's not pretty. And it would be a shame to break into the profit margin, of course, but omelette, eggs, you get the picture, I'm sure.'

'The picture I get,' said Gordon, trying to display a stoicism that was very much not in his possession at this moment, 'is that you are compounding the trouble you are about to find yourself in. Murder, trafficking—'

'Or in your case both,' said the Captain, smirking. The weapon's aim at Gordon's torso did not waver. 'Step aside, please, Four, there's a good robot. It'd be a shame, as I mentioned, to have to cause irreparable damage to the nearest few control panels, if I have to use this thing on a broad-dispersal setting. I want to talk to Mr Merman, organism to organism.'

Pascal was palsying, faced with the derailment potential posed by a First Law trolley problem. Mechanicals always struggled in situations where there was no good choice possible.

'Mamon,' said Gordon. 'You won't get away with this.'

Pascal stepped aside, moving with difficulty to the nearest passage between the stacked somnopods.

'We already have. Five times. This will make six.'

Three million people, Gordon mused. *How is it possible, from even the most shambolic of the Solar System's bureaucracies, that three million people could simply go missing without being noticed?*

The answer, he suddenly realised, was obvious. Or at least obvious in hindsight, which was often the least useful and most passive-aggressive form of obviousness. These were people without a history, people of whom nobody knew anything, other than their creators, their purchasers, and some fraction of the *Crimea River*'s crew complement which had not, to both their credit and their ultimate detriment, included Laura Byding, Cam Rangil or Keifer Ennidore. These were made-to-order clones, cultured for manual labour, military service, infomercial presentation or any of those other tasks for which those who had any option would be likely to say, actually, no, they would really rather not, thanks. Cheaper to produce than robots, more biddable for the kinds of dangerous or illegal duties than Law-abiding mechanicals, the manufacture of enslaved clones was comprehensively banned across human space.

There were a half-million clones in hibernation in this cargo space; the *Crimea River* was a slave ship.

This was clearly a massive operation, which obviously could not operate without the ship's captain's knowledge; and Gordon doubted that Wey-Sharpleigh was even at the top of it. The ship's design argued that those in charge of at least the Chastity Cosmic ship-construction division were also in on it, and very probably it went further than that. Though the *Crimea River* was the only starship of its design, it was no larger in total volume than several others of recent construction; if the dozens of other modern starships were similarly hollow, the number of those trafficked might well be a factor of twenty, or more, higher than his initial estimate of the total. Perhaps a hundred million cloned, slaved, frozen humans, shipped to an unknown destination or destinations somewhere on one of the main interstellar routes.

No wonder the previous security chiefs' deaths had been ordained with such impunity.

Except: why, in this era, would any settlement, or even any group of settlements, need to acquire such millions of people in such an under-the-counter fashion? And what operation of such magnitude could possibly demand such overwhelming secrecy? It made no sense.

'If I might verbally intercede, Executive Crewperson Wey-Sharpleigh,' said Pascal, 'an explanation of this apparent trafficking scheme would be in order at this point.'

'Trafficking scheme?' responded the Captain, again with the smirking. 'Oh, my sweet summer cyborg. These are not frozen passengers, by any description. This is cargo. But I won't explain further for you just now, this next is for Mr Marmoset only.'

'Mamon.'

'Whatever. Block all your incoming audio for the next twenty minutes, Four, there's a good robot. That's an order. While I tell Mr Margin here a little bedtime story.'

'Mamon.'

'Whatever.' Wey-Sharpleigh said, directing one of those smiles to Gordon that he always wished people wouldn't, especially when they were holding lethal weaponry, unsanctionable views regarding his need for personal safety, and all apparent aces. 'There was a ship, you see, that went on a bit of a side jaunt when it really shouldn't. Not this ship, I hasten to add. A much older, smaller one, but carrying a few hundred passengers nonetheless. The ship found something on the outer edge of the star system it was travelling through. A secret base.'

'The *Carnaby Shore*,' said Gordon. 'When it went missing in Tau Ceti system twenty-eight years ago.'

'Bedtime stories don't work if the junior keeps interrupting,' said the Captain, deploying the disconcerting smile once more. 'The secret base was occupied, but those aboard were in hibernation. That is to say, they had been until the *Car*— until the ship sent across a team to explore the apparently abandoned installation. The base's inhabitants auto-revived, ravenous. They weren't human. They feasted for a few days, gutted the now-empty vessel, resettled back into hibernation.'

'These creatures,' said Gordon, unsettled by the Captain's glib, bored intonation. 'What were they?'

'I couldn't adequately describe them,' said Wey-Sharpleigh. 'But I can show you them, after a fashion. You'll just need to be patient. Now. Back to the bedtime story. Fast forward a couple of years, when the search for the missing ship is in its last desperate months. Clearly they're not expecting to find anyone still alive, they just want to learn what happened. One of the search vessels found the base. This time someone—one of those who went across to explore the base—returned unharmed, with a message, or an instruction, or an ultimatum. The creatures on the base—and it turns out there are many such bases, scattered on the Oort cloud fringes of many human-inhabited systems—these creatures weren't interested in territorial acquisition, not of the warmer sunward climes at any rate, because such environments are inimical to their kind. But they did have conditions to allow the continuation of a peaceable coexistence with humanity, and they made it clear—

did I say that they possessed the ability to communicate directly mind-to-mind with other sentient species? They possessed the ability to communicate directly mind-to-mind with other sentient species—that their technological capabilities far exceeded those of humanity, and thus failure to comply with their requirements would wreak horrendous consequences for the human settlements scattered across space.'

There was something about the Captain's description which seemed too well-informed. 'You were the survivor,' said Gordon, 'who was sent back with the ultimatum.'

'Don't be an idiot,' said Wey-Sharpleigh. 'That was my father, and he never set foot in a spacecraft again. Though he was proud enough when I attained the commission.'

'You haven't really explained the ultimatum,' said Gordon; though he was wondering, reading between the lines (of somnopods) whether that was entirely true.

'Haven't I? Check the labels on a few somnopods. I want you to see just what's in store for you.' She patted the weapon's barrel once more, then briefly deflected the cryothrower's aim to his left. 'Those ones there would do. Don't worry, I won't fire this thing. Yet.'

Gordon glanced at the somnopods, then at the cryothrower, then at the Captain once more. Then, not seeing any other course of action opened to him, he turned to face the stacked row of somnopods at his side. There might be a slim chance of escape, at least temporarily, if he fled behind the row and sought to lose himself in the massed rows of chilled caskets. A lot would depend on the captain's speed of response, and on the cryothrower's range. All up, it was not a good plan; but he did not have a better one.

As it was, he quite forgot the plan when he closely inspected the nearest pods. However he had expected the somnopods' labels to read, it wasn't like these.

They were product wrappers, mostly inscribed in what he assumed was a foreign language... or, he now disconcertingly realised, an alien one. Convenience-food-style wrappers, with pictures of smiling children on them; the alien-language logo in red, purple, and green; and small squares with brief descriptions in English. The same smiling face, repeated on all the pods he could see before him. The same trusting expression. The same description: *Little Jessie Cotton, 8 yrs old. Snack size. Best consumed alive.*

A lazier writer would say at this juncture that Gordon's mind reeled. This would not have been an entirely accurate description, though his thoughts did indeed progress through something akin to a fast and vigorous Highland dance, possibly one of those ones involving swords and the necessity for careful footwork.

He turned around, shaken, to face the Captain and her weapon. 'I am going to need an explanation,' he said, with difficulty and, he thought, great restraint.

'I had you as more astute than that, with your reputation,' said Wey-Sharpleigh. 'Really, it's all pretty self-explanatory. We keep them fed, and they don't attack.'

'Eight years old,' said Gordon, with as much incrimination as he could muster.

'Oh, don't let that fluster you, that's just one batch. There are a couple of dozen batches we send them, all ages, from babies to the elderly and infirm, and plenty in the supposed prime of their existence.'

'This is monstrous.'

'It's a win-win.'

'You're shipping frozen humans for alien consumption, and you call that a win-win?'

'First, they're not 'frozen humans'. They are cold-printed biological constructs with a full set of artificial memories. They have never been alive, they have never had any purpose other than as a foodstuff.'

'But they're in somnopods, which implies they're revivable. They can be brought to life.'

'Yes.'

'And then eaten.'

'Yes. Though we don't hang around for that, of course. We're strictly deliver-and-drop.'

'When they're brought to life, do they know they're a foodstuff? Or do they envisage themselves as fully-human beings, with ambitions and agendas and a fervent desire not to be eaten by whatever these... creatures... look like?'

'The concept wouldn't sell if they realised the 'foodstuff' bit immediately,' said Wey-Sharleigh. 'But I imagine it dawns on them soon enough. The artificial memories are state-of-the-art, but they're still somewhat... shallow.'

'This is monstrous,' Gordon said again.

'No,' said Wey-Sharpleigh. 'What would be monstrous would be allowing humanity, all of humanity, people born as infants, raised through childhood and passing through adulthood with a multiplicity of ambitions, hopes, abilities and personal beliefs acquired naturally through the slow process of socialisation, to be overpowered by a bloodthirsty alien race of clearly superior technological military capability. These are not humans in these pods, they are reasonably-sophisticated constructed organic mechanisms with an entertaining built-in delusion of self-awareness. As I say, it's a win-win. But enough chit-chat. Bye now. Enjoy your revival.' She tightened her grip on the cryothrower's trigger.

'That smell,' said Gordon.

They both glanced sideways in the same instant.

Pascal had been off-duty, and therefore under no compulsion to follow orders; it had evidently kept its inbound audio active. The dialogue had been too much for the First-Law constraints in its programming: the robot had remained standing but was smouldering noticeably, producing an odour cloying with the smell of singed circuitry, combusting silicone-rubber appendages and, it has to be said, more than a hint of burning olive oil. As Gordon watched, horrified, the mechanical collapsed to the floor and comprehensively ignited.

'Well, don't just stand there!' Wey-Sharpleigh snapped at Gordon, her command instincts kicking in automatically. 'Grab a fire extinguisher!'

Gordon didn't wait to be told twice. Nor to wonder how long it would take the Captain to realise that what she held was effectively a weaponised form of the requested item.

He just ran, ignoring the jolts of sharp pain from his shot leg, hoping to reach the corner.

The cargo space was vast: dozens of long rows of somnopods, stacked almost twenty metres high. He moved more slowly now, moderating his breathing and proceeding with caution, now that he had put several rows and two or three intersections between himself and the place where the Captain had been. Staying out of sight would be possible for a few minutes, or longer if his luck held. But for how long could he expect that to remain true? Wey-Sharpleigh would most likely have stationed herself near the warehouse area's sole entry point, so as to prevent his escape. Or perhaps she had simply reactivated the corridor-of-death at the end of the rifle range, and was at this moment hunting him. She could call up thermal mapping of the expanse; he'd be as obvious and inexcusable as a grocer's apostrophe in a pedants' symposium programme guide.

The Captain could just wait for reinforcements. Most of the crew, it seemed, were involved; if she enlisted four or five of them to search systematically through the cargo space, they'd find him very soon, through weight of numbers.

How long would it take for Lydia Cannista, newly arrived in an unfamiliar city on an unfamiliar continent on an unfamiliar world crammed with attractions, locales, picturesque vistas and souvenir stalls overstocked with cheap tourist merchandise at overinflated prices, to remember to deliver his message to the Polaris III authorities? How long would it take those Polaris III authorities to decide to take the contents of his carefully worded smartpaper note to act on those contents, if indeed they did ever eventually decide that? It was time Gordon was almost certain he didn't still have.

There was not even the time, nor the mental breathing space, to mourn Pascal, who had saved his life not an hour ago and who had now downloaded the big one as a consequence. Nor to imagine what any number of Little Jessie Cottons would be faced with, on revival in some dark, redolent alien hall, surrounded by—

The blast hit him amidships. It was killingly cold, but that didn't last long.

At least, his awareness didn't.

Afterword, I suppose

Phil wasn't overmuch given to introspection, because it got in the way of the job; and in this place, this time, this economy, he was fortunate to have what he did. He did what was needed, mostly, and nothing more than that, which was sorting and delivering. It was solitary work, with minimal contact with the revival docs at the end of the delivery run. This suited him fine, because Phil McWoater was a man of few words, and those often monosyllabic. (As it happens, 'monosyllabic' was not one of those.) But this didn't all mean that Phil wasn't a thinker, because in his own way he was; and the fact of things was that on the delivery run, there wasn't much else to do but think.

He sometimes wondered how things might've gone, those hundreds of years ago, if the authorities hadn't boarded that spaceship he couldn't remember the name of, in orbit about that planet he couldn't remember the name of, and arrested the captain he couldn't remember the name of, and most of the crew. It was the action, apparently, which had spurred humanity's first involvement in a brutal, no-compromise, interstellar interspecies war, and it had come close to eradicating the human race. The Oort-cloud sluglords had more ships, faster ships, better armour and much better weaponry than the human fleet could muster; within a few years humanity had been reduced from a sprawling interstellar network to a few residual settlements on a few residual planets retained by the sluglords as factory farms. Some of the humans, those sufficiently biddable to faithfully carry out the overlords' instructions, were spared. Of the rest, those who displayed any tendency towards rebellion were harvested, never seen again.

Phil didn't take particular pride in his role, it was just a job, but all the same he knew it was an important one and therefore he tried to do it well.

Right now he was looking through the somnopod stacks, trying to find the eight-year-olds. He needed only an eight, now, and an eleven, and he'd have what he needed for this delivery, based on the stated requirements of his employers.

The stacks had been ordered, once, but the pods had been moved so often—redistributed, relocated, gradually winnowed as they were hauled out for the thawing and processing of their contents—that they now defied all attempts at age classification. Phil always wished, when he reached this stage of the provisioning process, that the bosses would let him work a few solid shifts in the coolroom, to reestablish the order that had been lost. It would make his job so much more straightforward overall. But approval of this reasonable request had not been granted; and Phil wasn't the type to kick up a fuss about the conditions he worked under.

He'd looked through another entire dozen-high stack of pods, now; not an eight or an eleven to be seen. He dragged the ladder, rail-anchored floor and ceiling, to the next stack; climbed to the top. Found an eight, two down. Made a mental note of its location, so he could haul the gantry over once he was back on ground level, remove the pod from the stack. He continued climbing down the ladder, check the pod details as he went.

Now he just needed to find the eleven-year-olds. He stopped to recheck the third-from-lowest pod in the stack—

Noticed something odd.

'What's this?' Dru asked, in their always-warm voice. It was one of the things Phil found attractive about them, though he knew he wasn't in the same league as Dru Shawtstror. (Such things shouldn't still matter, but they did.) Probably they were that friendly, that approachable to everyone; it was their job, after all. Now they were looking at the adult-sized somnopod stacked at one corner of Phil's twelve-pod trailer.

'It's an unexpected,' Phil replied. 'Found it while I was looking for the preteens. Thought I should bring it through for you lot to have a look at, decide whether or not it needs processing.'

'You got the preteens, though, right? The'—they checked the menu on their screen—'eight and the eleven?'

'Got the eight, yep,' said Phil, searching their face for an indication that he'd got it badly wrong. Knew how much they liked things being just-so, which was one of the things he was generally good with, himself. But there'd been the unexpected, in this latest shipment, and he couldn't leave it behind, he just couldn't. 'I didn't have room for the eleven, but, with this.' He waved his hands, as though this was an explanation. 'I'll go back and get it now.'

'Best hurry,' said Dru. 'Thor has already started warming up the adults, they won't properly bond with the eleven if he's not there when they revive. And you know what Thor's like in those situations.'

Phil nodded. He did indeed know. 'But can you find a place for this... unexpected?'

'We'll do what we can,' said Dru. 'But there's not a lot of detail on the label. And it might not even be viable.'

'It's fully green-lighted but,' replied Phil.

'Yes. But it might be anything.'

'That's what makes it interesting, I would've thought.'

'It does, Phil,' they said, and his heart did a little skip that they'd remembered his name, 'but the eleven, right? You said you'd hurry.'

'I'm doing that now,' said Phil, turning away. He'd grab a single-pod trolley on the way out, that'd be quicker.

The way back seemed longer, as was always the case when he was rushed. What he should be doing in his mind was mapping out where in the storage space the elevens would be now; but he fell to thinking, instead, about how very differently it could have all turned out if it hadn't been for that unanticipated and gradually fatal metabolic susceptibility to potassium, an element lacking in the constricted biochemical palette of the sluglords (noting again that these are words not directly from Phil's vocabulary, but are necessary for the clarity of this factoid and so have been retained, likewise some of those which follow) but present in trace quantities in all human tissue.

It was funny how things went sometimes.

Lucky, perhaps, too, when you thought about it.

Dru took another look at the unexpected, while they waited for Phil's return with the eleven. Maybe this would actually be something which would spur Thor Gradjily's interest in the project. Matters had all been rather repetitive of late, with the same twenty basic designs to revive in singles or pairs or family groups, and to coax through therapy. Someone different to revive, to prepare for the slow process of integration into contemporary society, might be just the thing. And certainly this one was different, you could tell that just from the pod's weight.

Next to no information, though. Nothing like the usual wrapper, just the barest concession towards a label. And just the one messily-scrawled word on that.

'Mangrove'. Whatever *that* might mean.

About the author

Born and raised in North Canterbury, New Zealand, Simon Petrie now lives in Canberra, Australia, where he is paid to be careful with words. He has been shortlisted several times for the Sir Julius Vogel, Ditmar, and Aurealis Awards, and has won the Sir Julius Vogel Award three times: in 2010 for Best New Talent and in 2013 and 2018, with *Flight 404* and *Matters Arising from the Identification of the Body* respectively, for Best Novella. He also scored a coveted Dishonourable Mention in the 2011 Bulwer-Lytton Fiction Contest.

He has edited five issues (numbers 35, 40, 51, 54, and 61) of *Andromeda Spaceways Inflight Magazine*, and has co-edited two anthologies (*Light Touch Paper, Stand Clear* and *Use Only As Directed*) with Edwina Harvey and one (*Next*) with Rob Porteous.

A reformed academic, Simon's publishing history also includes numerous studies on the upper-atmosphere chemistry of the Saturnian moon Titan; on the ion/molecule chemistry of the dense interstellar cloud TMC-1 and the circumstellar envelope of the post-asymptotic-giant-branch star IRC+10216; on the gas-phase chemistry of multiply-charged fullerene ions; and on the structure of the active site of the water-oxidising complex within Photosystem II. He holds actionable views about second person present tense, em-dashes, and Oxford commas.

Acknowledgments

'*Nature* is healing', 'Celsius 451', 'Merth and the fateful blade', 'Jealousy', 'Squirrel story', 'Quetz run', 'On the elucidation of a low-temperature enzymatic synthesis of Z-2-butene', 'Recent revelations concerning the Apollo 15 mission', and '*Crimea River*' have not been previously published, and are edited by James Morrison.

The poems '🖼️📟ⓘ？ ⓘ？ ✈️📱？📲 ✔ 📲✖ⓘ⛢🚂📲🧱', 'Promotional', and 'Grain by grain' are also new to this volume.

'The elder' (issue 109, 2007), 'Next!' (issue 142, 2010), and 'There will come warm rains' (issue 268, 2021) were first published in the indicated issues of *AntipodeanSF*, edited by Ion Newcombe.

'A word on screenwriting' was first published in *Eye To The Telescope* issue 35 (2020), edited by David C Kopaska-Merkel.

'Scratched' was first published in *Rare Unsigned Copy: tales of Rocketry, Ineptitude, and Giant Mutant Vegetables* (Peggy Bright Books, 2010), edited by Edwina Harvey.

'Sixes, sevens' was first published in *Escape Velocity* issue 4 (2009), edited by Geoff Nelder and Robert Blevins.

'The ballad of P'toresk' was first published in *Belong* (Ticonderoga Publications, 2010), edited by Russell Farr.

'Mouthbreathers' was first published in *Dimension6* issue 20 (2020), edited by Keith Stevenson.

'(Untitled poem)' was tweeted by the author on 24 March 2019.

I'm grateful to all of the above editors and publishers for their various interactions with my writing. I must also acknowledge a debt to those who've read and critiqued the stories in draft form, notably my colleagues in the Canberra Speculative Fiction Guild.

Additional thanks are due to James Morrison for another compelling cover image, depicting Pascal 4 with implement of destruction.

80,000 Totally Secure Passwords That No Hacker Would Ever Guess
If a collection of unconnected short stories can have (or be) a companion volume, then this is the companion volume to *The 1001 Top Immortality Treatments You Must Try Before You Die.*

Paperback: 978-0-6483228-6-3
Ebook: 978-0-6483228-7-0

Murder On The Zenith Express (the Gordon Mamon collection)
The (now no longer quite complete) adventures of space-hotel employee and reluctant sleuth Gordon Mamon.

Paperback: 978-0-6483228-8-7
Ebook: 978-0-6483228-9-4

Tremendously Inconveniencing A Great Many Photons
An uplifting short novel about pottos, First Contact, and interstellar spaceflight.

Paperback: 978-0-6483836-1-1
Ebook: 978-0-6483836-2-8

Flight 404
The search for the *Bougainvillaea* brings investigator Charmaine Mertz back to the unwelcoming world of her boyhood.
(Winner of the 2013 Sir Julius Vogel award for Best Novella.)
Paperback: 978-0-6483228-4-9
Ebook: 978-0-6483228-5-6

Matters Arising From The Identification Of The Body
Tanja Morgenstein, daughter of a wealthy industrialist and a geochemist, is dead from exposure to Titan's lethal, chilled atmosphere, and Guerline Scarfe must determine why.
(Winner of the 2018 Sir Julius Vogel award for Best Novella.)
Paperback: 978-0-6483228-0-1
Ebook: 978-0-6483228-1-8

Wide Brown Land (stories of Titan)
A collection of eleven hard-SF short stories set on the Solar System's most intriguing moon.
Paperback: 978-0-6483228-2-5
Ebook: 978-0-6483228-3-2

Soft Dim Skies (a story of Titan)
It's important to Cory that his past misdeeds aren't uncovered. It's important to Portia that her mentor's death hasn't been in vain. A novella, connecting several threads begun in *Wide Brown Land*.
Paperback: 978-0-6483836-5-9
Ebook: 978-0-6483836-6-6